CONFEDERADO

D1453567

OTHER BOOKS BY
Casey Clabough

CREATIVE NONFICTION

The Warrior's Path: Reflections Along an Ancient Route

SCHOLARLY

*Inhabiting Contemporary Southern and
Appalachian Literature:
Region and Place in the 21st Century*

Elements: The Novels of James Dickey

*Experimentation and Versatility:
The Early Novels and Short Fiction
of Fred Chappell*

*The Art of the Magic Striptease:
The Literary Layers of George Garrett*

*Gayl Jones: The Language of Voice
and Freedom in Her Writings*

CONFEDERADO

A NOVEL OF THE AMERICAS

CASEY CLABOUGH

INGALLS PUBLISHING GROUP, INC

PO Box 2500
Banner Elk, NC 28604
www.ingallspublishinggroup.com

Library of Congress Cataloging-in-Publication Data

Clabough, Casey Howard, 1974-
Confederado : a novel of the Americas / Casey Clabough.
p. cm.
ISBN 978-1-932158-98-4 (trade pbk. : alk. paper)
1. American Confederate voluntary exiles--Ficiton. 2. Virginia--History--Civil War, 1861-1865--Fiction. 3. Americans--Brazil--History--19th century--Fiction. 4. United States--History--Civil War, 1861-1865--Refugees--Fiction. I. Title.
PS3603.L335C66 2012
813'.6--dc23
2012006341

For my wife's people

Where any of Mosby's men are caught hang them without trial.

—Letter from General in Chief Ulysses S. Grant to General Philip Sheridan

The South is to become another Poland or Ireland—ruled by despotic strangers who can have no sympathy with us.

—W.W. Legaré, Immigrant to Brazil

Once fallen and crushed
We submitted to fate,
Then as pent waters, rushed
From our sad estate.
Fortune favors the brave
Cast down though he be;
His true heart will e'er crave
A noble destiny.

—James McFadden Gaston, Immigrant to Brazil

To feel *saudade* is to miss or to long for somebody or something; it is to be homesick, nostalgic. Sometimes Portuguese, as well as Brazilians, feel *saudade* even of a person they have never seen or of a place they have never been to. The national Portuguese song, the *fado,* is a sad music with melancholy lyrics. Sorrow is the keynote of the Portuguese poetry.

—Erico Verissimo, *Brazilian Literature: An Outline*

CONTENTS

CONFEDERADO

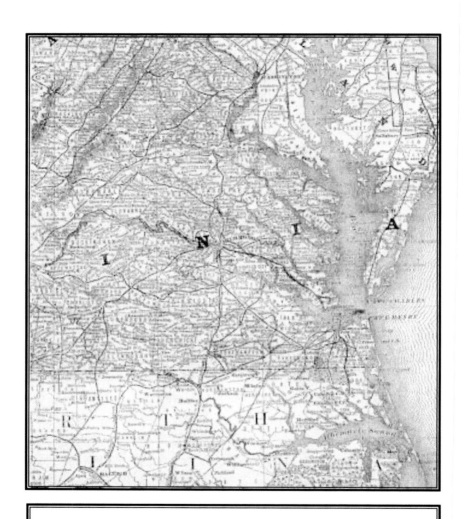

I. Virginia
APRIL, 1865

CONFEDERADO

II. BRAZIL

CIRCA 1860s

CONFEDERADO

PROLOGUE: THE FUGITIVE

Every time the hell-bent little mare took a curve of the narrow, wagon-rutted road, Alvis Benjamin Stevens felt she was a splinter's breadth from losing her footing and sending them both sliding and tumbling into the mud and puddles of brown water passing beneath. It had been hard riding for what he figured the better part of seven miles. But as the trail straightened out and firmed in the midst of ascending a bald rise, Alvis took a chance to wheel and consider his pursuers.

It was a graceful maneuver, man and horse turning as one, the man as much the animal as the horse the man. All the more remarkable since Alvis Stevens was tall and rode high in the saddle. He had the look of the countryside about him: sun-browned skin and tangled hair that stirred in the wind like stalks of wheat. Hunted though he was, there was no apparent panic in him and, indeed, one might remark that he moved with the natural ease of a hunter himself—that he likely had been a hunter of many things over the course of his young life, men not least among them.

The detail of five federal soldiers had closed significantly and they continued to press their mounts hard, sweat glistening on the animals' flanks, highlighting the rippling musculature of grace in furious motion. The mounts the men rode were beautiful, well-formed creatures seized from the Virginia horse country farms of Albemarle and Loudoun. Alvis' horse, borrowed that morning from Pastor Howell, was of a humble line of Morgans. Like its legs and hooves, the animal's stride was short and compact albeit strong and sure. The larger horses steadily gained, but the little Morgan's formidable endurance and sure-footed penchant for changing direction suddenly had spared them from being overtaken thus far.

The hill they found themselves atop stood in the shadow of Blade Mountain, really nothing more than a foothill of the Blue Ridge but the largest peak in that section of Virginia and home to a labyrinth of game trails amid thickets of gnarled mountain laurel, wild azalea, and stunted rhododendron. Alvis swung the reins and put his heels into the mare's flanks. They plunged down the back side of the bald, but at the bottom Alvis reined her in where the road softened and forded a creek. There they turned west and followed the water upstream beneath a stand of old hemlocks, the little Morgan lifting her hooves high as she splashed through the water at a steady canter.

Alvis had hunted this brook in his youth and knew that it welled from a dark hollow near the crest of Blade Mountain. He tightened his knees and leaned forward slightly as the streambed and the banks about them steepened.

By and by he turned them up a dry, rocky creek bed where it converged with the stream. The banks too were nearly all rock and when man and horse angled up the near side they left almost no sign of their passing. At the top stood a great mound of heaped stone from which Alvis once had watched for deer at pale first light and that overlooked the mountain stream some fifty feet below. Behind this outcropping he dismounted and tethered the mare to a sourwood sapling. He spoke to her softly and rubbed her lathered neck for a moment, then he checked the pistol and found the chambers full, minus one. He worked his way up the rock to a dim place between two slick mossy boulders from which he might peer downstream.

For some interval there was silence, and he took the opportunity to stretch his stiff muscles. The men, he thought, probably had overrun the place where he left the road and been forced to retrace their steps along the shoulders in search of hoof prints. A light mist snaked its way down the mountain along the creek bed. But then the sound of voices and hooves splashing against rock announced the searchers had identified his route and were ascending the mountain. On the creek they came into view man by man, a single file line, moving slowly, the horses casting their heads about them as though joining in the search.

Alvis Stevens had no illusions. These men meant to kill him. From his dark spot between the rocks he sighted his pistol on the first soldier, a dark-haired fellow with a red face and bushy mustache. When the man came to the place where the dry creek bed joined the mountain stream, he signaled for his comrades to halt. The soldier stared up the waterless draw before directing his eyes toward the ground. Then he glanced up about him at the high banks, his searching gaze coming to rest on Alvis' outcropping of stone.

Between the rocks Alvis' finger was light on the trigger, eyes intent but body relaxed—the reaction and countenance of one who has encountered such circumstances before, has killed before, and understands what it exacts. He might as soon have been preparing to drive a nail into a locust post as fixing to put a bullet in a man. The federal soldier's eyes narrowed. Alvis' forefinger began to tighten.

The war had been over for four months.

CONFEDERADO

I. Virginia
April, 1865

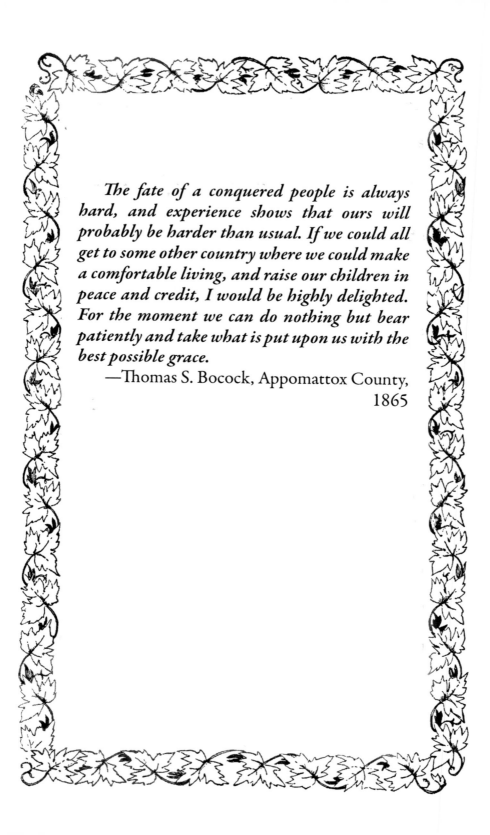

The fate of a conquered people is always hard, and experience shows that ours will probably be harder than usual. If we could all get to some other country where we could make a comfortable living, and raise our children in peace and credit, I would be highly delighted. For the moment we can do nothing but bear patiently and take what is put upon us with the best possible grace.

—Thomas S. Bocock, Appomattox County, 1865

I. VIRGINIA
HOMECOMINGS: APPOMATTOX

In the wake of Robert E. Lee's surrender at the little Virginia village of Appomattox Court House, Alvis Stevens bore his father home, some half-dozen miles, on his back. It felt to him as if the old man weighed almost nothing, and the labor seemed but commonplace after weeks of numbed marching with pistol, canteen, bedroll, and haversack.

They had not served together but during the war's closing days Alvis had received leave from Colonel Mosby's Rangers and sought his father out amid the haggard remnants of the Army of Northern Virginia as it limped westward from the broken siege at Petersburg.

More than halfway home, father and son rested alongside the road in a rolling wheat field from which they could discern the great cloudy shape of the Blue Ridge Mountains running northeast.

"Why don't you walk on, son," the father said, "and send for me directly."

"It is no burden so long as we are together," Alvis replied, his breath heavy but regular. "I did not ride all that way to Petersburg and march a sad retreat only to abandon you not three miles from home."

They rested on three more occasions, the last at the Tower Hill crossroads against the rock wall, warm with the spring's late-afternoon sun, before pressing on toward the farm. The fields were silent, no traffic upon the rutted muddy road, the quiet holding until they gained their own sloping pasture which fell away toward Stevens Run and the house, white against the bright green of hillside fields.

As he staggered down the slope Alvis spied the outline of a familiar figure along the creek. In a worn brown dress, his sister Anne, grown taller and leaner since the last time he laid eyes on her, was gathering watercress.

When she glimpsed their approach, she let out a startled cry, clutching her basket to her chest, her manner brimming with outright unfamiliarity and fear. As the strangely burdened figure came on, body on his back, she glanced quickly toward the house as if judging its distance.

Though he observed his sister's apprehension as he came to face her, Alvis Stevens at that moment lacked much idea of his appearance. His shoulders and back were bent with the weight of his father, his hair was long and tangled, and his beard uneven; the tattered, dry-rotted uniform hung over a body of skin and bones. Even so, his faded blue jacket was too small for him as were the pair of threadbare gray trousers, patched with blue, which also were much too short. And there remained both in the jacket and pants a number of tears which had not been patched at all. His feet wanted socks and were covered by frayed shoes held together by rotting twine. And set upon his head was an old hat the brim of which touched the tops of his ears. It had been shot and worn nearly all to pieces; one could look through the holes. Though he wore it low, it revealed a sliver of a jagged scar along his forehead.

So sister Anne believed for an instant this must be some army-dodging ruffian come to rob and spoil her, toting a prior victim on his back. Yet it was through his eyes, abnormally large yet soft with warmth at the sight of her, that recognition struck her at last full in the mind and she rushed to embrace him, dropping the basket of watercress in the tall creekside grass.

At the house Mama and Aunt Marcella waited to greet them, and Old January, who helped Alvis lower his father to the horsehair sofa in the parlor. Brief were the sobs and embraces as Mama, Anne, and Aunt Marcella immediately went to work in the kitchen, while Alvis drew up a chair to the sofa and January set off with a wooden pail to fetch water.

"Now you sit down too, young Mr. Stevens," said Aunt Marcella, returning from the kitchen to take Alvis' hand and guide him away from his father to a deep-cushioned flyback on the other side of the room. He collapsed more than lowered himself into it.

Any meat on the place, save three coveted laying hens, was long since gone, but in a short time there appeared on the kitchen table steaming fried potatoes and the delicious browned flour and fat grease of thickened gravy. Alvis and his father had eaten only parched corn since Saylor's Creek, the men marching alongside them having been glad to witness a horse die since it meant more ration for everyone.

When Aunt Marcella had filled the first plate and taken it to his father, Alvis loaded up one of his own and proceeded to gorge himself on the home cooking, sopping up the gravy. Halfway into his second plate however, his chewing slowed and his head began to droop, half dizzy with the warmth of the meal. He'd hardly swallowed the last mouthful of food before he was asleep at the table.

He lay in bed for three days, speaking almost not at all, except to inquire after Father. He awoke or floated away to muffled voices in the hall and the regular creaking sounds of motion in the house below.

"I've never known a man to sleep so long." It was Mama's

voice, just outside his door.

"Don't fret, Mizss Stevens," replied Aunt Marcella. "I've heard tell of others coming back and sleeping just as long."

Then they were gone or he slept again—he knew not which. Like a note in some carefully-keyed instrument, a certain board near the door of Alvis' room moaned without fail in answer to a footfall on a particular step in the stairwell, which gauged their comings and goings. For four years Alvis had lived almost entirely out of doors, exhausted by heat or tormented by cold, almost always hungry, dirty, and uncomfortable. Yet now, in his old room, Aunt Marcella tended him in the same manner she had once hovered ever near him when he was a child—as a speckled hen clucks about its lone chick, ready to cover it with a warm protective wing.

As she sat beside him, Alvis recalled vaguely the strange bitter soups she prepared when he was ill and the songs she sang at bedside. Aunt Marcella's voice droned on idly, reporting on events, the few favorable ones, that had transpired in the section during the war and lapsing into fond reminiscences of Alvis' childhood. She reminded him, for instance, of how he always loved the water and played along the creek in his boyhood, little Anne running from him as he splashed water after her.

And from these anecdotes she wandered on into the more fanciful stories that were her very own—that rang both strange and familiar from Alvis' childhood. Unlike the other servants in the family, Aunt Marcella had been taught to read so as to afford the family another voice to give utterance to the Bible. Her mind was an uncommon one, gifted with an extraordinary facility for quoting scripture and recalling recipes that had been related to her on but a single occasion. She always recounted her own stories with a vividness and warmth that spanned the boundaries of tales set in books.

"A very long time ago," she began late one afternoon as the shadows of the budding chestnut branches danced along the ceiling of Alvis' room, "Ananzi the spider had harvested all the wisdom in the world and kept it stored up in a huge pot. Niyame, the god of the sky, had given it to him. Now even though the spider had been told to share it with everybody, he was loath to do it. Every day he looked in the pot and learned different things, since that pot was full of most all the ideas and skills a body might think of. This made him even more bent on keeping that wisdom just for himself. Now to guarantee it would stay all his, Ananzi made up his mind to carry the pot to the top of a tall poplar. Setting it on the ground, he tied a sliver of string around the pot and wrapped the loose end around his waist so the pot would hang like he wanted as he climbed. But once he began climbing he found it a great trial since the pot of wisdom kept getting in his way, bumping against his tummy and the bark of the tree.

"Now from below Ananzi's son watched in fascination as his father struggled on up the tree. Finally, the son called out to him, 'If you tie the pot to your back, Father, it'll make it easier to hang on to that tree and climb.' Ananzi was so exhausted by then, he did what his son suggested and moved the pot to his back before continuing his climb, which went by with much greater ease than before. But then once Ananzi reached the top branches and recovered his breath, he got angry. 'A young one with a little common sense knows more than I do?' he yelled. 'And I the owner of the great pot of wisdom!' In his frustration and outrage Ananzi threw down the pot, and it crashed through the tree limbs, striking hard wherever it hit ..."

As Aunt Marcella spoke, Alvis gazed out the window, beyond the swaying branches, and into the sloping north field where the tops of old pasture grasses stirred only slightly.

"Alvis," she said quietly, "Do you remember what happened to the pot?"

There was silence before he spoke. "It broke open," he said slowly at last, his eyes still fixed on the field's expanse, "and the pieces of wisdom flew away in every direction. People found fragments scattered everywhere, and if they wished, they could bear a few home to their families and friends. That is why, to this day, no one person has all the world's wisdom. People everywhere may possess small pieces of it, but the whole of it remains the world's and not one man's."

Marcella watched him intently as he spoke, but when his words ceased she patted his arm and rose to depart.

Alvis was asleep when his brother McCain was brought home by wagon from Farmville. He had not been wounded but rather suffered from one of the many camp afflictions that tears at a soldier's insides and diminishes the body. Alvis slept through the considerable racket of Anne, Aunt Marcella, and Old January struggling to pull and drag his body up the stairs.

For two days McCain sipped soup and gravy and slept. On the third he was able to sit up in bed with the pillows propped behind him. By then Alvis was up and about and the long-separated brothers spoke both of the war and the immediate future.

"The farm is a wreck," McCain remarked when they had swapped accounts of their last days in the army.

"Yet the three of us have returned," Alvis replied, "and there can be no greater good fortune that that."

"What of Lavinia's fortunes?" McCain countered. "I heard her family left the country."

Alvis shook his head silently, his gaze straying to his father.

"Do you think he will recover?" McCain asked.

"Sleep now, brother," Alvis replied. "I am watching over you both."

When McCain was awake again Alvis brought out the old backgammon board and the two siblings played long into the night as they had done before the war, their conversation brightening somewhat in light of taking up an old familiar habit.

With all their men either wounded or weak Aunt Marcella, Anne, and Mama were quick about the house and garden. Mama's quiet countenance and steady, deep glance contained forceful, magnetic qualities: though she said little, under her eyes things appeared to move, noiselessly, into their proper places. Yet though she was by nature reserved in her speech and conduct, she had always existed in Alvis' mind as the epitome of love. From her seemed to emerge the very essence of devotion and family, which bound them each to the other, even in times of great suffering.

And all of them sensed there was more suffering to come for just as smoke continues to rise from the embers of a fire that is doused, so the war itself had been extinguished but its effects simmered and lingered on. Father's condition continued to deteriorate, the nature of the wound in his leg spreading to the other parts of his body until the inevitable outcome of the malady became plain. His responsiveness dwindled to the point they reckoned his passing was on the order of hours. After dinner all the family save McCain—who temporarily had been spared the sad news—quietly gathered round his bed, and when he awoke he considered them. He could no longer speak nor move, and it seemed as though all the remaining life he possessed had drained entirely into his eyes, which managed to communicate what his lips could not: that he loved them all. At three that morning the great grandfather clock in the downstairs hallway struck faintly the numbers he would never hear again. Cold took over and the night breezes received his spirit.

By candlelight at the long kitchen table Alvis prepared his father's necrology for the Richmond and Lynchburg newspapers while the others returned to their rooms, save Mama, who sat opposite Alvis, her elbows on the table and temples in her hands, gazing down into the heavy black family Bible. In the days ahead it would be commonplace to come upon her sitting immovable in the old three legged kitchen chair, hands folded in her lap, her dark eyes wide open, staring either at scripture or elsewhere into space. Alvis longed to comfort her but sadly realized he could never truly speak to his mother as he had before the war for reasons twofold: the boyish innocence that had bound him to her had been destroyed forever and accompanying it was the knowledge that within the deep soundings of her being were strange thoughts and passions directing her life of which he could never know a thing. When he had completed and sealed the necrologies he rose and rounded the table. Placing his hands on Mama's shoulders, he gently raised her up and guided her to her room.

Two days later it was Alvis' sad duty to dig his father's grave alone in the little family cemetery above Stevens Run since McCain had not sufficiently recovered to embrace such exertions and Old January could no longer perform sustained physical tasks. He might have sought assistance from their neighbors or congregation, yet Liberty Chapel already had offered to supply the coffin and it suited Alvis to perform the task alone since he and his father, the two of them, had been much together both during the war's last weeks and the final days of life. To the bond of father and son then was added that of hard-pressed brothers in arms when Alvis had secured from Colonel Mosby a transfer to the army for the purpose of seeking out his father, who had written him of his failing health. Selling his mount and uncomfortable cavalry boots, Alvis met the main army and located, with no small difficulty, his father's regiment as it staggered west in the wake of the broken siege at Petersburg. It was a proud, dying animal they found themselves sustaining as the worn Army of Northern Virginia moved on. Supplies trickled almost to nonexistence, as did reinforcement, the most recent replacements consisting of a few fourteen-year-olds and some old men who could have been their grandfathers, and in a couple cases perhaps were.

All, it struck Alvis, the army and indeed the whole war effort, had been given over to dissolution and death. Buzzards swooped and circled high above the thin column's tattered banners as collections of barefoot men limped and tottered down narrow country roads. In the wake of the Saylor's Creek engagement, Alvis glimpsed a hobbling older soldier, blood flowing freely from his face, abandon his rifle for a small live pig which he clutched to his breast greedily and whispered to incoherently as he walked.

"This day will be our last, and we cannot escape it," his father said to him in the midst of his fever as they sat along the Appomattox River on the morning of the impending surrender, "but remember that the safety of the vanquished lies in having no hope."

Alvis let the echo of these words fade even as his mind fancied they belonged less to his father than to the spring breezes that fluttered and then seemed suddenly to encircle them, like invisible fellow combatants, the ghosts of war, on some final piece of ground.

As in the contest's final days, Alvis and his father had been much together before the war as the son shadowed him about the fields or superintended the execution of his orders in his absence. He always listened closely to his father's friends as well and much of what they said stayed with him.

"Always keep a patch of sky above your life, little boy," one of them whose name he could not recall said to him one evening long ago before pressing a silver coin into his palm and mounting a fine white stallion to ride off into the gathering shadows. It was a philosophy of life he no longer was capable of embracing, but at the time he had pledged to make it his.

Anne and Mama prepared Father's meals and read to him from the family Bible during his last days, but it was Alvis who had conveyed to Father the contents of the newspapers and delivered reports on various matters of business just as Father had done for Alvis when he was a boy.

"You'll have to see about getting horses," Father said, "and watch closely the price of corn."

"Rest easy," Alvis replied. "You have taught me all those things. When I perform them it will be as with your hands, through your eyes."

Though it remained unspoken, they knew they were of a kind in a way McCain, much as they loved him, was not and never could be.

"I know you will, son," replied the dying man.

℘℧℘

Though the small country church appeared half empty, the turnout for the funeral of Mr. Stevens might safely have been considered strong given the pressing circumstances of the times in that section of Virginia: so many other families grieving deaths or awaiting news or the return of loved ones maimed, missing or captured.

Alvis himself had experienced no opportunity to attend church since his return, and when he arrived early to see about the funeral arrangements, he was greeted warmly by Pastor Howell, whose regrets and condolences spanned well beyond his ecclesiastical office. It was Alvis' father, along with Thomas S. Bocock, who, some years back, had led the preacher, a learned and eloquent man just out of English seminary, to conclude that the Lord had called him to this small country congregation and away from that of a much larger Richmond church.

Howell had never regretted that calling, though he had missed the good company of Bocock and the elder Stevens during the war—as much, truth be known, for their manly fellowship and apple brandy as for their lively scriptural and political debates. The "Blade Mountain Prophets," they had christened themselves at the conclusion of one evening which consisted more of brandy than of talk. Pastor Howell's dominant image of Stevens was of his face wrinkling as he laughed his unforgettable laugh and drank deeply before playfully seizing and attacking the ideas under discussion, not unlike a powerful, good-natured dog shaking and tearing his favorite toy. When the funeral hour arrived and Pastor Howell stepped to the pulpit, his spirit and natural heart spoke as one: a final sermon and treatise for his departed parishioner and his good friend.

"My friends," he began, "Second Chronicles: 'If Thy people go out to war against their enemies by the way that Thou shalt send them, and they pray unto Thee toward this city which Thou hast chosen, and the house which I have built for Thy name; then hear Thou from the heavens their prayer and their supplication, and maintain their cause.'"

Howell looked up from his scripture and, sweeping his gaze up and down the pews, noted sadly, as he had many times of late, the missing faces among the families of his riddled congregation.

"Friends and neighbors," he continued, "our world has changed forever since the autumn leaves of last year began to fall. The terrible conflict that came upon us has reached its conclusion, yet its dire consequences continue to ripple across our lives, disrupting the return to peace each of us craves in his heart. Yet that is why we must all draw near to God: so that we who remain, having been delivered out of the hands of our enemies, and all who hate us, might serve Him without fear.

"That war is an evil, and often a sore and terrible evil, and a thing at variance with the spirit of the Gospel, is something no Christian can for a moment doubt. But these facts do not place it beyond the employment of God, as a means of working out His purposes upon the earth. Sickness, suffering, famine and pestilence also are evils, yet God employs them in His way, and thus uses war to effect His designs among nations. Had there been no sin, there would have been no war."

Pastor Howell paused for a moment before continuing. "War, we have learned, is a vast demoralizer, and religious feeling threatens to wither under its baleful breath, as we ourselves mournfully have observed. Yet there likely has been no army since the time of Cromwell in which there was a more pervading sense of the power of God than our own. A crippled, decorated officer of my acquaintance remarked to me a few days ago, adopting the language of the scriptures, 'If it had not been the Lord who was on our side, now may Israel say, when men rose up against us, they had swallowed us up quick.' This was the solemn conviction of thousands, even the most wicked. The resources of that mighty organization, whose stupendous gage of battle we fearlessly took up, were so vast in men, money, munitions, forts, fleets and armies, that unless God had been with us we must surely have been crushed quickly. All history proves— Abraham and his armed servants, the three hundred men of Gideon and Sparta, Marathon, the Spanish Armada—that

God grants victory only insofar as He pleases to carry out His great and holy purposes in human history."

Howell bowed his head. "In our own circumstance the larger purposes of the Lord have yet to reveal themselves readily and we wait to see if we shall, as feared, become the vassal province of a colossal despotism which, having wasted our lands with fire and sword, might now compel it by military force to pay the enormous expense of our own subjugation: whilst the current owners of these lands must either remain as cowering factors for insolent conquerors and oppressive lords, or wander as penniless and homeless fugitives in a land of strangers."

He shifted slightly in the pulpit before assuming a more resolute, upright stance. "I tell you today that no such fate awaits us so long as we are true to ourselves and true to God. Battles may be lost, cities may be taken, many a gallant man and many a gentle woman may sleep in a premature grave, and many a home shrouded with mournful memories, and yet we shall be unconquered still; for in God we will continue to trust. Many a husband and son have fallen, and we grieve today for one of the finest in their number, but the reply of the Christian shall always be that 'if God has willed that I should be laid as a sacrifice on the altar of my country, I bow to His will with unrepining submission.' Amen."

When the singing concluded, a procession of horses and wagons creaked toward the farm, the mourners saddening the quiet country lane as the wagon carrying the body of Alvis' father led them on. At graveside Pastor Howell's words were lost to many on the late spring winds and the service was brief. It was a ceremony possessed of a strong sense of sorrow but few tears, the war having taken already man and tear alike in numbers beyond reckoning.

Of all the mourners Old January wept the most, for he

had known the elder Stevens the longest. They had played together as boys. The only male servant not to have departed the farm over the course of the war, January remained as faithful and inevitable as the month for which he was named, which in truth also was the month of his birth, though he did not know the exact year. On Mr. Stevens' modest tombstone were inscribed these words: "Loved among these fields and upon all others where there were men who knew him."

After dinner at the house concluded, the mourners departed, a few of them having lingered on to pay bedside respects to McCain. Alvis then took a long, circuitous walk about the farm as mottled clouds drifted eastward overhead, filtering the sunlight of late afternoon. He paused in the midst of his return beneath a great sycamore on a hillside overlooking the surrounding terrain. The whiteness of the house shone in the bottom against the green fields and weathered gray chestnut boards of the outbuildings. The fields had been neglected during the war and stood now covered in weeds, sumac and saplings, but Alvis, recalling all his father had taught him, could imagine how they would appear when he worked them again: how the furrows would open with a dark purple hue in the creek bottom while irregular shades of hard red clay would line the hillsides.

He placed his hand on the trunk of the old sycamore and fingered the flaking bark as he took in the view of the land before him. He had always been fond of trees, for beyond the warmth they provided to the hearth and the fences and buildings they made possible, he admired and liked to gauge the manner by which they spoke of the seasons through the shifting colors of the leaves and the rushing and receding of sap. It seemed to him as though the whole world changed when spring or fall moved along their branches, transforming also the canopy of his life.

Alvis patted the old sycamore and thought grimly, "There is this tree, of many one; this is the stretch of land that so many times I have looked upon. Both of them speak now of something that is gone."

Late that evening, as he sat on the bed in his room, he aimlessly took to going through drawers. They were mostly empty now, the garments they once held having been put to other uses, other necessities, during the war. He could recall now little of what their contents once had been, yet in the back corner of the bottom drawer he came upon a dusty oblong hand-mirror he had never seen before. A jagged crack inexplicably ran up the middle of the glass. Sitting hunched on the bed, he peered into his dust-streaked reflection and curiously felt nothing, as if some vast chasm stretched between him and the distorted face he beheld. To Alvis it appeared as though they were strangers to one another, the broken image before him and the face that was his own, just as it seemed to him he had grown a stranger to this place.

ഗ്രരു

Both during the war and in its wake the place that was the Stevens farm—the remote location it occupied, far from any town or city—proved a favorable circumstance for the family. In colonial times Lynchburg, the nearest municipality, some thirty miles to the west, was known as "the Seat of Satan's Kingdom" to servant and free man alike on account of its river bottom taverns and brothels, and so it had become again insofar as it was designated a central area of occupation and administration for the conquerors—a point from which they might monitor and direct central Virginia. And even the most remote of outlying areas in time would come to feel the presence of that force and direction.

"They're visiting all the farms in the section," said one of the Thornhill boys who had come to warn them and caught Alvis mending the roof of the main barn.

"What of it?" Alvis inquired.

"It's meant trouble for some," replied the youth, who had been too young to fight and, as a result, possessed a more fiery hatred for the occupiers than any veteran. "They're verifying Oaths of Allegiance, checking land titles, preying on the old and the womenfolk when they can."

"They're coming, Mr. Stevens," he concluded, about to spur his horse on toward the next farm. "They're coming."

ഇരു

Some two weeks following young Mr. Thornhill's warning visit, late one startlingly clear summer day, humidity having abated itself considerably in the wake of a brief hard shower, two federal occupation soldiers in a wagon came rolling down the lane and proceeded to enter the front door of the house unannounced. Ignoring the flurry of questions posed to them by Mama and Anne, startled in their dinner preparations, the pair tramped about the place, casually opening drawers and cabinets and peering behind furniture. As they moved from room to room, the enlisted man, a short spindly figure, began recounting to no one in particular a tale of two people in Amherst County who had been shot for resisting the lawful right of soldiers to go where they pleased and confiscate anything they might loosely consider war material or otherwise suspect property.

The officer, for his part, remained silent and sauntered about the house with a pronounced air of boredom. He was a man of middle height entering middle age, his crop of brown hair beginning to grey and thin. His eyes were set far apart, standing out prominently from shallow sockets. The nose was straight but the mouth weak and it wore a sullen expression. Either by virtue of birth or battle wound, his head drooped rather to one side.

The incongruous pair were preparing to ascend the stairs when Alvis and McCain noisily entered the main hall. They had come in from the fields and mud clung to the lower portions of their boots. A person who might have made their acquaintance in the days following the surrender would have been hard pressed to recognize the brothers now, the unrelenting toil of reclaiming the farm from years of neglect having tanned their faces and thickened their bodies. McCain was the slimmer of the two and, as a result of his wartime malady, would never regain his full weight or the extraordinary physical strength he had developed through his boyhood wrestling contests with Alvis; yet his hands, clenched at his sides, were finely veined and knotted with muscle. Alvis, standing a full head taller than his brother, affected a manner of casual disinterest—almost a bored contempt—yet his eyes were hard and the jagged scar across his forehead shone pale against his otherwise sun-darkened face.

Startled by the sudden arrival of the brothers in what they had taken for yet another forlorn household of widows and fatherless children, the soldiers introduced themselves formally yet awkwardly. Pressed by Alvis as to the purpose of their errand, they revealed their standard orders more readily to the brothers than they had to the Stevens women.

"It is our duty and lawful right," the lieutenant informed them, partially recovering his sullen air of disdain, "to search all land and holdings in the section and to verify the parole status of every war veteran.

"As you should know," he continued, "documented parole carries with it a loyalty oath to the union and is required of all men in order to vote, hold office, receive destitute rations, or draw up wedding licenses."

Alvis knew McCain had been issued his parole while lying wounded in a makeshift hospital in Farmville, but Alvis had not lingered long enough to receive his pass following the surrender at Appomattox. The necessity of delivering his father home took precedence over the formalities of organized capitulation.

While McCain excused himself to retrieve his parole, the lieutenant questioned Alvis on the particulars of his failure to secure the document.

"Don't matter the reason," chimed in the enlisted man at the conclusion of Alvis' account of his father's wound and subsequent death. "Any Johnny's not got one's a traitor."

"How do you suggest I acquire a parole, lieutenant?" inquired Alvis, ignoring the surly subordinate.

"You must report to the county courthouse and apply for it there," was the officer's curt response.

"Then I shall tend to it directly," said Alvis as McCain rejoined them and handed his parole to the lieutenant for inspection.

The officer afforded the small, flimsy rectangular piece of paper a cursory glance before nodding and returning it to McCain.

Beckoning his companion the lieutenant made for the door, yet when he had opened it he turned back to Alvis. "You'd best obtain a parole and swear the loyalty oath," he said, all traces of boredom vanished from his face. "And you may rest assured we shall be coming here again to see that you have."

The enlisted man flashed them a wide churlish smile by way of farewell before slamming the door.

When Anne returned to the kitchen she discovered two potatoes she had laid out for supper were missing.

ഗ©രു

Early next morning, new sun glancing off beads of dew and setting the hayfields all asparkle, Alvis walked the two miles to Pastor Howell's little house next to Liberty Chapel for the purpose of borrowing his Morgan mare. The only hoofed creatures left on the Stevens farm were a pair of ornery old nags and it had been the deacons of the church, after all, Alvis' father among them, who had secured for Howell a horse so that he might better visit the sick and the old.

Howell, fresh from morning prayers, was pleased to see Alvis and, allowing that he planned to spend the pre-noon hours in meditation and preparation for his next sermon, readily offered him "Little Betty" provided that Alvis would commit for him three letters to the post and pledge not to ride his beloved little Morgan too hard.

"It is true," continued Howell, "that pastors should have no truck with war, yet I am not so oblivious or ill-informed that I have not heard recounted a tale or two of Mosby's hard riding horsemen."

Smiling, Alvis agreed to Howell's conditions and, accepting the letters, set off for the small outbuilding which served as both the pastor's stable and woodshed. Little Betty, rambunctious in the cool damp of the morning air, stamped and jerked her head as her bridle was slipped on, and then bucked when Alvis tightened the girth. When he had mounted her he allowed the little Morgan to prance merrily about the church grounds before directing her to the road and settling her into a jaunty canter. Alvis had done little riding since departing the Rangers and taking up the saddle again felt like rediscovering some aspect of himself. He was tempted to break into a wild, joyous gallop, but remembering his promise to Pastor Howell, he resigned himself instead to alternating between walking and trotting the ten miles to Buckingham Court House.

The seat of Buckingham County consisted of the same post office, courthouse, and handful of residences that had been familiar to Alvis before the war, yet subtle changes struck him as he rode up the hill from the Slate River on the old Richmond-Lynchburg Stage Road and proceeded into the village. Most noticeable was the forlorn aspect of the buildings and lanes. A wagon creaked along the pike at the far eastern end of the little hamlet, but the buildings and homes appeared altogether silent, the ill-kept yards empty and ragged curtains drawn. The exception to the motionless silence was the old two-story tavern, which stood ahead of him to the left of the pike, just beyond the courthouse and opposite the little, pine-board post office. On the narrow, paint-chipped porch of the tavern, their mounts tethered to posts, a collection of men in blue, perhaps six or seven, on benches and in chairs, talked and laughed loudly. A couple of them went silent long enough to consider Alvis as he came up the road, but turned back to their companions when he brought Little Betty to a halt at the courthouse hitching rail and dismounted.

The courthouse building was by no means an opulent structure, yet it had been notably designed by Thomas Jefferson, who prescribed that four great columns built of brick and covered with plaster, their bases and caps made of stone, should support the Tuscan portico. Jefferson also called for the building to reach outward with stately wings, but these were never completed, though the structure contained an attractive feature not included in Jefferson's plans: a beautiful, grey-blue roof shingled in slate, the heavy cut pieces brought by wagon from the quarry at Arvonia, some fifteen miles to the northeast.

Between two of the columns, over the main entrance of the courthouse, hung a new union jack, its colors crisp and bright in summer's mid-morning sun. Inside, in the clerk's office, Alvis encountered a grey-haired colonel with bushy sideburns rather than a local official. The officer, seated at the clerk's desk, conferred with a heavy-set sergeant who stood bowed forward at his side, both of the men studying a document on the desk. Though Alvis suspected they were aware of his entrance, the pair ignored him for several moments as they continued to discuss a piece of property set for sale at public auction by apparent virtue of the owner's inability to pay taxes on it. When the colonel at last looked up, he affected surprise at Alvis' presence.

"Good morning, sir," he said formally, "and with what business do you come to our courthouse today?"

"Come to give up your land on account of taxes?" added the sergeant, before glancing down at the colonel and suppressing a smile. "Because if you—"

"I have come to receive parole," said Alvis in a cold voice, interrupting the sergeant and addressing himself to the colonel.

A sour expression flashed across the sergeant's face, but it was the colonel who responded, appraising his visitor more closely. "You certainly have taken your time in making your request," replied the colonel.

"Time is what I have had almost nothing of since the close of the war," countered Alvis and matter-of-factly related his father's injury and death, and the constant toil exacted by the attempt to make the Stevens farm a working enterprise once more.

The colonel studied the man as he spoke. There was an air of meekness or supplication in most all the veterans and citizens who came to call on him, but this man displayed neither nervousness nor deference. There was a certain directness, even a mild arrogance about him which raised the colonel's ire. Nevertheless, as Alvis concluded his explanation, the colonel wordlessly withdrew from a lower desk drawer a parole book and flipped it open to a blank sheet.

"Name?" he asked, and began filling in the necessary information as Alvis provided answers to the officer's subsequent queries in clipped military tones. Yet, when he identified his regiment—the 43rd Virginia—the colonel's pen paused and the sergeant started.

"Bushwhackers! Rebel wagon burners!" exclaimed the sergeant, pointing at Alvis. "Don't give this rascal a parole, colonel!"

"That will be enough, Sergeant Newman," said the colonel steadily, though his own inclination was not dissimilar.

He turned his attention back to Alvis. "As you may know, Mr. Stevens, there is little love among our ranks for the Confederate Rangers."

Alvis shrugged. "We did our duty and gave better than we got."

"Yet in the end you were beaten," the colonel said, pressing, "and your land devastated."

"That may be," said Alvis, "but it is still our land to love."

The colonel's irritation mounted. He was used to toying with broken-down rebs. This man disarmed him and he was struck then by the uneasy impression that Stevens had assessed the room and himself within a few seconds of entering it. Not only this, but that he had learned more of the colonel than the colonel had of him, despite the fact that he was the one undergoing interrogation. A sensation akin to fear tugged at the corners of his being and he suddenly wished to rid himself of the man.

"Your name is not listed among those wanted for war

crimes or other offenses," said the colonel, keeping his voice level, "and I see no reason why you should not have your parole."

Face red, the sergeant, who had remained silent and brooding, struck the desktop with his open palm and, rounding it, brushed by Alvis and stormed out of the clerk's office, door slamming in his wake.

"Sergeant Newman," the colonel said, having expressionlessly observed his subordinate's fiery departure and turning his attention now back to the parole form, "was a wagon drover during the war and suffered at the hands of your Rangers on more than one occasion."

"Then he should be grateful he is alive," replied Alvis, countenance equally expressionless.

With a sigh the colonel signed the bottom line of the parole and, carefully tearing the small sheet from the booklet, handed it across the desk. Alvis thanked him perfunctorily and turned to go, yet his departure was accompanied by an admonition from the uncomfortable, deskbound officer.

"A word of advice, Mr. Stevens," said the colonel. "You might play the part of the defeated with a little more grace, and I certainly would not make known the particular regiment you fought with during the war. You rebels are not the only ones who believe there to be certain matters left unsettled."

Outside the courthouse Alvis patted Little Betty before crossing the muddy stage road to the post office. As he did so, however, he took note of the fact that the men on the tavern porch were watching him now as a body and that among their number was the fat man from the clerk's office whom the colonel had called Sergeant Newman.

Alvis found the post office counter occupied by a tall,

balding, stooped figure he did not recognize and who spoke in a strange accent. Pressed as to the fate of Mr. Vaughn, the postmaster before the war, the man volunteered what Alvis already knew: that rebels could hold no government posts. The foreigner's tone was peculiar but matter-of-fact, and Alvis sensed in it no malice or disrespect. Having handed over Howell's letters and thanked the man, he turned to go.

Exiting the building he discovered Sergeant Newman standing next to Little Betty, looking her over and patting her flank. Alvis advanced as slowly and leisurely as he might across the stage road, coming to stand next to the occupation soldier.

"Not much of a horse," commented Sergeant Newman, glancing at Alvis, mouth twisted into a sneer, "but I figure there wasn't much left to steal when you settled on seizing this one."

"This horse is not stolen, sergeant," said Alvis matter-of-factly.

"I know how you devils operate," countered Newman, eyes squinting, voice grown low and tight. "Attacking in the dark like the cowards you are, burning wagons, taking horses.

"I don't figure anyone will question a soldier confiscating a stolen horse from a rebel thief," he continued, reaching toward Little Betty's halter.

As Newman moved Alvis raised his own hand, casually yet quickly, smacking Newman's fingers away from the horse, a quick motion not unlike swatting a horsefly.

Little Betty jerked her head at the sharp sound as Newman's eyes grew large with shining wrath, blood rushing into his face, affording it a pinkish hue. Yet when he drew his pistol Alvis was quick enough to close with the bulky sergeant and get his hands on the weapon. The sergeant was bullish and proved considerably strong despite his fleshiness. But his bulk also conspired to make him wanting in coordination. He leaned into Alvis, employing his weight in an effort to bring the pistol barrel around toward his adversary's stomach. Yet as the weapon came to right itself in the direction of Alvis' abdomen and the sergeant's finger sought the trigger, Alvis dropped a leg slightly and then shoved upward, using his powerful lower body strength to press the barrel up and back so that it lay flat against the middle of the surprised sergeant's breast, pointing toward his chin. As the big man awkwardly struggled to push the weapon from his chest his forefinger slipped and a resounding explosion echoed among the buildings accompanied by a crimson eruption from the top of Newman's head.

Cursing under his breath, Alvis received the pistol from the sergeant's limp grasp as the heavy body fell backward. Then—fluid reflex of a man accustomed to flight—he was on Little Betty, pistol in his belt, riding hard for the edge of the village as shouts rang out behind him. Plunging down the stage road, man and animal splashed across the Slate River at full gallop. Yet as they gained the opposite bank and left the road, bolting instead across the wide river-bottom field, the report of two pistols echoed across the flood plain and Alvis saw sod fly up from the damp ground ahead of him. Little Betty snorted shrilly and jumped sideways, lifting her rear and nearly throwing him. Either by virtue of drunkenness or an intention to check his flight, both of the shots fired at him had been high and wide right.

Betty was no war-hardened steed and the repercussions had caused her to spook, but the steadiness of her Morgan demeanor allowed Alvis to right her quickly enough, a wisp of mane lashing his cheek as he leaned forward and urged her on.

He kept the little Morgan at a measured gallop, slowing only when pasture turned to wood and the tangled way became less certain. At the edge of the second field they traversed, a quarter mile sea of alfalfa, Alvis glanced back to find horsemen just entering it in pursuit. He maintained the pace, skirting the north branch of the Slate River, embracing and forsaking game trails, crisscrossing the water in favor of whichever proved the more open bank. The federal riders invariably would gain on them in the wide, sun-drenched pastures and shady, wooded straight-aways, but then fall back again once Alvis and the hard-charging, little mare passed back among the thick forest and bracken—Little Betty adopting a trail, departing it, and then taking up another with a surefootedness more reminiscent of a mountain goat than a horse.

When, some two miles farther on, they struck the old roadway that ran toward Blade Mountain north of Meadow Creek, Alvis gave the mare her head and she assumed a dead gallop. As they ascended a bald rise Alvis dropped his hand to Little Betty's neck and then reached back and down to touch her flank. Though he could feel the muscles working furiously beneath her skin, the coat was not yet warm to the touch though they had been pressing hard now for miles.

What a magnificent little animal, he thought as he wheeled her at the top of the rise to consider their pursuers. The detail of five federal soldiers had closed on them significantly and they continued to press their mounts hard, sweat glistening on the animals' flanks, highlighting the rippling musculature of grace in furious motion. Alvis grimly swung the reins and put his heels into the mare's flanks, plunging them down the back side of the bald.

ഈ)(രു

When the searching eyes of the red-faced soldier glanced away from the dark hiding place between the boulders where Alvis crouched, he carefully eased his finger's pressure on the pistol's trigger and allowed his thumb to slowly return the hammer to its resting place. Signaling his fellows, the soldier reined his horse, a lanky creature of indeterminate breed, up the rocky, dry creek bed. As they disappeared into the draw Alvis could hear hooves scraping upon stone and the scattering of dislodged pebbles while the contingent proceeded past the spot where he and Little Betty had ascended the bank.

When the sounds of the enemy's passing grew faint, Alvis wiggled down the rocks, untethered Betty, and, rather than returning to the creek, led her directly into the thick mountainside forest, wiry branches scraping their sides and mountain laurel and decaying boughs snapping and crumbling beneath them as they waded through the underbrush.

Man and horse walked on for some time, changing direction, zigzagging among thickets and rocks, Alvis so engrossed in the intricacies of their path that he failed to notice the thickening of clouds above them until he discerned a rumbling to the southwest and caught the heavy scent of rain mingled with a barely discernible odor of sulphur. The storm's bearing might have been uncertain to a traveler unfamiliar with that section of Virginia, but having lived there his entire life, Alvis recognized the whimsies of the weather in the way one expects the reassuring gestures and sayings of a cherished friend. He knew how the storm would approach them: drifting along the James River, just two miles to the north, and darkening the sky only in part while offering the mountain but the very edge of its southern fringe.

They had about rounded the mountain to its western steep slope—an inhospitable place where bluffs of stone swelled outward and rocky crags leaned precariously over deep gullies. Beneath a shallow overhang he tethered Betty to the thick trunk of a great gnarled mountain laurel bush and sat down on a bed of moss to wait out the summer shower.

It was the first opportunity Alvis had experienced to think ahead and as the thunder broke over them and scattered droplets tapped upon the leaves of the forest canopy high above, he worried now for his family. He knew when the soldiers gave up searching for him on the mountain they would seek him on the farm and likely keep watch over it.

He knew too that he could not go home. Indeed, where, in fact, could he go? And was it not ironic that the single meaningless death of an obnoxious bully of a man in the wake of the war should count for more than all of those duty-bound men—more of them good than bad, he suspected—who had fallen before his pistol in combat? Alvis gently shook his head and as the rain applied itself in earnest, a dark, vague future filled his mind—all charted and arranged for him in the confused action of a few seconds and the single round of a pistol.

The storm lasted perhaps a quarter of an hour, and when it had passed Alvis stepped out from beneath the overhang and walked among the rocks, his boots making barely a sound upon the dampened leaves. When he saw that all was clear he returned to collect Betty and together they walked to a place where he knew a spring seeped forth from the rocky side of the mountain. The scent of water elicited a soft nicker from the tired horse and man and animal drank deeply. Alvis splashed water on his face and hair, rubbing it into the back of his neck. They slept that night beneath the overhang, Betty swaying on her tired, hobbled legs. The piercing tune of the whippoorwills at the foot of the mountain serenaded Alvis into slumber as he lay against the saddle on a warm bed of heaped pine and cedar needles, the bristles of which pricked his hands in the dark.

In the wake of his new trials he dreamed that night of dim before times. He had thought in the aftermath of the war to shut away his past just as he had thought to sow and gather again on the land that had borne him. Yet slumber spoke to him now through his bed of pine needles in the voice of mountainside stone. The sound of the utterance was beautiful but the message grim, bearing old wounds and future impossibilities. And so he slumbered uneasily beneath the overhang, amid curious night sounds and the nearness of rock, accompanied only by dreams he would not remember and the unrelenting pitch of mountain dark.

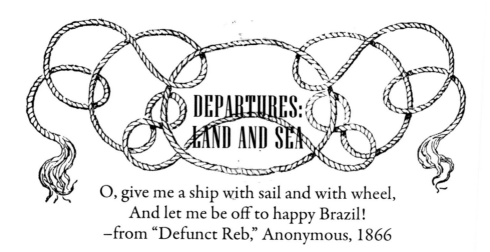

DEPARTURES: LAND AND SEA

O, give me a ship with sail and with wheel,
And let me be off to happy Brazil!
—from "Defunct Reb," Anonymous, 1866

Alvis drank from the mountainside spring at dawn and watched as the early morning sun, like some great knife of light, gradually pared away the edges of darkness and shadow in the hollows below.

As he made his return to the overhang he heard distinctly the clear crow of a rooster from the thicket of mountain laurel below him. Alvis' pistol was out and leveled down the slope almost before the tail end of the shrill unlikely cry had faded from the thin mountain air. But even as he peered into the underbrush another equally unlooked for sound met his ears: human laughter, followed by a familiar voice.

"Don't shoot, Mr. Stevens! I got breakfast for us both!"

This declaration was followed by a shuffling within the thicket, not unlike the sound a squirrel, unmindful of his racket, creates while foraging the forest floor, and from the tangled laurel emerged the shape of a slight, weathered man all clad in homespun.

"Stenson!" exclaimed Alvis, lowering his pistol.

The woodsman laughed again as he advanced up the hillside. "You look like you just seen a haint or the devil himself."

"Truly I hadn't figured on encountering man or devil on

this side of Blade Mountain," Alvis countered.

"And I do believe you picked a good spot not to be spied," said Stenson, who came to stand at Alvis' side before turning to survey the terrain with an open-palmed gesture, "but you might say this mountain here is as much me as my own body. No track led me to you, but I rightly had an itch as to where you might be."

Stenson laughed again as Alvis' features, which had met the morning still bearing traces of the night's fitful anxieties, relaxed into an answering smile.

At the overhang Stenson produced from his haversack two freshly killed rabbits and set about cleaning them, his rust-flecked blade deftly flashing in the morning sun, while Alvis gathered dry branches and boughs for a smokeless fire.

In appearance Silvanus Stenson was nothing more than a youthful wisp of a fellow of just below middle height. His weak jaw and expression were careless, though his gray eyes were hard and sharp. His lank brown hair reached almost to his shoulders and from his thin-lipped mouth, streaked brown by tobacco juice, it was not uncommon for there to emerge a curious story or whimsical verse of song. It likely would not enter the mind of the casual observer that Stenson was in fact the section's greatest hunter who, before the war, had helped Alvis to adjust the way he held his rifle, and how better to account for wind and arc when considering distant targets.

Alvis had become a fine marksman under his tutelage, though not so skilled as to rival the keen-eyed, wiry master. Stenson was expert in his use of knives as well, having deepened his knowledge while hunting across the river among the Monacans, and this knowledge too he had imparted to Alvis and his brother when they were all younger.

"So the news is that I have viciously assaulted and murdered an occupation soldier?" said Alvis, chewing a stringy sliver of cooked rabbit meat.

"They tell it for true," replied Stenson grimly and went on to inform him that the farm already had been searched and patrols doubled on the main roads. There was talk too of a bounty.

"Such a reward would carry a man a long way in these times," observed Alvis.

"I'll admit as much," answered Stenson, "but I don't reckon it's the kind of pay any decent fellow would accept."

They ate on in silence. When they had completed their meal Stenson took up a chew of tobacco and leaned back contentedly while Alvis sat cross-legged on a bed of moss, staring into the fire.

After a few moments Stenson turned to his side and spat loudly. When he resumed his careless reclining position, he spoke. "Tempting as it may be, Mr. Stevens," he said, "a body can't hide on this mountain forever, especially when folks have a mind to look for him. Throw money into the bargain and they'll find you for sure."

"I have been thinking of that," replied Alvis quietly, "and I don't have any intention of staying here, though it is yet unclear to me where exactly I should go."

The men were silent for a time, Alvis continuing to stare meditatively into the fire and Stenson having sat up and taken to whittling a pine knot. Then, as if sensing Alvis' subdued despondency and hoping to alter it, the woodsman lapsed into one of his oblique impromptu tales, this particular one stemming from his time in the army, while his busy hands continued to shave and shape the shard of sweet smelling pine. Stenson's lips moved amicably, albeit with increased urgency, as thin streams of tobacco juice began running slowly from the corners of his mouth. The account went on for a good while, as it no doubt was meant to—a salve to pass the time, ease the mind. He related in more detail than necessary the marching and camping of his infantry regiment leading up to the struggle for Williamsburg—a campaign with which Alvis possessed little familiarity—before Stenson arrived at last at the inevitable drama of battle which served also as the meandering narrative's conclusion.

"Major was a good man and a fighter," he said, "not like some of the other officers. Like I say, he was a glass-half-empty fellow, but he'd earned his good name for always leveling with us, good times and bad.

"So Major calls us together like he's fixing to pray over a dead man and says, 'You're going to have to fight, boys. We're outnumbered: four men of theirs for every one of ours. And I do believe we're likely to retreat no matter how many blue bellies we plant in the ground today. But, by God, let's make 'em fight for every piece of sod and bleed on every patch of grass they set foot!'

"We figured part of Major's sermon was his natural doom and gloom talking and things weren't as bad as he said, but come battle time the blue bellies come on just like he told it: a whole mess of them, filling a field the size of Mr. Thornhill's river bottom pasture. I swear I fired and packed and fired and packed until my barrel was so hot I couldn't rightly handle it, even with the rags I'd knotted round my paws. So I dropped back behind the main line, down in a bottom, to have myself a smoke of rabbit tobacco and wait for the steel to cool. I'd have given most anything for a twist of dark leaf right then, but I reckon I had myself a fair enough smoke considering. But then, just as I'm set to tap my pipe and go back to killing, here comes Major riding up on his big dapple gray and commences to holler.

"'Stenson!' he yells, and I can just make out his voice over all the racket from the line, 'Why ain't you fighting?'

"I start to tell him about the gun being too hot to handle, but then I change my mind. 'Major,' I says, hollering as loud as I can and making my hand into a little play pistol, 'I already got my four!'"

As Stenson delivered the concluding lines of his tale he pointed the shard of pine, hewn now into the rough likeness of a pistol, at Alvis while his face broke open into a wide smile that began of course at his tobacco stained mouth, but proceeded to grow so as to cover his entire countenance, not unlike the rippling effect of a stone cast into still water.

Alvis' unchecked laughter echoed off the rocks as the sun of midmorning lazily streamed down upon them through the low canopy of wind-stunted oak and hickory.

When Stenson departed he left with Alvis some strips of venison and several ears of dried corn from last year's harvest for Little Betty. The combination of the meal and the woodsman's visit had left Alvis somewhat heartened and a plan formed in his mind to seek the counsel of Thomas Bocock, his uncle and the man generally regarded as the most educated in all the section.

Having napped throughout the middle of the day and walked Betty about so as to limber her up, Alvis followed a rocky draw to the summit of Blade Mountain, where gnarled oaks and pines hunched against the high winds, many of their crowns broken and all more or less meager and stunted. Setting his back against the base of a dry pine stump, he let his gaze wander northwest toward the distant hills, the far Blue Ridge where the late afternoon shadows thickened. Having looked upon these peaks over the course of his life, Alvis knew how the mountains, in conjunction with the nature of the weather, changed their character many times during the course of the day, sometimes appearing very close and at other times quite distant.

When evening fell, sun having retreated down into the horizon, it seemed to him as though the peaks underwent a process of flattening and smoothing in the failing light, as though they were stretching and spreading themselves for the long night ahead.

The moon that evening was only half full as man and horse descended the mountain, Alvis guiding the mare but little, allowing the animal's instincts to choose the most favorable route as he squinched his eyes and leaned forward in an effort to avoid barely visible branches and twigs. When they had gained level ground they eschewed the roads altogether, cutting instead across pastures and fields. They encountered but a single herd of close-pressed cattle and a couple of fleet, skittish deer, as Little Betty cantered on in the direction of Wildway, Uncle Bocock's estate.

As they passed over the quiet, dim countryside Alvis' thoughts turned to his uncle. He had not seen Bocock since before the war, but heard he had returned home when the Confederate government had been dissolved, having served for some time as the Speaker of its Congress. On that last occasion they met Alvis had been sent to Wildway by his father to seek advice on which college he should attend. He smiled grimly into the dark as he called to mind those innocent days of hope and change. Intuitive for his years, he had sensed even then his country youth—its genial blues and greens of sky and meadow—passing him by, which made him cherish all the more those times he knelt to drink from the spring on the hillside above the house. Cupping the water with his right hand, he savored its peculiarly sweet flavor, which stemmed in part from the small patches of mint growing here and there in the moist ground surrounding it.

Even as he knew he was losing his youth, he was certain parts of it would stay with him forever.

Alvis recalled that when he went to see Bocock about the prospect of college, the news of life on Virginia campuses which had reached him had little to do with education. In those last weeks before the firing on Fort Sumter students had raised secession flags at the College of William and Mary, the Virginia Military Institute, Lynchburg College, and many other schools. He remembered the tension hanging over the entire state despite such flurries of activity, as if all action and preparation, regardless of the degree of time and energy invested, could neither harness nor even articulate the hulking presence of the indefinite thing to come. At home, though, the talk had remained genial and reserved, in keeping with family custom and the routine of country life.

"I want you to speak to your uncle about college, my son," his father had said, as if all in their world were normal.

Alvis' uncle's home had never ceased to impress him and he enjoyed visiting it, even though it and the man who owned it tended to intimidate him a bit. One of the finest houses in Piedmont Virginia, Wildway was built of deep red brick and stood two stories high, though it appeared much larger on account of the fourteen-foot ceilings which defined its spaciousness both upstairs and down. The home was lent additional grandeur by its situation atop a gentle rise of ground with the foundation set in such a way that any individual peering out through a front window looked full upon Piney Mountain, a small shapely peak resting some three or four miles to the southwest. Across Wildway's front stretched a beautiful portico formed by four massive Doric columns, supporting a heavy roof of Arvonia slate. Opening upon this portico and facing the marble steps was the front entrance, over the door of which spread an ornate fanlight, and on either side of which glimmered curious broad lights formed by numerous small diamond shaped panels. The brass knocker represented the family coat of arms while the door's massive brass knob spoke of another time. Inside, a spacious hall promised comfort to the newly-arrived guest; a long stairway ascended, on the side of which hung several skillfully-wrought portraits of family personages, some of them bearing more than a slight resemblance to Alvis. The great room lay beyond a wide open entrance to the right, its mantle-framed fireplace flanked by inviting mahogany chairs upholstered in black horsehair. Yet the piece of furniture that most attracted Alvis' attention on that day as he was ushered into the room by Bocock's favorite house servant, Perkins, was a large, marble-topped table upon which stood a considerable candle stand, distinctive for its richly-figured globe and cut glass pendants. As Alvis took his place in one of the chairs, a gentle methodical sound drew his gaze away from the candle stand and toward a corner of the great room where stood the large, dark-polished grandfather clock from England, whose quiet constant tick and melodious periodic chimes measured out the lives of all the Bococks and their people.

"So, my boy," Mr. Bocock had announced, his voice echoing as he strode into the great room, "I understand from your father that the bewildering prospect of a liberal education lies before you."

Bocock was not a large man but the imposing sound of his voice, so used to oratory both inside the courtroom and at the public podium without, had brought Alvis to his feet. He came to stand beside the other mahogany chair, resting his elbow upon it in fact, and smiling at Alvis warmly. He was just entering middle age then, but his face was of a ruddy hue produced by virtue of an active life marked by prolonged bachelorhood and a strong appreciation for brandy. Bushy sideburns descended from a handsome head of graying hair. The expression upon his long open face was not unlike his dress: proud and sharp, but without affectation.

"Well sir," Alvis remembered beginning timidly, having risen to shake his uncle's hand and resumed his chair, "I had about narrowed it to William and Mary or Lynchburg College, but Father thought I should take the matter up with you."

"Alas, I may claim no authoritative expertise on the subject," said Bocock, maintaining his good humor and flinging himself down in the seat opposite Alvis. "But let me urge you not to rule out Hampden Sydney, which was very good to me in my period of youthful learning and, from what I am given to understand, still promises much even in these uncertain times."

Alvis recalled how he had nodded in silent agreement though in truth he had no wish to attend Hampden Sydney, in part for the simple fact that his uncle had been educated there and served on its board of trustees. While he had been determined to keep his demeanor diffident and respectful, Alvis remembered how deeply determined he had been to go his own way and how he had viewed the meeting more as one of familial duty than professional counsel. He fingered the reins absently as he rode on through the night, recalling how his fingers had nervously played about his lap that day, fidgety in his uncle's authoritative presence.

As Bocock held forth on his undergraduate days, Perkins entered the room with a tray bearing a bottle and two glasses.

"A unique blend of apple cider, arrived only this week from George Johnson in Nelson County," observed Bocock with a smile, breaking away from his educational address as Perkins filled the glasses.

When uncle and nephew each held a glass, Bocock rose and offered a toast. "To the brightest of futures for both of us," he said, "and especially for you, young nephew."

Alvis smiled at the memory of how, having risen for the toast, he drank deeply and almost immediately felt his cheeks flush. If there had been a mirror available he would have witnessed his face take on a ruddy color not unlike his uncle's. It was his first encounter with liquor and he remembered too how he had swayed slightly on his feet as his uncle chuckled softly and motioned for him to resume his chair.

Bocock then moved on to detailed informed accounts of William and Mary and Lynchburg College: of their endowments and faculty and the prominent men he knew who had attended them. As his uncle's voice droned on, Alvis, head light with the cider, gazed beyond Bocock's face to Piney Mountain, visible in the distance through one of the enormous parlor windows, which stood large enough for a tall man to step through. Piney Mountain rose on the horizon, a great faraway thing. Like the future, Alvis thought.

A shift in the timbre of his uncle's voice brought Alvis back from his mountain reverie. "If it occurs, Brother John plans to join an infantry regiment as chaplain," Bocock said softly, "though I fear his health will not sustain him long."

Alvis had nodded though he was uncertain then of where the conversation had drifted. The atmosphere of the room suddenly grew subdued, as if this small intimation of military matters had cast a shadow over everything and, indeed, as if following the conversation, a cloud glided just then over Piney Mountain, darkening the top half of the peak. Alvis, fidgety again in the wake of the brandy's effects, was uncertain how he should fill the space of Bocock's silence. But then his uncle, as if sensing the pall that had come over them, laughed suddenly and rose to refill their glasses. The talk turned to matters of family and other leisurely topics.

When Alvis made mention of his need to depart, Bocock

had been speaking at some length of his friend, Dr. William Christian, and stated by way of conclusion, "He is among the most brilliant men I know, but has never made a profession of faith, though the subject continues to interest him."

As he accompanied Alvis to the door, Bocock placed his hand upon Alvis' shoulder. "I know I talk a great deal, nephew, and I fear the nature of my office has exacerbated that unfortunate habit, but I send you on your way with this advice, for your education as well as for whatever else may come amid the strangeness of this life: fear not the zeal of the opinions of those who surround you, your father and uncle included. Weigh their words carefully, my young friend, but keep your own counsel."

⊱⊰

Horse and rider reached Wildway just before midnight, its white paint, chipping now in places, glowing softly in the dim moonlight. As Alvis dismounted and approached the once formal white entrance, he noted that boards had replaced the decorative, fan-shaped window above the door. His knock was answered after a short span of moments by Bocock himself who, cracking the door, squinted out into the dark while holding forth in his right hand a heavy pistol. Yet hearing Alvis' voice quietly address him as Uncle, he quickly lowered the weapon and bade his kinsman enter.

In the great room, uncle and nephew seated upon rough pine benches, Bocock lit a candle which immediately served to illuminate the older man's tired countenance, aged by the war, and the unkempt quality of the house, which possessed all the habiliments of decay: the velvet carpet marked by tears and burns and much of the furniture Alvis remembered either broken now or departed. After Bocock served as Speaker of the Confederate Congress, he had worked as a liaison officer between the Confederate government and the Army of Northern Virginia. Those duties had conspired to keep him from home almost constantly, the upshot of which—as is often the case with domiciles during times of prolonged conflict—was the sad neglect, robbing, and thorough vandalizing of Wildway.

Yet despite his worn, aged appearance and that of his surroundings, Bocock managed a wan smile at Alvis in the candlelight. "I learned today the truth of your troubles, nephew," he said, "and was hoping you might pay me a call."

"Well sir," Alvis replied, "I regret to trouble you with my misfortunes, but you have always been credited for your good counsel, and I surely find myself in need of some now."

"Our trials and misfortunes are all shared in these times," observed Bocock, "and even if they were not, the bonds of family would still compel me to offer you my aid. In any event, your visit is a joy and a comfort, for it is good to see you alive and, as has always been the case with you, possessed of some forethought.

"Now, as to this pressing matter of the moment," he continued, projecting a measure of his old pride, "you realize, of course, you must depart this section and do so without tarrying. To that end it happens that since the conclusion of the war, and perhaps even a little before, an associate of mine in Lynchburg named John Nounnan has been organizing passage to Brazil for individuals interested in resuming their lives elsewhere. There is need there, it is said, for advanced agricultural practices. Moreover, the government is issuing land grants to immigrants and, by all accounts, appears particularly desirous of attracting Southerners."

"Brazil," said Alvis as if trying out the word. The utterance emerged awkwardly on his lips and, indeed, it seemed to him as though his uncle might just as soon have mentioned immigrating to the moon.

"I am aware it is a very curious proposition," said Bocock, as if reading Alvis' thoughts, "but I fear you are not privy to many options, dear nephew, and time is of the essence. Late this afternoon a detachment of soldiers came asking after you. They worry, I gather, your actions may inspire similar episodes. We cannot blame them for that, but we must move quickly to secure your safe departure."

Alvis appreciated now that his uncle was directly endangering himself in order to aid him. "What would you have me do?" he asked simply.

"Leave," said Bocock in a voice suddenly tired, his face appearing grayer and older than before. "You must set out tonight for Norfolk harbor. I will secure your passage to Brazil through Mr. Nounnan. Be mindful, however, a journey across war-ravaged lands lies between Buckingham County and the salty air of Hampton Roads. I do not believe you will be sought in the course of your travels, but to move with both alacrity and anonymity should be your aim. Do not linger at the harbor but ask for your Brazil-bound vessel and seek it out quickly. Your name will appear on the ship's passenger roll as James Cook."

From a small notebook Bocock withdrew a parole with Alvis' assigned name printed upon it, barely discernible in the wavering candlelight. He also imparted to his nephew, following considerable resistance on Alvis' part, a small sum of silver which he removed from a space behind a loose brick in the empty, soot-stained fireplace.

"Take it," Bocock insisted, "for my recompense is the prospect of your safe passage and future health.

"And one thing more," he continued, straightening himself in his former manner and eyeing Alvis closely. "A good thing, I believe. I received word some time ago that Lavinia's family had removed themselves to Brazil."

At this name Alvis' heart leapt in a way it had not for months, perhaps years. Lavinia. He had not spoken the name for what felt like an eternity, though he had learned of her family's departure from Virginia upon returning home. The sad constellation of circumstances regarding his family at home, along with the haunting ravages of the war, had blocked further thought of her from his mind. But she had been his love before the war and likely his wife if war had not come.

Bocock smiled at him, noting his heightened color and for an instant it seemed they stood together again as they had on that day long ago as uncle and nephew brimming with future hopes while holding their glasses of moonshine.

"So you see, nephew," said Bocock, "all is not without hope. Perhaps you will find Lavinia in Brazil. It is, at the least, a notion to entertain."

Alvis nodded. It most certainly was.

"As strange as it may seem," Bocock continued, "I do not know who most to pity: we that remain or you that must undertake such a journey. But take it you must and, in doing so, you must never give up hope."

When the time soon came to depart Alvis was moved to deliver some grave words of gratitude to his beloved kinsman but Bocock only shook his head, smiled, and extended his hand. Uncle and nephew shook hands for the final time in the ruined hall of Wildway, and when Alvis exited the house the candle in the great room fluttered.

As Little Betty's hoofbeats faded into the night, Bocock resumed his place on the rough bench and stared motionlessly into the candle's small flame for some time before at last rising with a sigh and, after extinguishing the candle between thumb and forefinger, returning to bed.

ℰↃↃↄ

In the early hours of morning, grass slippery with dew, Alvis quietly led Betty into Pastor Howell's small stable. He removed her saddle and bridle and brushed and patted her for several moments before placing an ear of corn in her trough and transferring his haversack from the worn English saddle to his shoulder.

Departing the church grounds, he walked briskly cross country, amid stray fields and open woods, in the vague direction of Stevens Run, which lay perhaps some three miles distant, its course running through heavy forest toward the James River. Once, approaching a road, he heard fast hoofbeats and hastily took shelter behind a tree, yet night cloaked the rider when Alvis peered and the horseman's identity and purpose remained as anonymous as the darkness.

What you're trying to do is mad, he thought, heart still aflutter from the near encounter. They're going to catch you and then you'll be like nearly all your friends: dead.

Alvis shook his head in an attempt to dismiss the dark thoughts. He knew that to have a chance it was important for him to reach the creek that bore his family's name before dawn, since it would be dangerous to be observed by early rising farmers or unanticipated fellow travelers. Once he gained the stream he believed it possible to reach the river unmolested, though the prospect of encountering a woodsman like Stenson was not altogether remote. He aimed, of course, to follow the river to Richmond and from there on to Norfolk, yet he knew from experience that it was a fool's errand to plan too far ahead. War had taught him that chance and contingency are recurring combatants in life, and that to align oneself too firmly with one or the other is to willingly invite the darker aspects of fate.

His pace was brisk and alert. Speed was important but

so was careful observation, and it was crucial he conserve his energy if possible. When he reached Stevens Run, having descended a bluff so steep that it forced him to his side and compelled him to lower himself by means of exposed hillside roots, Alvis knelt on the rocky bank and cupped the cold morning water in his hands, drinking. He stood and looked upstream to where the creek rounded the high wooded bluff and disappeared. Dawn was only beginning to arrive and the forest was still, save for the occasional piercing notes of an awakening songbird scattered somewhere among its fellows in the branches above. He knew he could follow Stevens Run upstream to the farm, to within a few yards of the house in fact, and for a moment was powerfully tempted to do so. But then he thought of his family—of their distress at the loss of him, of the needless pain and potential danger a final, lingering visit would impart. Alvis was not afraid of pain. He had endured it in many degrees and incarnations, and knew he could do so again, but he would go to great lengths, sacrifice his life even, to spare his family any more.

When he turned downstream he did so resolutely, hopping now and again from rock to rock, avoiding the slick mossy ones and leaving no track, before taking up the more open north bank and picking his way toward the James.

As dawn broke in earnest, Alvis' heavy thoughts turned again to his family: to Mama, Anne, Marcella, January. He had confidence that McCain would look after them, for his brother had always been more domestic-minded than he— better attuned to the local requirements of life, both pleasant and painful. Alvis dimly recalled an occasion upon which he and McCain had been gathering dried alfalfa for the horses following a journey to Lynchburg. A field mouse had darted out of the agitated hay pile and McCain had stomped at it quickly, attempting to crush the rodent underfoot. He cursed as he missed, even as Alvis deftly tossed his hat upon the zigzagging creature. Leaning forward and removing the hat in a flash, Alvis swept up the confused, terrified creature in a gloved hand.

"Kill it!" McCain had exclaimed.

But instead Alvis had rubbed a finger over the creature's soft pink muzzle before setting it down behind a pile of old, gnawed fence rails. His brother had shaken his head and departed with his armful of hay. Such had been the nature of their relationship for much of their lives.

"You have always been a stranger among your equals, brother," McCain had observed in the midst of one of their quarrels before the war. "You never take much pity on our friends, be they ever so unfortunate in life and love. Whenever Father sends you to sell a horse or a mule you fix your price and stick to it, no matter the social or political connection to be gained by making a bargain of it to the right man. Yet whenever you trade with one of the servants, it seems as though you must give him what you have for nothing. However good your name may be in the servant quarters, you don't need me to tell you such behavior creates little affection for you among the people of our circle."

"McCain," Alvis murmured softly as he trudged on along the creek bank, and his voice startled him, the name it had formed sounding of finality, as if somehow the utterance had just closed a chapter of his life. Of the next, Alvis knew almost nothing—it stretched out before him not unlike the war once had: large yet indefinite. He knew only that a long exile likely lay ahead of him and vast sea reaches beyond his imagining. He had been to the war and acquired from it a terrible body of knowledge, but it remained that he knew precious little of the world. Yet the understanding that he might be condemned to forever walk alone upon it pierced his heart more woefully than any wound of battle had.

When he came to the James around midmorning, having passed out of the forest and into the sandy flat, tree-scattered flood plain, Alvis removed his shoes and thin woolen socks and waded across unobserved, the soft river-bottom sand oozing between his toes. On the opposite side he seated himself upon a massive driftwood bow, wedged against the bank during some forgotten flood, and allowed his legs and feet to dry in the sun before redonning his footwear and scrambling up the embankment. Before him, mirroring the river, ran the James River and Kanawha Canal, upon which bateau traffic of times past, bearing hogsheads of tobacco and supplies had once drifted. Beyond the canal, paralleling it in like, albeit on higher ground, was the railroad, its steel lines gleaming dully in the late midmorning sun.

A curious evolution of progress lay before Alvis' field of vision, not unlike dots upon a time line or the ascending highwater marks along the walls of a seaside cave. And it struck him as ironic that it was the most primitive of these avenues of travel, the river, that would be his, eschewing all other available modes. He realized he likely could board a train or float down the James on a boat, yet he knew too it was safest to avoid both. No, he would follow the river on foot, going down it just as his distant ancestor, Thomas Stevens, had once come up it in search of the six hundred acre tract granted him by the King of England, having disembarked at Gloucester from the ship that had borne him across the Atlantic.

Alvis took his time now, speed no longer of the essence. Paramount now were the prevention of discovery and conservation of energy for any unanticipated trials. The railroad and canal remained silent as he journeyed east along the serpentine course of the river. It was likely, he mused, the line had not yet recovered from its war damages. Once, amid the heavy, sundrenched haze of mid-afternoon, he saw a boy up ahead on the opposite bank fishing and sought the low cover of the canal bank, maintaining his eastward course in defilade until it carried him well past the young fisherman.

Toward late afternoon he began sweeping the terrain to the north beyond the canal and railroad for a likely place to make camp. He wished to get up out of the flood plain if possible. It would make for warmer, drier sleeping and, he hoped, afford him a view of the river bottom as well. After perhaps a half hour of walking and looking, a grove of pines in a small valley which sloped toward the river presented itself as an attractive candidate, and he waded across the canal, shoes tied over his shoulder, and crossed the tracks, before making his way up the long draw. As he did so he stopped periodically to listen, wary of any sudden undesirable encounters while moving away from the river. He saw the tracks of deer, raccoon, possum—even the old prints of a large bobcat—but no human markings.

When Alvis reached the pines, he was greeted by the sweet odor of sap. As he walked on, searching for a likely sleeping spot, the bluffs on either side began to steepen. He had just about settled upon a place of heaped needles near a shallow spring, and was preparing to remove his haversack, when a curious flash of light caught his eye through the trees further up the little valley. He had transferred the army pistol from his belt to his haversack sometime back so the weapon would remain unobserved, but now he drew it out and, noiselessly dropping the haversack on the needle-littered ground, walked softly through the pines in the direction from which the unnatural light had emanated.

As he proceeded, the glare announcing itself suddenly at indeterminate intervals, the pines thinned—giving way to sumac, saplings, and other typical occupants of abandoned fields—until at last Alvis arrived at a place where the draw became one large open bottom area containing the heaped, burned ruins of a great house and several outbuildings. Beyond it stretched a sad, unkempt landscape, resembling an overgrown English park: shoots, copses, and shrubbery mingled with overgrown weeds and grasses. As he approached the wasted homeplace, Alvis came upon the source of the flash that had attracted his attention through the pines: a large shard of mirror-glass propped against a charred, axe-hewn beam.

He circled the ruins of the house and as he did so was struck by a powerful sensation of recognition: a blow that nearly staggered him. Alvis looked all about him—at the pine-covered hills, the arrangement of the obliterated buildings in the small valley bottom and softly curving, yet deeply-rutted drive—and pain accompanied his comprehension, for he knew this as the place he had first encountered his love Lavinia in those now-distant prewar days and danced with her all the long evening before kissing her on the lawn after midnight.

What prominent family of those before days had dwelt here and given that opulent dance? The Warrens? The Tappscotts? The Warminsters? He could no longer recall and, as he surveyed the ruins once more, he realized it hardly mattered. With a forlorn sense of emptiness, Alvis circled back round the wreckage of the homeplace and looked once more upon the large fragment of glass. Vaguely he recalled a great bronze-framed mirror from the night of the dance, which he had used to follow Lavinia's movements across the room while appearing occupied by events in the opposite direction. He mused now idly upon all the images that mirror had held, before narrowing his thoughts in an attempt to summon those forms which had gracefully moved across it that warm spring night when hoop skirts of every color twirled, flying outward, as if animated by a will of their own, from the prettiest girls of all the surrounding counties. How many of them now danced no longer, their partners, beaus, husbands, perhaps even themselves, taken by the war? The shard of glass returned Alvis' image alone when he knelt to gaze into it amid the failing light: hard, deepset, penetrating blue eyes staring searchingly into themselves.

Lavinia. He had not spoken the name for months. The constellation of circumstances to which he had found himself subjected had blocked it from his mind and heart. He sat a little away from the ruins, legs crossed, dwelling upon a fire he had scraped together with remnants from the corpse of the great house. Absently he fashioned a walking stick out of a maple bough, stripping it of its little twigs and then slowly smoothing the knots with his knife as the shadows of flame played upon it. When sleep took him it did so uneasily, tugging at him while he struggled against it. Disjointed images and memories conspired to suffocate him like smoke from a fire of wet poplar until at last he gave way to an earnest slumber, and that which tortured him crystallized itself into dream.

It is said that men beset by hard times often endure dreams that reflect those times. They toss and mutter and awake in sweats which dampen their garments and hair and leave them feeling more spent than when they had first shut their eyes. Perhaps it was the nearness of the ruined house or the songs of the whippoorwills that echoed down the draw or the great heaviness in his heart, but the dream Alvis dreamed that night—was blessed with—was a dream of love.

During that feverish period just before the war, Alvis half-heartedly had accompanied McCain to a dance held on a large farm along the James River between Wingina and Scottsville. And it was of this he dreamed, the image of the sprawling house whose ruins he now slept beside forming in his mind in all its festive glory. Its torch-lit lawn ranged to the edge of the dip in the small valley, where the pine wood began. A strong spring wind bent the tops of the evergreens on the slopes that night but Alvis felt barely a breeze when he paused on the front steps prior to entering the house and the flames of the torches burned steady.

He recalled how he sensed the spacious interior of the home, the windows having been pushed half open and the night air bringing with it the lush, damp smell of the lawn. Furniture had been pushed against the walls in anticipation of the dance, and the murmuring guests mingled freely, the men, clad mostly in dark coats, smiling beneath their mustaches, and the women, moving gracefully in their wide skirts, some of which were printed handsomely in colorful varieties of flowers. The intricate bodices of the women were cut low and framed with lace, and many of the younger girls wore flowers in their hair just above their ears, placed there by an admirer or perhaps a loving sister or mother. Alvis smiled in his sleep. It had been years since he had seen women attired so.

In the fashion of the country, the dances that night would all be square and, corners balanced, youthful couples standing in readiness, the servant fiddlers struck up the "Virginia Reel" in quick time, the room suddenly spinning into a kaleidoscope of color, couples swinging and weaving, while at the windows the wide-eyed faces of servants could be glimpsed marveling at the spectacle.

Unlike his brother, who plunged into music, Alvis stood back against a wall, taking in the festivities, while next to him two elderly gentlemen sat contentedly on a small sofa a little inside the great room, sipping bourbon and taking in the motion of youth before them with perhaps a little of the melancholic superiority of age. In the quiet lull between dances they spoke of old unfamiliar scandals involving familiar Old Dominion names, many of them having their beginnings at similar such social occasions of Virginia's long ago. They spoke too of their dwindling common friends and political matters long since resolved and viewed now as matters of historical inevitability. Alvis found himself listening more to them than to the din of youthful gaiety pervading the place.

But then the present realities of the occasion penetrated the musings of the elders in the form of a young woman. "What a lovely creature!" exclaimed the venerable gentleman nearest Alvis in his weathered voice.

Glancing down at the old men, Alvis followed their shared gaze across the room to a circle of youths among whom stood a slender figure in a black bombazine, cut low in the neck and possessed of long angel sleeves which fell away from her arms above the elbow to the hem of her dress. Her naturally curling tresses were raven black and glossy, and around her neck was a band of black velvet with a black onyx cross. The conspiracy between her dark beauty and unusual attire afforded her an otherworldly quality which captured Alvis' attention in a way that forced him to stare longer and harder than he intended, so that when she suddenly turned her eyes full upon him, it was apparent she had sensed his watchful look for some time. His slumbering, watching mind recognized her, but in the dream he saw her for the first time, and his sleeping lips smiled again.

Having been discovered in his staring, there was nothing for it now but to approach her and make his introduction. She had turned back to her circle of friends, but when Alvis came to stand at her side she cast her frank, disconcerting gaze upon him once more. Up close she was beautiful to be sure, yet it was her eyes, her grey-green eyes, that chiefly denied Alvis attention to everything else. Their expression, though soft, blunted all inquiry or analysis. Cleopatra might have had such eyes, he thought to himself.

"Alvis Stevens," he said, bowing slightly. "May I have the honor of the next dance?"

"I do not make it my habit to dance with men I do not know," she replied coolly.

"Then, by all means, let us dance and come to know one another," countered Alvis with a smile.

"Poor, poor provincial," she mocked, but her own slight smile was inviting. "Is this what passes for cleverness among your acquaintances?"

"I confess I have little cultivated imagination or wit," said Alvis. "I am only a plain, simple fellow, but one who can see to the end of his nose with extreme clearness."

At this she laughed warmly and placed her hand upon his offered arm as the next song began. She moved gracefully and, in the middle of the room, danced upon feet so light as to make her appear to drift at times. Alvis, for his part, though a passable dancer, was made to feel like a clumsy draft horse by comparison. The concentration her dancing exacted of him foiled all conversation, and when the song concluded he had gotten no further than her name.

She declined to dance with him a second time though she smiled at him warmly. When pressed as to her reason she grinned mischievously and replied, "*Caprice de femme enceinte*!" before turning from his uncomprehending face to take up the arm of a red-haired confidante whom she addressed as Arabella. Walking across the busy room, heads leaned together, they giggled suddenly and looked back at him before continuing on into another part of the house. He shrugged and made for the nearest tray to collect a glass of bourbon.

When he asked for another dance some time later, La-

vinia relented and the two spent much of the evening in each
other's company. As the night wore on, her singular yet placid cast of beauty and low musical voice made their way into
his heart by stealthy and steady paces, while around them
other minds and voices grew more impassioned, stoked by
liquor and song.

"We're going to whip 'em quick, by George!" a boister-
ous voice exclaimed between songs in another part of the
house and was followed quickly by incoherent shouting.

Sometime later, as Alvis retrieved a drink for Lavinia at
the great crystal punch bowl, he overheard a tall, dark-haired
man solemnly intone to McCain, "To train the horse to war
is not an easy task."

He winced in his sleep at these fragments of conversation, yet in the dream they remained faraway as he danced
on with Lavinia. When the fiddlers struck up "The Dear
Virginia Bride" he peered searchingly into her grey-green
eyes, yet she only smiled at him. But when the piece had
concluded she offered him her hand to kiss.

"Is not this a fair hand?" she said, donning again her
mischievous smile and arching an eyebrow. "The mouths of
many fools have kissed it."

Later, when the music had ceased and many of the guests
had departed, Lavinia's own carriage having been summoned
from the stables, Alvis kissed her in the dark upon the lawn
while a pair of rabbits grazed from the edge of the still pine
forest. The high breezes of early evening had died down to
the point the deep night appeared almost bewildering in its
silence and peace, as if something magical and invisible–or so
it seemed to Alvis—had mysteriously occurred in the world.
How could he have known these pleasures were merely the
prelude to his grief?

He tossed upon the cold ground but did not awaken, and the dream moved on beyond the dance to find him writing Lavinia a passionate letter to her address at the Buckingham Female College Institute. How he had waited those anxious three days only to receive a very cold and formal reply, which nonetheless invited him to call upon her on the afternoon of the Saturday after next.

He departed early on the appointed morning, riding the promising young saddle gelding McCain later would have shot out from beneath him at Brandy Station, the three hour cross country ride a leisurely one. The slate-roofed, brick Institute building sat atop a rise surrounded by old tobacco fields, its two breezeways affording the structure a receptive, airy aspect. Inside, however, in the entry area known as Lyceum Hall—a great room paneled in walnut with Ionic pilasters painted white—Alvis was greeted by a severe matronly instructor of classics named Miss Shepard whose duty it was, he was crisply informed, to serve as Lavinia's chaperone.

He knew in the dream he would not be permitted to see Lavinia until he had answered several questions from Miss Shepard concerning his connection to Lavinia and the nature of his family. When at last the matronly chaperone arrived at a state of grudging acceptance, she retired through a side door and returned with Lavinia, who entered the hall a little behind Miss Shepard, walking with an affected pose of nonchalance. Yet when Alvis greeted her, he discerned in her face a degree of heightened color and a nervous smile which made his heart jump.

Later, walking about the grounds attended by Miss Shepard, who followed a few paces behind them, Lavinia, speaking quietly, made him to understand that all incoming and outgoing mail at the Institute was read by the president or governess.

"Often," she said, "one is put upon to write things in such a way as to appease the censor more than the reader."

At this Alvis' heart beat faster, for he knew now her frigid letter had been a point of necessity rather than an accurate profession of truth and feeling. As a result of Miss Shepard's proximity, their talk remained measured, while their eyes and smiles said more.

Though the conversation was oblique, it served to give Alvis an idea of how Lavinia spent her time there at the Institute, while also affording him a glimpse of the daunting quality of her mind. Lavinia owned she was much given to reading in the Institute's three-thousand volume library, though she confessed to a recent reprimand for having been discovered reading fiction. Such texts were forbidden since it was widely known they adversely affected one's morals. Being caught with such a book, she explained, violated the Institute's Bylaw Number Seven, which stipulated that a young lady could "not read novels or stories or tell stories which would excite the imagination or call forth feelings of fear and apprehension." Thus, Miss Shepard had been horrified to come upon her impressionable protégé perusing a copy of Poe's *Tales of the Grotesque and Arabesque*, the small book deftly set inside a large volume of Cicero in a bid to keep it hidden.

"Mr. Poe's is a peculiar intellect," she commented quietly when Alvis inquired about the book with the strange title. "There is a girl here whose father worked with him for the *Southern Literary Messenger* in Richmond and attended the University while Mr. Poe was there. He is fond of recounting a walk they took with a group of students in the hills around Charlottesville during which Mr. Poe informed them all that a great war among ourselves would one day descend upon the land. Some of the young men laughed and called him a drunken fool, but this girl's father did not."

She paused to glance back at Miss Shepard before making her voice quieter still, almost a whisper. "Another time, Mr. Poe confided to him that often in the evening he distinctly could hear the sound of nightfall, of darkness, rolling toward him over the horizon. This man believed him, for he knew him and had read his poems and tales. I think I believe it, too."

"I have yet to experience much education," confessed Alvis with some embarrassment, before turning humorous, "and I had no idea one's reading could result in such scoldings as you describe."

"Well," said Lavinia, "Arabella informs me one may be permitted to read novels at Hollins College. Perhaps I shall quit this place and join her there."

Her laugh was like music as she took in Alvis' sudden expression of concern at the prospect of her transfer to a more distant women's repository of learning. Finding the combination of whispering and merrymaking not to her liking, Miss Shepard closed in upon them so that she followed almost at their backs.

Sobered by the proximity of her chaperone, Lavinia shifted her talk to academic subjects as they retraced their steps toward the Institute building, traversing remote areas of the moral, physical, and mathematical sciences until the dizziness in Alvis' mind came to match the confused and enamored beatings of his heart.

"You must read Jamieson's *A Grammar of Logic and Intellectual Philosophy, on Didactic Principles*," Lavinia instructed him as he stood next to his mount, Miss Shepard having remarked upon the nearness of the dinner hour in order to hasten Alvis' departure.

Determined to remember the title, Alvis nonetheless

could not recollect it by the time he reached the crossroads at Mount Rush. The intimations of looks and expressions, that which had remained unspoken, occupied his mind instead.

He did not visit the Institute again but began courting Lavinia as regularly as he might, riding to her family's farm in Prince Edward County on those handful of days she was home, most often Sunday afternoons. Though she had attracted the attention of many admirers, Lavinia was fond of the fact that, unlike so many of her other boy suitors, Alvis always listened to her and evinced an interest in what she thought. This trait in his character quickly became very precious to her, perhaps more so than she realized. Other suitors, her girlfriends, her family would become fidgety, doze, or simply depart when Lavinia began expounding at length upon some academic subject or classical narrative. Yet Alvis always listened, not out of politeness, but attentively, without interrupting, as Lavinia recounted a Greek tale or the nature of a recent scientific discovery while the two of them walked along the edges of her family's rolling fields or took up rockers in the cool of evening upon the porch. She learned he had been told many stories as a boy and fancied he merely had acquired an overdeveloped ear for the spoken word, yet it delighted her vanity nonetheless that he enjoyed listening to hers.

It pleased Lavinia too that the children and servants quickly grew very fond of Alvis, partially because his visits always included something for them. Indeed, it seemed as though he was constantly arriving with some variety of fruit, vegetable, nut, or hard candy—the manner of gift depending on some combination of the season and his elusive whimsy. When a servant reported Alvis coming down the lane, the hopeful house servants and children, some of whom had been hiding from their work and study assignments, all appeared suddenly from their remote tasks and quarters with piping cries of "Alvis is coming! Alvis is coming!"

It was from such little things that the opening chords of love made themselves palpable. Not as a tune is struck up suddenly, but rather as the low hum of an orchestra gradually rises from silence into song. As Alvis' visits became more frequent, Lavinia came to anticipate his smile and the sound of his voice when he arrived and inquired of her, "Where shall we walk? Do you have a story for me today?"

Sometimes, in the midst of their walk, they rested beneath a tree, on a bed of moss or dry leaves. As Lavinia recounted her narrative, Alvis would lie on his side, listening and watching her, clear eyed, from beginning to end. Despite her superiority in learning, he generally kept better account of the tale than she. In fact, the only times he interrupted her would be to say something on the order of, "You said that same man had died sometime near the beginning, didn't you? But no matter, it is of little consequence to the tale."

Through his responses she discovered that Alvis was fond of narratives that involved journeys and mysteries, for she rightly took him for both a wanderer and wonderer.

"I am fond of this Stevens boy," her mother told her one evening when he had departed, "yet don't you think there is something about him that is like the wind? Sometimes, even when that young man is here, it seems as though he isn't. As if he has drifted away somewhere else and a body couldn't hope to grab onto him even if it wanted to."

Outwardly, Lavinia had laughed dismissively at her mother's observation, though in truth she was troubled by the shadowy measure of its accuracy. When she shared her mother's perspective with Alvis out of curiosity as to how he would respond, he was silent in thought for a moment before replying with an enigmatic question of his own.

"Who has ever seen the wind?" he asked her, smiling gently. "But when the trees bow their heads, we know he is passing."

In the midst of one of their walks, perhaps a month following the dance at Scottsville, they rested near a stream, she sitting upon a great rock in a pool of sunlight along the edge of the water and he resting upon an old sycamore log in the shade of the trees. It pleased her that he always chose to sit where his eyes could most easily rest upon her. The air was cool along the stream and a generous sweetness hung upon it. When she asked him what he was thinking, he paused before replying, looking first upstream and then down.

"I was thinking of the people who dwelled here before us," he said. "How they lived out their long days when this entire land was a great forest and wolves roamed the hills."

"Indians," she intoned.

"Yes," he said, "or whatever ancient people whose tools and weapons reveal themselves to the plow each spring in every field. How long they must have lived here to create such a great litter of shaped stones."

Lavinia regarded him silently; she had no wish to interrupt his words when he spoke from his heart. She became aware of an answering warmth rising within her, and feared her expression might give away more than she felt willing to reveal.

"But all of them are gone now," he continued, "save a few Monacans in the hills beyond the river. It makes one wonder how long our own kind will dwell here."

Lavinia sensed that behind such musings lay the vague shadow of war, for it was in her mind as well, darkening and making uncertain the prospect of all things. Rather than replying, she held out her hand and Alvis rose to take it, kissing it before seating himself by her side on the rock and regarding her intently. They sat in this fashion for a full moment before Lavinia blushed and told him to stop looking at her that way.

"What way?" he asked, his look intensifying even more.

Many suitors had loved Lavinia for her beauty and charm, but she had come to realize that Alvis cherished her for the soul within her and thus loved even the sorrows on her changing face. Something enabled him to see beyond the others, and he loved what he saw.

The sweetness of the surrounding creek and forest and their own deep silence amid the closeness of their hearts became one for the lovers, and together they sank into them unresisting.

A while later she said, "I must go," and did up her hair.

₧₧

When Alvis' marching orders arrived, including the date of his departure, he and Lavinia began to speak to each other as though the future did not exist. Her eyes gazed far away on their long walks through field and forest and, watching her intently, Alvis attempted to take in the landscape through her eyes, as if only through her could he know that it truly existed and held among its undulations the wondrous secrets that occupied her.

It was not in Alvis' nature to worry, and he tried to make light of Lavinia's distress about the war. She spoke of it only indirectly. Like many of the women in those before days, she had taken up the needle and pin, and had become especially adept at knitting shawls. Into them she was fond of weaving elaborate patterns. When she had shown several pieces of her work to Alvis, he complimented her on them but did not perceive many of the patterns until she taught him how to notice them.

"They are like the forces that guide our lives," she told him, "barely discernible yet underlying all we do."

"And do you know anyone who can read life's patterns as we do those of shawls?" Alvis asked, attempting to jest, shaking a shawl in his hand as he did so.

"Only God may do that," rejoined Lavinia solemnly, "for the patterns of life are a different confusion to each of us, viewed as they are from different places and positions."

At such times, rather than offering a reply, Alvis usually elected to sit down beside her and take her hand. Often they remained in this fashion for an hour or more, as if they were the children of silence and time.

When Alvis at last went away to the war he did so riding Tamerlane, a magnificent black stallion reared from the stables of Lavinia's father. Their grim parting was one of silence and tears, Lavinia's cheek and kiss cold against Alvis' face as they embraced one final time. Then horse and man disappeared into the early morning fog of late summer, as Lavinia stood listening to the dying echo of hoofbeats, a shawl wrapped round her.

Of all they had shared, it was the little things she most missed and recalled in the months that followed. How when Alvis came to visit he sometimes would stop in the door to look at her, believing her to be unaware of his presence. Yet she always knew he was there, his silent gaze itself announcing the presence of love.

"What happy days!" she exclaimed to herself in thought on the wood and pasture trails she now walked alone. "The happiest of my life and yet so soon over."

Lavinia did all she could to keep her formidable mind occupied. At the Institute she had become accomplished on the piano beneath the expert tutelage of Professor Arnaud Préot, a French born composer of romantic songs and sprightly dances, who had noticed early Lavinia's agile mind and sought to translate its talents into the cascading labyrinths of musical formulae. Now she took on those difficult compositions she had shunned while working with Professor Préot, laboring at the piano for hours, occasionally even missing meals.

The true salvation of her health was her daily turn about the farm, during which she made up stories in the hopes of recounting them to Alvis when the war was decided and he returned home. Yet, as the months passed and the lengthiness of the conflict set in, she began instead to write them down and mail them to him. From the brief and hurried letters he wrote, she determined he did not always receive her dispatches. But it comforted her to think of him reading her letters and tales somewhere in the great, war-torn expanse of Virginia, imagining her face and hearing her voice in the words. Lavinia's most treasured letter was as simple and as short as the others he had sent her and she kept it folded in a secret space behind the mahogany headboard of her bed, reading it only before retiring at night.

"Dearest Lavinia," it read. "I have been with you every day of the war. You know that it has been so. And I shall be with you every day that is left to me. Every evening when I lie down upon the earth in pasture or wood, you lie down with me. Together we count the stars. Ever and Always, Alvis."

He awoke before dawn, body drawn into a ball, a rock jabbing into his shoulder and bits of leaves and dirt clinging to his dew-dampened hair and clothing. Gathering his things, he staggered back in the direction of the river, careful not to let his eyes fall on the ruined house again.

He continued his journey eastward toward Richmond for a number of days and nights without incident, skirting around the occasional hamlet, frequenting overgrown fields of briars, sumac, and young sassafras, but always more or less shadowing the course of the James. Scenes and patterns repeated themselves as he wandered on: stunted crops planted hastily by returning veterans; the hewn appearance of many an old forest cut by the armies or individuals for heat or raw material, or, most recently, he suspected, for the erection of new split rail fences, since it was old Virginia custom that unfenced land could be traveled, hunted, or grazed on regardless of the damage incurred. In many a field nothing had been planted at all and the packed red soil, peppered by weeds, lay unturned by horse and plow. Here and there a lone woman peered out from a wretched hovel or half-clad former servants lounged upon the porch or overgrown lawn of some ruined house, the sagging upper story of which sometimes created the impression it was peering down sadly upon the faded grandeur of the wreckage surrounding it.

As he neared Richmond the frequency of destruction and desolation increased: burnt chimneys standing alone or in pairs like tired, darkened sentinels over barren fields, blackened groves and weedy gardens. Approaching the outlying area of the old capital, it seemed to Alvis as if the world itself had become a great, forsaken house, and his errand was to pass through it room after lonely room, noting not so much what he saw but rather imagining what had once occupied the now empty spaces.

He struck upon the busy old river road as he neared the city, strewn with as many aimless wanderers as men and wagons bent on commerce. Burying himself among the directionless, shuffling brood, he reduced his purposeful stride to a careless saunter and loitered about the roadside among his derelict fellows on those few occasions an occupation contingent marched or rode by.

In the city itself there lingered confusion and the remnants of sorrow, many a house lying charred next to homes of old red brick or pale gray stucco, inexplicably left untouched. Most of the mighty sycamores had been cut to fuel the hearth but the majority of the old magnolias had been let alone, the brown, dead leaves of last year glimpsed just below the thick, shiny new growth. He wandered about the city noting forlorn sights everywhere he passed: on Grace Street by St. Paul's, the Ballard House, the Spotswood, and on Shockoe Hill near the old President's House. Loafers lounged in the streets—by turns gaunt, stricken, surly— and here and there blue soldiers patrolled, self-important yet bored. On designated blocks the war-ravaged populace crowded about the American Union tents, waiting to collect their destitute rations.

Dirty and weary from his unremitting outdoor travels, skin peppered by marks from mosquitoes and ticks, Alvis resolved to help himself to a meal and a good night's sleep in one of the city's taverns. Yet he was determined to make Bocock's silver go as far as it could and, having purchased from a butcher a sizeable amount of jerky he hoped would sustain him on his journey to Norfolk, he selected a cheap tavern amid the darkened warehouses and gambling dens of Shockoe Bottom. Having made arrangements for his supper and room with the tavern keeper—a husky, squint-eyed man lacking the forefinger on his right hand—Alvis took up a corner table in the smoky dining room among rough, battered men who made their meager livings along the railroad or the river and spoke in low tones of various grim prospects. At the table nearest him there was loose talk of carpetbaggers having taken up residence in some of the city's finer homes and of Mayor Mayo's capitulations to the occupation authorities, with more likely to come.

"I heard tell of railroad building in Southside," commented a spindly, red-haired fellow.

"It's no better outside the city," a hoarse-voiced man replied, sipping from his mug.

These and other sentiments drifted to Alvis' ears on voices from which the war had exacted the capacity for outrage or even significant emotional expression. Indeed, the collective atmosphere of the smoke-filled room was one of resignation: a great horde of hard-earned knowledge bereft of any measure of hope.

In silence he ate his meal of cold roast pork and butter beans and turned in early, the sagging bed in his little room only marginally more comfortable than the heaped leaves he had grown used to sleeping upon as he traced the river. In the early morning hours he came to his senses sitting up in bed, shaking and sweating, his pistol pointing into the darkness. Yet all was silence, and he did not know what noise or dream had jolted him from slumber wild-eyed and battle ready, as if Death himself had forsaken the killing fields of some present, foreign war and returned that night to Richmond.

Next morning he departed the city by way of New Market Road, shuffling bleary-eyed amid the loafers, wagons, and occasional lone horseman. His fellows paid him little heed, the dirty, unkempt figure he presented marking him merely as another one of their own. The traffic thinned considerably as the miles unfolded beyond the city and eventually he walked alone, encountering only the infrequent traveler. Periodically he noted homes pocked by shell holes and jagged, earthen breastworks smoothed now by the elements. He passed also ambiguous quiet lanes, some of which he knew curved and drifted in the direction of the river toward some of the Old Dominion's most storied homes: Shirley, Berkeley, Evelynton, Westover.

He spent his first night beyond Richmond this side of Charles City in a lesser known place of former grandeur just off the road, its roof partially collapsed and the flooring stripped in a number of rooms. Mingled together were the odors of earth, of humans and animals, of fires and meals made long ago. Curious things remained: a faded purple sash tied about an upstairs brass doorknob and, downstairs, rusty steel engravings of Virginia's distant glory bolted into a rock wall. Water had seeped down from the roof bestowing upon the steel a streaked, orangish hue. But Alvis recognized the scenes: the 1619 House of Burgesses, Governor Spotswood gazing westward high upon the Blue Ridge attended by his knights, Jefferson at work on the Declaration of Independence, and Washington receiving the sword of Cornwallis. He slept that night beneath them on a pile of rags, a living bygone thing in complement to the cold historical images hovering above him.

Across the flat, marshy expanse of eastern Virginia he drifted, a landscape of crumbling ruins and lapping tides. He skirted around Williamsburg and on down the peninsula, flanked now by the York River to the north, like some misplaced leftover being from a world that no longer existed.

Seagulls cried and wheeled against a vast, golden sky on the afternoon Alvis entered Newport News. The same evening he managed to secure lodging as the sole occupant of a squalid boarding house run by an old woman who had lost her sons at Gettysburg and the Wilderness. Her face was lined, yellow and hard: a molded wooden visage of the variety that only may be earned reluctantly over time. Her knotty fingers, half closed by rheumatism and hard as the claws of lobsters, popped oyster shells and carved long slivers of skin from potatoes with a broken kitchen knife as she prepared their supper. To aid her and hasten the meal's arrival, Alvis gathered the skins and took them, as she directed, to a bare-ground chicken pen in back of the place. He watched as a rooster and two hens, moving hesitantly forward and back in their jerky manner, pecked at the discarded skins. Occasionally one of them would grasp a sliver in its beak and run away with its prize. When Alvis returned to the kitchen his dinner was laid out for him, but the old woman had vanished.

He thought it better to put off journeying across the water to Norfolk until he knew more about the particulars of his South America bound vessel, if in fact there was even such a ship in port. He made inquiries of his host, and she in turn gathered what news she could from the fishermen at the dilapidated wharf where she regularly surveyed and poked among the daily harvests from the Chesapeake Bay and the sea. At first she learned nothing. Two days later, however, a boat just come from Norfolk brought news of the harbor and of a weatherbeaten vessel which lay in anchor bound for Brazil.

Before the war in Norfolk harbor there had fluttered the flags of many nations. Yet, as had been the case inland, the effects of the recent contest were still palpable as the bracing breeze waxed afresh and the schooner bearing Alvis across Hampton Roads sailed into the old port: wrecked docks; charred, crumbling buildings and the skeletal remains of crippled vessels presented themselves along the shoreline. Alvis, hat in hand, took in both the scattered wreckage and the surrounding open expanse of water as the breeze swept his brow. He knew he was close to realizing Bocock's plan for him, but would a description of him have been issued to the soldiers who worked among the ships? Likely they had enough problems of their own here, but he could not discount the possibility. He set his jaw against the wind.

He oriented himself once he set foot upon the sharpodored, tarred planks of the docks with the aid of instructions from the schooner's coxswain, who he learned had served aboard the ironclad *CSS Virginia* during the war and later endured capture at Saylor's Creek. The seaman had heard of the Brazil-bound ship—the *Aristides*, she was called—and its description did little to hearten Alvis: a venerable, leaky vessel employed by the Confederacy for smuggling purposes during the war.

"I wish you luck and Godspeed," said the veteran coxswain, "though I've seen little of either in these parts of late."

When Alvis glimpsed the *Aristides* at anchor, following a brief stroll along the rope-entangled and barrel-cluttered docks, the portrayal of his former brother-in-arms was confirmed. Though he was by no means a mariner, Alvis readily noted the ship's antiquated lines, the weathered quality of her wood, and the disconcerting fact that the hull appeared to rest low in the water. He loitered about the dock for the better part of an hour watching the harbor traffic and various passers-by before spying two mates clambering unsteadily into a dinghy. When he called out to them their responses were slurred, their apparent drunkenness and strange accents conspiring to splinter their expressions into tenuous fragments of meaning. Yet Alvis discerned enough—more from their hand signals than their speech—to gather they shipped aboard the *Aristides*, and that he was welcome to join them in their small boat. Once they were all seated and the seamen were about to take up the oars, the smaller of the two, shiny-eyed and grinning broadly, brought out a bottle from a rat-gnawed, woolen sack, and the sailors drank deeply before offering Alvis a swig, which he accepted out of courtesy.

"*Tonto,*" said the little seaman, chuckling as he clumsily leaned forward to return the bottle to its sack before seizing his oars.

Activity bustled and hummed on the deck of the *Aristides* as the dinghy drew near her, rocking gently on the harbor waves. Onboard a half dozen motley men sat on crates busily mending a sail, not unlike some unlikely buccaneer sewing circle, while other members of the crew moved about on sundry errands of their own. Once the dinghy was fastened and all were aboard, Alvis made signs of thanks to the inebriated sailors who responded with largely incomprehensible words of heavily accented drunken goodwill before ambling away in the direction of the poop.

The *Aristides* was not scheduled to put out for two days, but Alvis resolved to pass that time onboard, wishing to avoid any chance encounters with occupation officials on the busy docks or along the dank, narrow streets of Norfolk. Using the name ascribed him by Bocock, he made his arrangements with the captain—a gaunt, bearded fellow who most often could be found seated atop three great coils of rope puffing smoke rings from a long curved pipe as he oversaw the crew's activities—before finding himself conducted by a mate to the small, dingy cabin that was to serve as his chamber: a stuffy, confined little room with a canvas stretcher for a bed that opened into the dining room. Such was the customary design, he was informed, of all quarters occupied by single men.

He spent the majority of his time on deck, sitting where he could find patches of shade and gazing about the harbor or watching the sailors as they readied the ship for departure. He noted too the periodic arrival of his fellow passengers—families for the most part—some handsomely dressed and others bearing the palpable evidence of their wartime losses. He studied them closely as their chests were brought aboard, noting the manner in which they looked at each other and about themselves uncertainly. As he considered them, it seemed to Alvis as though for these travelers a thin mask of hopefulness sought to conceal the sorrow in their hearts; or did he merely ascribe to them the feelings lurking within his own breast? He thought too of Lavinia and wondered how her family had fared in their voyage. Were they safely situated in that foreign land?

Shortly before dawn on the third day, they were at last hauled out from the harbor while most of the passengers still slept. When she was free of her escort, the *Aristides* drifted silently eastward through a gentle mist, the long shoreline to the south dark and shapeless in the dim light of early morning. As they departed the Chesapeake Bay and entered the Atlantic the sun peeked over the gray-blue line of cloudless horizon and the vast expanse of the sea, creating a glorious, golden, blinding aura unlike any Alvis had before witnessed.

By the time the ship turned its prow south, most of the passengers were up and about, and Alvis joined them at breakfast before returning to the deck. Many of the men talked among themselves in low voices or, like Alvis, looked out over the waves. Most of the women conversed in like manner, while those who did not sewed or read or attended their children, many of whom piped with merriment at the magnificence of the Atlantic and the drama of the voyage.

Alvis kept his distance from his fellow travelers, standing off to himself near the crew quarters. Though he suspected his lot would be thrown in with some of these passengers once they all reached Brazil and set about attempting to acquire land grants, he had resolved to pass the voyage as anonymously as possible. He wondered idly too if there were others aboard who felt as he did—who traveled laden with secrets in the hopes of beginning life anew. To one who has never looked upon it before, the sea appears vast and empty beyond all reckoning, and as Alvis took it in, sunlight glittering on the morning waters, his mind reluctantly wandered back to home and that which he had been forced to forsake. Marveling at the stark, open beauty around him, he ached nonetheless for familiar faces, rolling hills, the murmur of freshwater brooks and the lonely echo of the woodpecker in the hollow.

His thoughts were interrupted by the approaching peculiar notes and words of a foreign melody and Alvis looked up from the waters to discover the smaller man from the dinghy sauntering toward him, singing as he came. Assuming a conspiratorial position next to Alvis, he surveyed the waters before shaking his head and glancing up at the Virginian.

"Nothing to see, nothing to see," he murmured sadly in English, his breath reeking of stale liquor, before taking up his foreign tune again.

Alvis looked curiously at the little man. He was short and stout and, either as a result of drink or natural predisposition, was possessed of an expression that suggested something of the reverie of a poet set against the complexion of a pirate. Indeed, when he considered him in detail it struck Alvis that this little sailor was a person at whom one might turn to look again, having passed him in the street, so startling was the peculiar contrast between expression and complexion.

Taking note of Alvis' preoccupied stare, the sailor ceased his singing again and studied Alvis in turn, squinting up at the Virginian.

"You are no family man, I gather," he said matter-of-factly, flinging a hand dismissively in the direction of the other passengers on deck, "but a loner like myself: a stranger among men."

Alvis did not speak but smiled down at the little man by way of reply.

"It is said the sea accepts all who come to her," said the

little sailor, "but it is known among those who travel with her that she loves especially lone men and strangers."

Turning, he belted out a line of verse and ambled off unsteadily across the deck.

Alvis became acquainted with the strange singing sailor during odd moments over the course of that day and the next. There was little to do on the ship and something in the little man's nature, perhaps his simple willingness to sing drunkenly and defiantly into the seaborne winds of the world, amused and interested Alvis. The sailor was known among the crew simply as El Pinho in light of the fact he served as shipwright and worked only with yellow pine, the wood typically employed in the planking and decking. He was at once a benign drunkard, a master craftsman, and a self-styled bard, each of these capacities overlapping with the other as he hammered on the ship and hummed his Portuguese ballads with a bottle of cane liquor never far out of arm's reach.

"Most all the songs of sailors are sad, Confederado," El Pinho elaborated in a melancholy voice as they sat perched atop the poop early one morning, the sea breezes rustling their hair and clothing.

"And why is that?" Alvis rejoined, smiling at El Pinho's over-dramatic solemnity.

"It is because they are like the lives we lead," said El Pinho wistfully, the sentimental sadness in his voice accentuated by his lingering drunkenness from the previous night. "Yet we sailors will never stop loving the sea. Never have I been tempted by the land and its large cities with their illusions of wealth and adventure. The sea is real. It is always before us—like destiny."

He brought his hand up in a fist. "It remains a mystery not even the oldest of sailors understands."

El Pinho went on to speak of the ocean's awesome capacity for anger—how it shook its foamy mane at those bold enough to brave its wrath—before entertaining Alvis with a fantastic rumor of some great apparition a number of vessels had sighted deep at sea over the course of the past few months: a strange unidentified thing larger and faster than a whale and giving forth sometimes a curious glow.

Alvis looked out over the sea smiling indulgently, but El Pinho continued. "For all your smiling, I believe I rightly take you to be a man who has been witness to curious things in life," said El Pinho. "Tragic things; things not to be expected. But don't stare out over the morning waters like that, Confederado! The sun will eat up your eyes!"

Alvis laughed and considered the little man. "Indeed I do smile at the bafflement of life," he said, "for I have learned that is the best thing, the only thing, a hard-pressed man may do. I have witnessed the deaths of a multitude of friends and loved ones and likely will never see my home again, yet the powers of providence and the kindnesses of people have delivered me here to this ship so that I find myself sitting by your side, where I count myself fortunate and without any cause to complain."

"That is a good and rare thing," said El Pinho, rubbing his forehead with his thumb and squinting at the morning horizon, "to have suffered so much but find yourself still capable of smiling at life. As for myself, I was raised homeless and parentless upon the waters of the world. I can ask for the nearest whore and wharf tavern in many languages and have witnessed all manner of storms and sea creatures. Mind you that when I ran away from the orphanage at the age of thirteen or fourteen or perhaps fifteen (for it is true I know not in what year I was born) and all its monotony, it was the sea that embraced me. For five years I did not return to the village of my orphaned youth. When at last I went there, I had grown strong, powerful in the hands and with keen eyes to square a board. I felt nothing in that place. If it ever had been my home, it was my home no longer."

"A man of the world to be sure," observed Alvis, smiling briefly before turning serious. "Yet it seems the places we come from remain loath to let us go," he said. "You will always remain from that place after all, my friend."

Then it was El Pinho's turn to be silent and the unlikely pair turned their attention back to the inscrutable sea.

The sea, whether one gazes over it in full daylight or sleeps upon its rocking lullaby of waves during the dark nocturnal hours, is a great conjuror of memory. It summons up things from its depths, brings them back round with its invisible currents. It forces men to take stock, whether they wish to or not. Seated upon the transom, Alvis had grown fond of peering into the sun-kissed, rippling waters or at the gliding shadows cast by the gulls that wheeled high above the ship. And as he sat perched one clear evening, the salty winds and vast loneliness of the open waters brought to him—offered up—the recollection of the first life he had taken.

He had spent most of his time during the war locating and identifying enemy supply wagons for Colonel John Mosby's Rangers, soldiers known also as Partisans or scouts or bushwhackers. The work of such men was a detached service, roaming where intuition and rumor directed, and reporting the information they gleaned directly to officers. It suited Alvis' wayward disposition and he delighted in coming to know the country at hand—every hog path and cow trail—and determining quickly whatever its relative condition might reveal to him: an enemy's numbers and inten-

tions, for example, reflected by a messy collection of foot
and hoof prints in the mud.

For Rangers haste was always a priority, thus it was that
mud, as much as the enemy, had been among Alvis' chief op-
ponents—slowing his progress, caking his horse's hooves.
And the longer the war went on the muddier the roads became. Plodding through the soupy red clay of some backcountry thoroughfare, coat wrapped about him, it sometimes seemed to Alvis as though the very skies rained mud
upon him. It was this experience with mud that led him to
conclude that the country around Richmond was the worst
for war: marshes, swamps, thickets, hidden roads, narrow
black creeks that sometimes appeared fordable but were in
fact often head deep. For this child of the Blue Ridge foothills the atmosphere of that thick, wet wilderness remained
strange and unpleasant. The clammy air of the place made
one uneasy, irritable, and on edge—a condition which wears
upon a soldier over time.

Even the ways in which features were described in that
landscape sounded peculiar to Alvis. Local folks, for instance, described Malvern Hill as something akin to a mountain while in fact it was really nothing more than a sloping
bluff above the north bank of the James River, rising to meet
the rest of the low-lying Peninsula plain. Cultivated fields
and a smattering of homes served its crest, a few patches of
woods populated mostly by elms, and overgrown ravines defined the lower part of the long grade.

Rangers and cavalrymen generally lived for the close-
pressed jostling of horses, the outer steeds scraping the walls
of houses, as they rode through a town just taken, cheers and
flower petals fluttering down from the hands of women old
and young, who smiled upon them from their windows. But
Alvis favored the obscure routes, little more than game trails,

which barely stood aside to let the narrow path creep and curve through deep forests where no moon shone and the thick leaves remained perpetually damp. He lived for those late nights when the pike was cool and hard, the rising moon hovering nearly full in a cloudless, star-scattered sky—fields of wheat, clover, and corn and stands of shadowy forest stretching out on either side—as he rushed on to share some shred of critical intelligence or join the Rangers in a raid.

Such were the things of Alvis Stevens' war. Yet before all of this—the mud, the hard incessant riding, the reading of a landscape in the way a scholar pores over a rare and crucial manuscript—before the realization of his true calling insofar as war claimed and concerned him, Alvis had served in an unremarkable Virginia infantry regiment—one that was not even uniformed initially and that appalled him in terms of the lack of education among the men assigned to fight alongside him. How curious, he later recalled, that in those early days he had felt himself a misplaced participant in some uncouth mob or rabble destined for disaster. He had yet to discover, but would learn very quickly, that when the barrels of battle grow hot, one's background and education count for less than nothing.

The occasion of his awful lesson was also his first action as an infantryman—a brief, vicious engagement, unremarkable in the war's vast bloodbath of clashes, in which his regiment, positioned along a hill crest above a wood with a sloping pasture of alfalfa between, received a determined enemy advance.

As news of the impending attack spread along the line, the men, the majority of them as green and raw as Alvis, looked at each other uncertainly, as if asking the same question and then gleaning a common answer, which arrived to them all in a sinking, empty feeling that some horrible end had been foreordained and lay in the nature of all things. Their eyes, shifting from the uneasy glances they exchanged with comrades, fixed themselves upon the line of the wood below them.

When movement came, however, it was not charging, blue-clad figures but rather a scattering of rabbits and fluttering birds, even a doe, bursting forth from the edge of the trees and hurtling toward them, only to veer aside, left or right, once they apprehended the peculiar, unnatural line of men along the hilltop. Following the eruption of forest creatures occurred a strange, heavy stillness. Alvis' heart jumped involuntarily and then momentarily seemed to cease beating. A chill passed along his spine and through his hair. He felt as though, even if he wanted to, he could not cry out or utter even a whisper. The only sound was that of his own pulse, steady in his head like the loud ticking of the grandfather clock in the hallway outside the parlor when he napped on the horsehair sofa after Sunday dinner.

"May God give us victory," someone muttered, the men pressed so close together it was impossible to determine who.

"And may all glory go to Him, and none to man," Alvis rejoined, thinking of his mother, his voice sounding stronger than he felt. A soft chorus of Amens followed and those whose heads had bent briefly now raised them back to their rifles, a single hope housed within many wills.

It was then the figures in blue emerged from the woods, running already, charging in a long ragged line, their entry into the open pasture met and announced shortly thereafter by a barely audible command and a thunderous volley from the hilltop, the sound and smoke of which echoed across the sloping pasture and rolled into the wood. Figures fell here and there, while others rushed on and still more bled forth from the trees.

It is a combination of fantasy and indolence which makes us endure uncomfortable situations and delay the necessity to act. At first there had been a coldness in Alvis' belly, a tightening, followed by a wish not to do anything, accompanied by fragments of memories. Then anger or a thing like anger came into his head, until something else cracked and abandon seized him. Yet it was a letting-go curiously accompanied by calm, for when he fired upon the first figure in blue, his hands were steady and as true to the purpose as his heart. He squeezed the trigger and the man's head became a crimson smear against the landscape.

It ended shortly thereafter. The assault never reached their position in force. The line held, no counterattack was ordered, and the enemy retreated back into the wood. At last there ensued a deathly silence, the smoke of the battle drifting across the field in a vague easterly direction. Then a tall, stately colonel, every thread and button in place, materialized out of the mist like a wraith. He surveyed the littered field and the wood beyond it, before focusing his grey expressionless eyes on the men about him. He offered them his encouragement and his gratitude, and to the aide who emerged beside him dictated matter-of-factly that the casualties were in number the weeks of the year: fifty-two.

Alvis volunteered to serve among those aiding in the collection of the dead, the air about the strewn carcasses already beginning to buzz with the presence of bees and flies. Here and there the blood-stained haversacks of the fallen lay open, disclosing some keepsake or a letter fluttering in the breeze. He would never forget the expression of one dead boy who appeared younger than himself: an enigmatic look—neither surprise nor resignation—which promised the impossible intimation that death somehow had not yet caught up to the dead. Indeed, the look suggested the boy's heart had been

seized and silenced by some powerful force. His face bore
the beginnings of an incredulous, though aborted, reaction.
In another part of the field Alvis discovered a miniball upon
which bone and lead appeared to have been fused, the pro-
jectile apparently having passed through someone and taken
a part of him with it.

The memory of that first battle continued to unfold in
Alvis' mind as if it were its own eternity while the remainder
of that day and week passed. He discovered that time slows
and compresses in combat. It might be said there is no time
save the immediacy of the lived moment which constantly
threatens to perish suddenly, like the soldier's existence. In
the wake of his first battle and the man he had killed in it,
Alvis felt not only as if he might have perished that day, but
as if he had been born that day too—as if he had been born
that day to perish that day.

Yet he was seized too by the exhilaration that he had
lived, lived to fight again and add to the body of his awful,
newfound area of knowledge. Indeed, how could he know
then that he would in time become a gifted killer? How
he would learn it is best to catch an enemy alone and un-
horsed if possible so that the animal cannot bear him away
to safety, how not to approach a body right after a man falls.
He would have found it hard to believe he might learn such
things, that there would be time to. Many had said the war
would be over in a year or two, but Alvis, having seen the el-
ephant and marched beneath enough cold rains, eventually
discerned that war really is like farming: it requires time and
patience, despite its awesome moments of rushed, crushing
brutality. So it was that the war grew up about him slowly,
like a field of corn, and he cultivated it, awaiting its fruition:
the indistinct future time of harvest.

CONFEDERADO

II. BRAZIL

*What dream came with you
that you came through
bitter tide of foam white feet?*
—W.B. Yeats

ARRIVAL:
ESPIRITU SANTO

Dry, gusting winds filled sun-drenched days of open water as the ship sailed past Puerto Rico, Saint Thomas, and the island of Guadaloupe with its beautiful mountain scenery, like and yet not like that of Virginia's Blue Ridge, the pinnacle of the highest peak gently interrupted by fleecy clouds.

Peering through one of the mates' spy glasses, Alvis could discern Guadaloupe's walls and curving streets, as well as its long rows of palmetto trees. Based on the sailors' favorable descriptions of Barbados, he had hoped to take in that island as well, but the *Aristides* sailed past her on a moonless night and her shore remained but a vague, graceful shadow off the bow.

Alvis had grown pleasantly drowsy amid the staid predictability of life on the boat, the veiled shadows of each night melting away into languorous days of idle water-watching and even more idle chatter with the likes of El Pinho, the routine of which was broken only by the vagaries of the weather or the morning services on the Sabbath. El Pinho had made it possible for Alvis to take his meals with the crew and in addition to listening to his friend's stories at supper, Alvis enjoyed hearing the rough, oath-laden sea tales of the other sailors, which reminded him of war stories in their frequently senseless brutal nature, outrageous boasts, and pervasive fraudulence. As an uncouth seaman invariably gestured with his calloused hands while passionately holding forth on some matter of great importance to him, the main portions of dinner would be brought out from the kitchen in large tin pans—one containing boiled potatoes, another bean soup, and a third pickled beef—sometimes even accompanied by light bread and butter, dried apples, and pickles. The fare was not wanting on the whole, though the inexplicable oatmeal coffee was worse than anything Alvis had tasted in the army.

After dinner, on gentle evenings when the sea grew quiet and the winds were low, a few of the younger passengers, too young to have been in the war and only now tentatively approaching adulthood, sometimes danced on deck to the music of accordion and triangle. Their families watched, calling to them and applauding at intervals. The crew often became captivated by the performance as well, a sailor abandoning his game of dice or some curse-strewn tale to watch the foreign dancers or simply close his eyes and drowsily take in the unfamiliar music. Perhaps the spectacle of witnessing these young refugees moving to their strange melodies reminded these rough seamen of their own faraway families and distant youthful days in Brazil or Argentina or Chile. When asked to dance, Alvis always politely refused, yet it touched his heart with a curious sense of hope to watch these young people swaying together as the ship rolled gently beneath them, graceful and seemingly oblivious both to the uncertain future before them and the long nightmare that sprawled out behind.

The *Aristides,* for passengers and crew alike, had become its own little world. People argued and expressed affection, the sailors went about their tasks, and day and night arrived and passed them all by. Life went on, but it was as if all life had been compressed, reduced to a small intense canvas, aboard this little boat upon the ocean. Its mild uniformity afforded Alvis a measure of comfort he had not experienced since those quiet, leisurely years before the war.

But then, suddenly, as in life, the course of events changed. The weather, which had smiled upon them thus far, began to alter its expression to that of a frown. As Alvis walked the deck with El Pinho during the early morning watch, the breezes turned baffling and variable before settling into strong sweeping gusts which made the ship seem constantly on wind, heeling to leeward. Alvis retired to his cabin for a time and, when he emerged on deck again, did not tarry long, the wind singing in his ears even as the rain soaked his hair.

When the gusts further intensified, everything was made snug as possible and the ship lay to, at length, under spanker and foretopsail, both double-reefed. In the passenger cabins, sea sickness struck several of the children, as well as adults plagued by weak stomachs. Even some of the crewmen bore grim, pale expressions as they hurried about their tasks.

Despite its favorable trim, the best that could be arrived at under the circumstances, the *Aristides* began taking on water, and as the gale freshened into a hurricane, the aftersail was split into ribbons. Mountainous waves ran one on top of the other. A particularly large swell crashed into them without warning, sweeping the deck and collecting a crewman in the caboose—a cumbersome, slowfooted Brazilian named Baleia. It claimed also nearly all the larboard bulwarks. By then the foretopsail was shredded into tatters and the crew raised a storm stay sail, its short term effect palpable for a time though ultimately for naught. The rigging strained and the mizzen mast went crashing by the board to windward.

The nerves of the passengers grew frayed at the ocean's wrath and the ship's pitching and tossing as they crowded together in the dining area. Some appeared numb and huddled against each other glumly, while others uttered cries of

alarm and desperate prayers each time the vessel heaved and
water washed over the deck. As Alvis stood among the passengers listening to the storm, arm braced against a wall, El
Pinho burst in from the deck and, seeking him out, reported
in a whisper that four feet of water stood in the hold and the
pumps were thoroughly choked.

A nearby eavesdropping passenger groaned loudly at this
news. "Lord Jesus," he sobbed, "I fear all of us will be in heav-
en or hell before this storm is through!"

A number of women gasped at this declaration even as El
Pinho roughly boxed the man's ears and growled, "Shut your
mouth, fool!"

Alvis returned with El Pinho to the deck, where efforts
had been initiated to lighten the ship. Struggling to keep his
footing, the Virginian and three other sailors thrust their
shoulders against a massive cargo crate, pushing it overboard.
Sending two more large crates plunging into the angry waters
left Alvis both winded and thoroughly soaked. As he leaned
unsteadily against a broken mast to peel off his drenched
shirt, he spotted a pair of frolicsome porpoises leaping from
a wave almost at eye level, perhaps thirty yards from where
he was standing. Only then did he realize just how low the
Aristides had dropped amid the turbulent waves.

Even as the two remaining masts were cut away, the water level in the hold continued to rise. The intensity of the
waves lessened somewhat, but whether this was a pause or
permanent abatement no one knew. The crew took advantage of the storm's lessening to get the long boat over the
side, though it threatened to jerk free of the ship once it
struck water. Calling out the women and children first, the
crew, their hoarse foreign shouts tenuously translated into
English, began herding passengers into the long boat. Once
it was full, its gunwale low enough so as to be almost in the

water, the first mate joined them and ordered it cut free from the mother ship. When the lines were loosed, the boat shot away over a near swell and disappeared from sight beyond the next.

Alvis remained onboard with El Pinho and the crew, fourteen men all told. Though the storm's fury now clearly was dissipating, waves continued to crash across the deck, the vessel bobbing precariously just above the long rolls. At last, knowing there was nothing more to be done, the gaunt bearded captain ordered them all into the jolly boat. On account of the *Aristides'* low position in the water, the crew did not have to lower the boat far, yet once upon the waves it crashed hard against its maternal vessel before a swell nearly carried it up onto the very deck of the larger ship.

Several of the crewmen, El Pinho among them, hastily scrambled into the jolly boat, which continued to jerk and pull against the sinking *Aristides*. In a desperate voice the captain called for more rope; yet even as he did Alvis saw El Pinho's eyes grow large at the prospect of something behind and beyond those who lingered onboard. Turning, Alvis beheld a great wave looming above them, about to break upon the ship. His cry of alarm accompanied the water's arrival and he felt his legs go out from under him as the current swept across the deck from stem to stern. He lost track of the captain and the others as brine filled his eyes and mouth. The force of the wave jammed him awkwardly between the stern post and the rudder. As the ship rolled leeward he sought to regain his balance, yet even as he righted himself, a trailing wave struck him, knocking him down and washing him overboard. Cold water enveloped his body and he was sucked under in the ship's wake. Ripped this way and that, his body twisted in circles, Alvis' arms lashed out for something—anything. Then he was on the surface again, riding the gradual swell of a surging wave, his eyes stinging with salt. He could see neither the ship nor the jolly boat, and he gasped and choked even as his legs kicked beneath him. Around him were the broken timbers of cargo boxes, yet when he reached out for the nearest collection of debris, the chaotic ocean currents bore them away from him. The top of the next wave, however, brought him together with a fragment of box consisting of four or five boards bound together. Taking hold of it, he clutched it to his chest as if it were the most precious thing on earth.

The sea pummeled him remorselessly. At the top of each new wave he raised his torso from his fragment of crate and peered all about him, but failed to discern either the *Aristides* or the jolly boat. His arms cramped as he clung to the broken boards, and he worried how much longer he could endure the unending swells and spray. He was rolled and sucked under, but always he emerged, some inner force compelling his arms not to let loose his wooden buoy. Yet as the dashing and tumbling went on and on, Alvis' outlook dissolved into despair as he considered his lonely place amid the dark, punishing waters and bleak, gray skies. He felt his bruised and water-laden resolve weaken and relent at last beneath the exhausting onslaught.

But it happens that the ways of God in nature, as in Providence, are not as our ways. As rapidly as it had come, the remnants of the storm moved on toward other seas, taking their wind and swells with them, to wreak their vengeance on other ships and foreign nations. As the skies cleared and the sea calmed, Alvis became aware of a hulking land-mass, a coastline, to the west, toward which the general current carried him. Too weak to swim or paddle, he merely clung to his precious fragment of crate and watched as the shore steadily came closer.

It was almost nightfall when he reached the crashing waves of the surf and found himself borne faster and more violently toward the beach. As he struggled to ride a swell, a frothy, curling wave caught him up and slammed him forward, wrenching his makeshift buoy from his cramped, benumbed arms and filling his mouth with brine. But as he came up choking, one of his naked feet brushed sand and he stumbled forward to a place where he could at last stand upright.

From this shallow sea he discerned a thick grove of forest, above which flew an assortment of water haunters, their colorful plumage bright against the glow of early evening. He stumbled up onto the beach and fell forward on his side. His arms, bereft now of their burden, ached and dull pain throbbed in places where his body had struck the ship and been jerked to and fro by the sea's wrath. He lay in such a fashion that allowed him to gaze down the beach, and as far as he could peer into the failing twilight, birds, opportunistic harpies of the ocean, lit and flitted among broken crates and other wreckage, gorging themselves on various food stores and snapping at each other with their beaks. He thought to rise but instead the exhaustion in his limbs conspired with the sand, still warm from the afternoon sun, and the constant drone of the sea to plunge him into unconsciousness.

He awoke before dawn to the gentle sound of the surf. He rose stiffly, stamped his feet and peered about in vain before touching himself tentatively in the places where he ached. Though chilled, he was grateful for his life and to feel firm soil beneath his salt stained legs. Yet he knew his outlook remained cheerless. He was friendless here, wherever here was. And it struck him at that moment that his life, all he was, the sum of his being until now, had been reduced to naught but a shipwreck. He laughed in the dark: a parched, hoarse sound as he sat down to await the dawn.

When the bright light of morning arrived, Alvis could at last discern the bruises visited upon his body. Of greater significance, however, were the things his person had given up or lost. In the midst of the storm, he had removed his shirt and, once in the water, kicked off his boots. Moreover, he had lost everything that had been in his cabin: his travel bag, his pistol, his hat. Notwithstanding all he had forfeited, he had his life, though his mouth and stomach reminded him that he would need water and food ere long to sustain it.

He set off down the beach, occasionally pausing to inspect the ship's strewn wreckage for anything that might prove useful. The birds appeared to have thoroughly picked through and stripped anything edible. He came across some boxes of nails and a torn strip of sack cloth, which he wrapped about his head and shoulders in an effort to protect them from the sun. He proceeded for the better part of three miles and still found nothing to drink or eat. The heat was unlike any he had endured, and he began to feel as though he were walking in his sleep, a sensation he had experienced in the war during those times when lack of food and rest conspired to make reality appear as though it were some dream unfolding within the mind of someone else.

Indeed, it was the experience of the war which helped him to understand what his body was suffering now as reality outran apprehension in the race toward occurrence in his sun-drunk brain. The ship's detritus on the beach reminded him of how rotting rations sometimes would languish on a distant wagon train while the men they were meant for starved, or important supplies were burned or broken so as not to be used by the enemy. And then there was the sheer madness the futility and exhaustion of war invited, such as the man Alvis witnessed at a crowded crossroads, whipping his crippled horse while showering it with screams, flecks of spittle flying from his mouth. When the animal went down, the man drew out his pistol, yet as his finger touched the trigger a flailing hoof struck his shin, sending him tumbling forward. He fell heavily and as he hit the ground the pistol fired. Those who witnessed the spectacle alternately laughed or shook their heads at the gut-shot knave. It was as if the horse, so abused, had called out for its master's blood, and the prayer had been answered by the gods of war or perhaps its demons.

He remembered how in the army camps there evolved a slower, more leisurely madness, wafting about amid the perpetual smell of excrement as men suffered from the flux. Huddled about open fires gamblers, drunkards, and other fools laughed in the faces of each other and the deaths that awaited them. From such company Alvis endeavored to keep his distance; experience had taught him it was better to fight and sleep alongside sober heathens than drunken thieving Christians. Time seemed to collapse the days' events into each other. When he lay down at night, his eyes sometimes closed so quickly that he had not time to dwell upon Lavinia—not even time to think, "I am going to sleep."

Alvis recalled these wartime trials and thus possessed the advantage of knowing his body was entering such a condition now. He struggled to recall if El Pinho had imparted to him any knowledge of the Brazilian coast, but nothing materialized in his shaky mind. Periodically he was jolted from his stumbling stupor by the violent ache of stomach cramps, brought on through a combination of his hunger and the saltwater he had swallowed. Yet on he went, staggering along the beach, weak and fatigued; he had been hurt, tired, and hungry before and knew how best to greet his old friends: to afford them his attention but keep them at arm's length. He paused to rub his eyes with his palms whenever the giddiness threatened to overpower him. He was careful not to sit down.

In the late afternoon he spotted fishermen casting nets out beyond the breakers in a rough vessel vaguely resembling a jolly boat. He waved to them weakly but the busy men onboard, three dark forms in vigorous motion against the horizon, either failed to see him or collectively ignored his gesticulations.

Alvis' thirst bordered nearly on desperation as he gazed hopelessly toward a mass of dark clouds assembling far out over the ocean. Uncertain of whether to continue following the shoreline or take his chances searching for fresh water in the dense inland forest, his dilemma was solved for him a mile further when his nose detected the rich damp odor of freshwater marshland. Turning his course away from the sea, he scaled a series of small dunes, slipping to his knees twice, before entering a stand of exotic, wind stunted trees, squatting upon great gnarled boughs.

Thunder broke close behind him, the forest darkened, and the ground grew soggy underfoot as he journeyed on, tripping occasionally over a concealed root and scraping his sore toes on shells and rocks. A hard rain was falling when at last he came upon a spring feeding into a murky lagoon along the edge of which strayed a footpath.

Kneeling, he tentatively brought water to his chapped lips in a cupped palm. The spring's offering tasted stale and brackish but he appraised it as drinkable and gulped it down greedily. He rested for a moment and drank deeply again. When he had his fill he found a tree to lie back against, the earlier intense heat of the beach and present cool barrage of rain bringing an overpowering drowsiness upon his exhausted body.

He awoke shivering, splayed out next to his tree, to discover three men standing over him. It was dark now but the rain still fell, and he could make out little about the men other than the fact that they were small-bodied fellows clad in hooded cloaks.

"Nome," the figure nearest him was saying. "Nome."

The accent of the man resembled that of some of the sailors on the boat which he had known to hail from Brazil.

Rising unsteadily, still shivering, Alvis tried a few sentences of English to no avail, he and the group's speaker bouncing their mutually foreign words off each other as the others looked on. After a few moments of this the speaker turned away from Alvis and consulted his companions. They spoke rapidly in low voices, one of them gesturing casually with his hands.

At last the original speaker turned back to Alvis and motioned for him to follow.

It seemed they journeyed an eternity in the rain, though the duration likely was no more than a couple of hours, Alvis frequently stumbling and continuing to shiver as they walked on. The cloud cover and tree canopy conspired to make the surroundings almost indiscernible other than the form of the man walking directly in front of Alvis on the forest path.

Eventually they came to a cottage in a clearing. When the man who had attempted speaking with Alvis knocked on the door it opened but a crack, and a rapid conversation ensued, the voice inside belonging to a woman. They spoke for some time, the woman raising her voice at one point followed by an emphatic string of words from the man.

When at last the door was thrown open Alvis beheld the woman's shadowy figure, which proceeded to address him in near-perfect English.

"Come in," she said in a tired voice, motioning to him.

"Come in."

Once Alvis was inside, the woman spoke to the cloaked men a final time in the language Alvis had identified as Portuguese before closing the door on them.

The interior of the cottage was cast in firelight and appeared rigorously simple: a round table with a lamp sitting in the middle of it, and a few wooden chairs—one of them possessing a slight lean—and a rocker. It was a small, dim place but the floor, gleaming in the firelight, appeared polished.

The woman motioned Alvis to the rocker near the fireplace, above the flames of which hung a black cauldron, and brought out a patched blanket from a dark corner for him to wrap about himself. She had grown wet herself during the exchange in the doorway, and now bent above the cabin's fireplace, grasping and shaking her long dark hair where it fell about her eyes. Only when she straightened could Alvis finally glimpse her face, though it remained faint and shifting in the firelight. She was slight and somewhat above the medium height, her eyes black and deepset. Her skin was stretched about the eyes and temples as if it had endured a great many gales along the shoreline, which in fact it had. Her age was indeterminate, though he doubted she could be much more than thirty, yet the ravages of time had done her an ill justice.

Bending again above the fireplace, she dipped a bowl into the cauldron and handed it to Alvis. He did not heed the steaming contents but consumed it immediately, burning his tongue and chapped lips in the process. Only halfway through his second bowl did he think to identify the flavor, which struck him as some mixture of oysters, bay, basil, and perhaps other herbs or spices.

The hot soup warmed Alvis' body and sharpened his mind. He suddenly remembered his manners.

"A thousand thanks," he proclaimed, returning the empty bowl to the woman. "To whom do I owe the honor of this hospitality?"

"I am Aletheia Landora," she said simply, in the same well-enunciated English she had employed earlier. "Those fishermen brought you here because you are an Englishman and I am the only person along this part of the coast who speaks your language."

"Alas, I am no Englishman," said Alvis, "but it seems I am fortunate indeed to have found one in this land who knows my language. And if I may infringe upon your hospitality but one step further, could you tell me what land this is?"

Aletheia regarded Alvis silently for a moment. Her proximity to the fire had caused her hair to slide slowly out of its wet tangles.

At last she said, "You are a stranger indeed to have no notion of your whereabouts. We are in the Brazilian state of Espírito Santo, one of the wild provinces north of Rio de Janeiro."

"Then I have arrived in Brazil," Alvis muttered to himself as Aletheia regarded him intently.

"What brings you here?" she asked. "To this particular place?"

Alvis laughed suddenly. "If I knew that," he said, "I would be privy to a great secret indeed, but alas I do not, and my only answer is the question, 'Why are we brought anywhere?'"

"I have known such unhappy people," said Aletheia, "who wander from place to place for no particular reason other than to escape their suffering. Perhaps you are one of them?"

"No," he said, shaking his head, "I am not of their number, but rather a simple man pressed or drawn—I can hardly tell which. It seems to me in this life there are those who are pulled toward something as a piece of iron to a magnet, and others who are driven by something which lies behind them, as the bowstring makes the arrow fly. I am one of those kinds of people, or perhaps both."

"You play a game with me," she said, smiling slightly.

"That was not my intent," said Alvis, a bit chastened. "Indeed, I ask pardon if I have. But I am weary with travel and travail, and my country lies far beyond the tumbling of this tide. My name is Alvis Benjamin Stevens and I come from a place called Virginia, if that name means anything to you, driven over strange seas, only to arrive in this place unknown and needy."

"Bad luck seems to have followed you," observed Aletheia grimly, "as it has followed me. We are what is called caipora. But even here there are words of praise and tears for those who suffer."

Alvis thanked her again for her hospitality and the conversation drifted toward the nature of his ocean journey and the particulars of the shipwreck. Aletheia brought out a pottery jug of wine, a curious fruity variety, which made Alvis' head light and warmed the jagged scar on his forehead.

Noting the wound's glazed quality reflected in the fire's flames, Aletheia inquired how he had come by it.

"A terrible grief you ask me to live again," Alvis replied, turning somber and sipping from his cup of wine, "a nightmare time when Horror and Fatality roamed my homeland, one trailing the other or side by side in tandem. But as a brilliant woman of my acquaintance once observed to me, 'Misery is manifold and the wretchedness of the earth is multiform.' Yet you are my generous host and I will deny you nothing, though I ask you to make yourself at ease, for I am a slow study and a poor raconteur, and all worn out to boot.

"Even here," Alvis began, lowering his voice, "you must

have heard of the awful storm cloud that broke out far to the north: the war between the states of North America. It is that which accounts for all my scars and has driven me, like a great tidal wave, across oceans and beaches in search of lost friends, a harbor, a home, where I might find rest at last. At night sometimes, when I close my eyes, I see the spent lives for which I once sought to lay down my own on those faraway battlefields. The wars men fight, one comes to understand, are a struggle between the best and worst aspects of our humanity. In battle the laws of civilization are abandoned utterly—to the point that the rare man who manages to honor them while doing his duty generally is deemed either a mad fool or a hero. For a man to emerge from a battle is to grope for the thing he has cast away in order to survive the contest. He seeks again articulation where before there existed among the combatants only hoarse cries and grunts, uttered for reasons no one knows, least of all himself."

Alvis had been speaking quickly and gazing intently into the fire, almost as if his words were part of a recitation, but he caught himself to glance at Aletheia, who watched him wide-eyed, lips slightly parted.

"I apologize if I have disturbed or baffled you," he said, his voice softer, "and for talking so much. It seems long since I have spoken to anyone and war is a poor topic for two who have just met. But I will try and make up for it by recounting a brief, curious tale of love and devotion insofar as I can grasp those notions, which may help also to explain this war I speak of so ineptly and perhaps a little of myself."

She nodded her assent.

"There was in one of the companies of soldiers I fought in a boy of fourteen who had hitchhiked to the city of Richmond, the capital of Virginia, to join the army. Deemed too young to fight, he was assigned the duty of ridge runner or messenger, carrying dispatches behind and along the lines with exhausting regularity, usually whistling a tune as he came and went. He was a cheerful boy and the men naturally were fond of him and called out to him and requested a musical number as he passed, for he reminded them of their own young brothers and sons, left far behind them at home.

"Eventually a battle came when re-enforcements were few and, being a brave lad, the boy slipped in with what men could be gathered to send to the front. Once there, he fought—as well as many of his elders and better than some. His fate, I am sorry to report, was a sad one. He should never have gone into battle and thus, when he died, he died of a wound meant for another. Yet his heart was such that he never would have complained of that fact. When his moment came, life and blood flowed out of him together.

"Following the battle, we buried him a little apart from the others since it was agreed he should be afforded his own place, having given and lost more than the rest as a result of his youth and all he did not live to see. There was sadness and the men missed his cheerful whistling form rushing along the line, but the war wore on and we all moved on, each of us dancing again and again to that great silent tune of death, until the melody arrived that was to be one's last.

"After a few months, however, the boy's mother came in search of him, with great difficulty, since it was winter by then and the roads were mush and not altogether safe. Her husband had perished before the contest and the boy was her only child. She wished to bury him in the family cemetery. Some men from our company organized a detail to dig him up for her and wrap the body in sackcloth. Though wagons were scarce she was afforded one, along with a man from that section to see her home directly. I admit it was a poor comfort for grief so great, but it was all we had to give her.

"Years later she was spotted among refugees, for enemy cavalry had passed through her section burning farms. But God or some other intimation had spoken to her. She had not buried her boy after all, but kept him wrapped in the sackcloth in one of the empty rooms of her house, as if somehow she knew the enemy eventually would come. And so when they did she was already gone, and she had taken her son with her, carrying his bones in a plaid satchel."

There ensued in the wake of the story's conclusion an interval of silence. The wine and the light around Alvis' face and shoulders had returned to his haggard features the bloom of youth and he yawned suddenly, as a boy might, before remembering himself and apologizing.

"Forgive me," he said, "I am near spent and have lived nearly all my life in the country, where few sleep past the sun's rising or keep awake long after dark."

He thanked Aletheia again for her hospitality and prepared to depart, but she would not allow him back out into the rain and instead afforded him a warm corner to lie down in. Once he was stretched out on the floor, slumber took him almost immediately as heavy rain drops struck the thatched roof overhead and dim dreams stuck out slowly their tentative feelers from the cottage's dark walls.

Aletheia moved to the rocker by the fire where she sat long into the night, rocking softly and gazing meditatively upon the sleeping form of the curious foreigner.

DEPARTURE AND ARRIVAL:
ESPÍRITO SANTO AND LINHARES

There is a time for departure
even when there is no certain place to go.
—Tennessee Williams

ALVIS Stevens had arrived in Brazil, yet had no certain place to go. He remained with Aletheia Landora at her urging, though something in her manner troubled him and left him uncomfortable at the prospect of sinking too far into her debt.

Clinging to her remote little cottage, she shunned all society and, in fact, said very little to Alvis. In the small space of the cabin, she sometimes shied away from him, without apparent reason, and he suspected she purposely kept the fire low in order to conceal the subtle lines of age upon her face. On those rare occasions when her eyes caught the light, they seemed to Alvis deep like the sea, and, like the sea, they continually changed.

He recovered his health quickly, dining mostly on dishes Aletheia identified as farinha, a slightly bitter starch flavored with various fruits and nuts, and a chicken soup she called canja. As he ventured out in ever greater circles about the cottage's clearing he discovered abundant banana groves and well-trod game trails amid a forest that glistened and dripped with steam almost constantly. Clad in tattered, moth- eaten garments Aletheia had brought out from an old chest, Alvis made himself useful about the place as best he could: gathering dry wood, filling the earthen-made talha with spring water, and casting leftovers into the little swine pen behind the cottage at the edge of the forest.

For the first time, he possessed the leisure to truly sense the strangeness of the place. The peculiar sounds of the insects and animals, especially at night, troubled him, and the period of twilight was of shorter duration than the daily interval of dimming he had known to the north. His favorite and most comforting spot was the beach, which lay less than a mile to the east. Even in foul weather the rare fisherman who trudged along the shore afforded a curious sense of reassurance in his daily pursuits. There was also the generous measure of simple delight in the smell of the ocean and the freedom of the great Atlantic. When the weather was good, Alvis would journey to the sea and sit upon the sand watching its undulations of water, the open sky, and the sizzle of tide on sand soothing his mind. He stared far out over the waters, toward the blue line where everything ends, or he would clench a handful of sand and sort it in his palm until only a grain remained. Then he would stare intently at that single grain as if it were home to a world, and as if he, in turn, might hold infinity in the palm of his hand. He treasured too the sudden weather changes, the whimsies of the sea, and learned to pay attention to the wind when it began to run.

In contrast to the sea, the setting of Aletheia's cottage was a forlorn place, and following an evening dinner he finally inquired of her, as tactfully as he might, how she had come to live there.

"The heart," she replied mysteriously. "The human heart is what throws us into all our miseries."

Her husband, a sailor who frequently had carried trade from Havana to New York, had been killed along with others of his crew by pirates at sea, surprised before dawn while in route to Port of Spain.

"It matters not," she said, when Alvis asked her how long ago he had perished. "He sleeps deep beneath the waves, where time is never counted."

This tragedy, it became apparent, was but one of the reasons Aletheia Landora despised the sea. Hers had been a wanting childhood in a fishing village where the men spoke in gruff tones and reeked of salt and the tar that clings to the ropes of the boats. There were women in the streets there, young widows, whose somber, lined expressions bore the grim tales of husbands perished in gales. Her own father had been a fishermen, and eventually there came the storm from which he did not return, leaving her to join her mother and elder sister working in various domestic jobs.

Both she and her sister were considered attractive and pleasant in temperament so people were glad to hire them. Eventually her sister married a bachelor lawyer for whom she cleaned and who was new to the village, and who took her away to Portugal after a year. As Aletheia moved into her sixteenth year, the men began to flirt with her more. Seafaring admirers would bring her fish or strange fruits, or even birds from the exotic places they had sailed. She kept the birds in a rusty old chicken cage and fed them moldy bread crumbs and leftover skins of fruits and vegetables. Among her suitors was one who owned his own trading vessel, seemed most likely to offer Aletheia escape from her poverty, and she consented to wed him before the village priest.

For a time after she married and when her husband was at sea, she was able to attend school in the small, crude building behind the docks. It was there she learned to speak English from a British missionary woman. As they practiced their English and performed their lessons, it seemed that everyone in the school constantly spoke of the sea: the teacher rhyming her maritime sonnets, the boys making wagers on the boat races, and the girls giggling about which of the young sailors they thought most handsome. By then Aletheia had convinced herself to hate and reject everything about the ocean: its winds and storms, the waterlogged ships, the very bows of the sloops, and especially the rough houses of the fishermen—so like her own. But beneath all these things and her passionate disavowal of them, loath as she was to admit it, the sea steadfastly remained Aletheia's confidant and lover—as it must to anyone who is born beside it. True, it was a love tinged with fear, bitterness, and hate, but unlike mortal men, the sea would never betray or abandon her. Deep within her, she knew that at the end of her days she would answer her lover's call and lie down to sleep with him.

Following her husband's death, there was a local man named Miguel who occasionally brought fish to Aletheia. He was a soft-spoken, older fellow, but his forgotten past was a dark one and in truth he richly deserved the hanging that would one day bring his life to its end. Aletheia took him for another suitor until one night there was a loud banging at the door and Miguel entered, drunk and red-eyed, muttering incoherently. He struck her twice before taking her roughly, muttering all the while, his body rank with the sour odor of rum and the docks.

When Aletheia discovered she was with child, she knew she must leave the village, since her husband was dead and she would never wed Miguel. After three days of walking along the coast, she turned inland and came upon the remote lonely cottage, its floor dirty, the dust long undisturbed. There she endured long lonely days with the sun and the breezes. Her favorite pastime was to lie upon the moss beneath the great banana tree at the edge of the forest, her eyes lifted to the bright yellow fruit amid the deep green foliage. She wondered at having a child and felt a warmth in her breast.

How she longed to leave the cottage, but the fear of someone glimpsing her in her condition was greater than her longing. So there were the days of waiting, the last few a torment—the terrible pains and then the endless, awful night. What misery she endured only to find the thing that emerged at last had neither breath nor life inside it. How she moaned and screamed even more at this new convulsion in her heart: the discovery that she had been deprived of the precious thing she had protected and endured for so long. When she was strong enough, she carried the little body to the beach and buried it beneath the sands.

Alvis had recovered entirely, his body, tanned now by the subequatorial sun, having regained much of its strength and thickness. He now swam in the ocean rather than merely gazed upon it, gliding over the swells with his strong, long-armed strokes. Outside Aletheia's cabin he no longer paced the edge of the forest, but plunged into it following game trails on journeys of increasing distance and duration.

Aletheia professed ignorance of the region's geography, but from the occasional fishermen he encountered who could speak a smattering of English and were willing to pause in their work to sketch maps in the sand, Alvis was able to assemble a rough understanding of the countryside surrounding him. Espírito Santo, he was informed by more than one seaman, was considered by Brazilians the smallest and poorest province in the entire empire. Wild and sparsely populated, it lay bounded to the north by Bahia, east by the ocean, south by Rio de Janeiro, and west by Minas Gerais. Its western border was traversed by low ranges of mountains, forming a northward continuation of a range known as the

Serra do Mar. To the south, he was told, the ranges were more broken and extended partly across the state toward the seaboard, while the eastern portion of the province in which Alvis found himself, the coastal plain, constituted the largest region—in many places lying low and swampy, while in others sand barrens, broken by isolated hills, purportedly stretched as far as the horizon. With the exception of these sandy plains, the country lay beneath heavy forest, even on steep mountainsides.

Alvis was especially interested to learn that beyond the coastal region existed a fertile plain, well suited for agriculture. There was, he regretfully was informed by the fishermen, only one good bay on the coast: the port of Victoria. All the other river mouths were obstructed by treacherous shifting sand bars and thus admitted small vessels only— a fact that concurred with what El Pinho had maintained as they discussed how best one might travel inland. Yet the lower courses of the state's rivers, he learned, generally were navigable. The greatest among them, the Rio Doce, the mouth of which lay less than three days' journey to the south, was friendly to man and boat for a distance of nearly one hundred miles.

Based on this rough knowledge he cobbled together from the fishermen, Alvis eventually established his plan of departure. The Rio Doce was familiar to him, for he had heard on board the *Aristides* that a number of Confederados had journeyed up it and that the land they had acquired was good, though the work and nature of their lives remained exceedingly difficult. Might they know something about acquiring a land grant? Could it be Lavinia was one of their number? It was mostly the urgency of the latter question which made him resolve to follow the shoreline to the mouth of that river.

He began making his preparations by steady degrees, but

thought better than to inform Aletheia of his intentions. If nothing else, he told himself, I owe her my kindness, though I know my destiny lies elsewhere.

Yet the tragedies of Aletheia's life had taught her to fear the worst even as all appears well. Though she had been reluctant at first to accept the foreigner from the fishermen who had borne him to her, she gradually came to view Alvis' arrival as something akin to a miracle: the eye in a storm of unhappiness. The sea had swallowed up her loved ones, just as it had swallowed up her dreams, and so she anxiously gauged by subtle signs his imminent departure, intimately knowing that he or she who has lost, and who fears the more, remains always the inferior and the sufferer.

Following a long day at the beach, during which he finally had resolved to take his leave on the morrow, Alvis returned to the cottage to discover Aletheia seated before a raging fire, plucking single hairs from her head and flinging them gently into the flames. She did not look at him, but the profile of her mouth turned ugly as she spoke with dog-voiced harshness.

"Did you think you might sneak away without so much as a word!" she exclaimed. "You men of the land know nothing. The very mother of the waters, Iemanjá, sent you to me!"

Alvis was silent, feeling not a little ashamed. "Your name," he said quietly at last, "whatever land I travel to, will endure so long as I have breath in my body and conscience in my spirit."

Aletheia did not reply and Alvis chose that quiet moment to depart the cabin with his humble provisions, returning to the beach and traveling a short distance south along the shore before lying down to pass the night.

Aletheia, sleepless with bitter wrath and sorrow, visited the beach herself in the dead of the low tide hours after midnight. Standing upon a high dune she cursed Alvis' name to the dark waves.

"Let him forever be driven by war, an exile," she prayed to the sea. "May he never find peace nor home! Let his remaining days be days of sorrow!"

The open glare of sand and vast ocean weighed heavily upon Alvis as he journeyed southward along the white-shelled beaches. The lonely openness of the landscape cultivated within him the feeling that he had strayed forth from his native land only to become a stranger everywhere he roamed. Birds of all colors fluttered and drifted on the coastal winds, and fish occasionally leapt from the water just beyond the swells, but he glimpsed no human as the miles steadily unfolded.

These unpeopled open leagues reminded him of his dispatch riding days near the end of the war, when he had returned to duty following the wound that nearly killed him. It was to regain his horse legs, he later learned, that Colonel Mosby had assigned him to run dispatch and the long hours, sometimes days, of riding without encountering another soul had aided him in regaining his mind as well. Ranging wide and free, he discovered the condition of the vast countryside, or his memory of it, significantly altered. Virginia had served as a battlefield for so long that nearly everywhere he journeyed bore evidence of the waste and extravagance of the war. Thus he witnessed many curious things alone, such as the excursion in the Shenandoah Valley during which he made camp on a night of heavy downpours in a little run-down shack amid a grove of oaks and beeches next to a creek, the trunks of the trees black with rain. When the showers ceased and he emerged with a hollow stomach shortly before dawn, a half dozen partially exposed corpses greeted him in the moonlight, the heavy rains having washed them from their shallow, sandy creek-side graves, revealing the grisly

smiles of their skulls in pale lunar relief. It was one of the
few times his solitude had seemed a burden, for he remained
little different than the next fellow in wishing to avoid encounters with death in lonely places at night.

Yet he preferred that occasion, awful as it was, to his dispatch duty during the Wilderness Campaign. He recalled
the hot, high winds that accompanied the days of battle and
how the news of Jeb Stuart's mortal wounds at Yellow Tavern was accompanied by a terrible lightning storm that same
evening which was said to have blown down the steeple of
St. John's Church in Richmond. He recalled the tangled
chorus of cries that arose from the wounded as he rode along
the battle line in the wake of the Bloody Angle, the trench
walls and floors slippery in places with the communal blood
of the fallen. When the rain began, water ran down the
muddy walls in red and pink streamlets, collecting along the
earthen floor in dark puddles. There had been, he was told,
perhaps four thousand men defending the salient and somewhere between twice and thrice as many hurling themselves
against it. Pistol, bayonet, and hand thrust and recoiled at
close quarters. Amid that confinement, the smells of the defenders, drifting here and there along the line, and coupled
with those of their enemies, proved nearly suffocating. Feet
slipped in the bloody mire or became entangled with the
limbs and parts of the corpses strewn beneath. Everywhere
the ground wore a film of detestable putrescence. Yet for all
this Alvis had borne and delivered his messages calmly and
matter-of-factly, most often at the behest of a youngish brigadier. He recalled the manner in which the sandy-haired fellow would hand Alvis his dispatch and cordially inquire after his intended route of delivery as though the two of them
were sitting amicably in a quiet Richmond dram house.

The empty beach, as he knew it must, eventually gave way to signs of habitation. When he arrived at the place where the Rio Doce emptied into the sea, its mouth yawning perhaps a mile, Alvis noted an assortment of small fishing boats beyond the clashing currents and breakers. He then turned inland, following a narrow riverside path in search of Povoacao, the little fishing village described to him as a promising place to secure a boat headed upriver. What he found however was less a village and more a loose assortment of a dozen or so poor structures with muddy footpaths passing between them, all set against a low, marshy landscape of tall grass stretching away from the river. The dwellings were very old and constructed of rock and mud with dingy tile roofs.

Alvis' cursory survey of the place was interrupted by a bustle unfolding along the nearby leaning river dock as fishermen, returning from their morning labor, glided their boats in and commenced to unloading the day's catch.

Trying his best to act as though he were on some errand, Alvis approached the nearest party of boatmen and, through a combination of hand signals and English words, attempted to make known his desire to travel upriver. The fishermen paused in their labor to peer at him with dull-eyed speculation, either not comprehending his intentions or choosing to withhold their responses from a strange foreigner clad in rags.

Abandoning his attempt, Alvis moved on to a big bald fellow farther down the dock loading wooden boxes into a collection of tethered canoes. Wordlessly joining the man in his work, Alvis proceeded, over the next half hour, to help load all the boxes, after which he repeated his meager combination of words and gestures, pointing several times upriver. At last the man appeared to understand and led Alvis off the dock and over to a group of fellows who sat resting on the riverbank beneath the shade of a great tree which vaguely re-

sembled a willow. The big man spoke rapidly in Portuguese
to the three men who sat together, motioning at Alvis several times. They afforded him a series of bored, appraising
glances as their river brother addressed them and, when he
had concluded, answered in short, clipped phrases. The big
man, turning to Alvis, lightly slapped his shoulder and nodded, and the boatman and foreigner sat down among the
others, who, Alvis gathered, were catching the last of their
rest before their journey.

Later that afternoon the party of stoic, rough-clad rivermen, Alvis among them, climbed into the three canoes they
had loaded earlier. Motioning him toward the front section
of the far tethered craft, his benefactor, whose name he had
learned was Bernardo, joined him in the boat. Sliding Alvis
a heavy oar, the big riverman loosed the mooring with a jerk
and shoved them away from the dock.

The Rio Doce is a deep, slow-flowing river which makes
it possible for strong men to make progress rowing against
the current. But the going of the boats remained a tedious
undertaking all the same, and before midday Alvis' back
ached and his hands, despite their callouses from the hard
toil of farm labor, began to blister. Yet he rowed on, aiding
their progress as well as he might, as they passed numerous
islands but no domiciles, the low-lying, sandy shores quickly
giving way on both sides to the stillness of dark, impenetra-
ble forest.

Though he had mastered a few words of Portuguese, Alvis had not the vocabulary to speak with his canoe mates,
but the simplicity of their undertaking and destination made
verbal communication of little moment. Bernardo, rowing
steadily behind him, would pause to tap a side of the canoe
with his oar to indicate on which side Alvis was to row. And

the need for this system became less frequent as Alvis gradually caught on to the maneuvering of the little vessel and the boatman's navigational style.

It was the custom of the rivermen often to break out into song toward late afternoon, to celebrate both their day's progress and the prospect of rest, the chorus of their voices echoing off the banks as they made landfall. Their meals consisted mostly of some variety of black bean, coupled with whatever strange-looking fish could be caught in the shallows. Lemon groves grew sporadically along the river, and the rivermen employed the sour fruit to flavor both the beans and the day's catch. In the evenings after dinner, the boatmen would stake all their paddles in the ground, oars up, and spread a great sheet for the night. Next morning, they would rise early at first light, nibbling at leftovers and breaking camp quickly.

Alvis found the simple work and speechless camaraderie reassuring. The rivermen were crude young fellows, yet they were not so different from the men Alvis had ridden alongside in Mosby's Rangers. In fact, he remembered his initial impression when he joined his regiment that nearly all the men riding with him were very young, perhaps as many as half of them younger than himself—a fact that, in the beginning, seemed to him ill-advised and perhaps even foolish. Once, while they were all bivouacked in a hollow of the Blue Ridge, one of these youngest fellows brought out a secret invoice of whiskey and it was not long before almost the entire party had fallen rollicking drunk. Colonel Mosby, having discovered too late the mischief, angrily paced to and fro among them, boxing an ear here and kicking a prone moaning body there, savagely cursing their inebriation all the while in the manner a pirate captain might berate his motley crew.

Later, after some weeks' service, Alvis finally realized Mosby had chosen these hard riding, reckless recruits on purpose: precisely because they were so young and thus heeded no danger. The dominant challenges of Mosby's style of war, Alvis came to recognize, were to keep awake during long sleepless periods and stay ready to fight at most any moment, whatever the odds and conditions. So these young brazen men, boys really—wild and drunk with their own youth and vigor and as yet untouched by mortality or defeat—served best Mosby's purpose despite the inevitable foolishness that occasionally entered into the bargain.

The days on the river proved long, their hours measured by the passing current and the circuit of the sun as its unremitting heat moved from Alvis' neck and back to his side and at last, toward the conclusion of the day, to his forehead and eyes so that it sometimes felt as though he was rowing into a blinding furnace. One night the mosquitoes became so thick and unbearable that their party wrapped the great sheet about them and huddled together rather than spreading it over the oars. The next night, mosquitoes diminished, they dispatched with the sheet altogether, making camp in an abandoned riverside cottage with a thatched roof and a muddy yard. A small herd of shaggy goats standing familiarly beneath the eaves waited patiently for the next bean shell or banana peel to come flying out the open doorway. Alvis slept that night in one corner of the cottage while a speckled hen set upon her nest in another.

Midmorning the following day, they emerged out of heavy river fog to glimpse the dilapidated wharf of Linhares, which, like the dock at Povoacao, listed rather to one side. Alvis helped the boatmen unload their cargo of salt and did his best to make known his thanks before slapping Bernardo on the shoulder by way of farewell and taking his leave. As he wandered up a slick, eroded trail, he glimpsed exposed beds of white and red clay in the riverbank. It was not until he reached a crest at the outskirts of the village that he realized Linhares was built upon a bluff, an orogeny which stood higher than the rest of the Doce's shoreline. Below him the river lay obscured by a pale mist, but the opposing bank revealed itself in the dark form of a great forest and, beyond it in the distance, the vague outline of a chain of shrouded mountains.

Turning from this prospect, Alvis entered the village and walked casually about its muddy streets, trying to establish his bearings. It was a significantly larger place than Povoacao and in better order, most of the houses appearing newer and built simply of clay with thatched roofs. The buildings, laid out in rows, formed a square around a large green common. Tile-roofed adobe dwellings appeared sporadically among the clay buildings, and there were open-doored structures as well which had the appearance of serving as stores or public buildings. The largest construction in the village resembled a half-built church, one of its sides open-ended and the beginnings of a steeple ascending slightly, its uppermost jagged reaches clutching at the sky.

People, women mostly, bustled about, occasionally affording Alvis curious, furtive looks. Indeed it seemed to him, as he walked and looked about himself, that women performed most of the work, even carrying great heavy vessels of water upon their heads, while many of the men he glimpsed loafed about, smoking on doorsteps or just inside windows. Most of the women wore lace-trimmed chemises or charming bodices with colored skirts. Near a back row of houses, standing out from the villagers and apart from everyone else, Alvis spied three figures he took to be Brazilian Indians, all of them nude save for the knives hanging from their necks, suspended by string. The heads of the Indians were shaved bald and though they appeared larger in body than the villagers, their limbs were quite small, affording them a peculiar, unbalanced appearance. The villagers, he noted, were well-formed and seemingly healthy, except for a little idiot girl he spied, possessed of a harelip and two long tusks protruding from her mouth, who tottered barefoot in an alleyway between cottages.

Behind the large building which had the appearance of an aborted church, Alvis paused to consider an old gravedigger at work on a fenced-in plot which served, he gathered, as an unmarked community burial ground. He watched as the stooped laborer, encountering an obstacle to his digging, reached down into his hole and tossed out bits of old femurs or skulls, clearing the remains of the long dead for the new set of bones in his charge. Something in this spectacle recalled in Alvis his time in the war, and he wondered idly as he stood there how fared now the bones of his friends and enemies alike, laid beneath the ground years ago in so many unmarked fields and groves.

"It is their custom," said a rich voice in English behind Alvis, interrupting his reverie, "to treat their dead in this manner."

Alvis turned to discover a bald, corpulent priest, of medium height and dressed in black robes, had joined him in considering the old man's work.

"Once in this graveyard," the priest continued, peering at the gravedigger, "I saw a little boy run over to a partially unearthed skull and, having studied it closely, call out, 'My old Aunt Calmou!' before tossing it back into the mud.

"Such is not what the church would fain see," the priest explained hastily, glancing at Alvis, "but it is of little moment to the commoner. Indeed, the Doce Brazilian may disturb his relatives from time to time, but he is always happy to see them."

The priest chuckled at his own jest before his fleshy, intelligent countenance relaxed into an expression of bemusement. "You are the newly arrived Confederado, I gather," he said, fixing his eyes full upon Alvis at last and affording him a speculative look.

"News in this village travels quickly, I see," observed Alvis, nodding and giving his name.

"I am Father Adelir," said the priest, now shifting his scrutiny to Alvis' rags, "and it will interest you to know you are not the first Confederado I have encountered, though certainly you are the most worst-for-wear I have yet seen."

"It is a condition I have grown used to," replied Alvis matter-of-factly, "and, indeed, one that should serve me well as preparation, if I am fortunate enough to join my countrymen and discover them in as poor repair."

The priest laughed heartily at this, belly jiggling beneath his robes. When he had mastered his merriment, he drew out from a pouch that hung from his rope belt a red handkerchief to mop his brow.

"It is always a joy to hear English," he said, "even if it be of the Confederado variety, and you speak well for one so shabbily attired. But shall we get out of this accursed sun?"

With that the priest led Alvis to one of the nearby open-doored buildings which served as a modest café, only a couple of its rough tables occupied. Alvis was wary of the man but wanted to learn what he knew of other Confederados and he struggled to quell in his heart the hope that Lavinia might be among them.

Once seated inside the café, Father Adelir ordered tea for them before inquiring of Alvis how he had come to arrive alone in that forsaken village. Eager to ply this priest for information in his turn, Alvis proceeded to recount the tale of his journey, leaving out the specific circumstances which had made it necessary and omitting the name of Aletheia Landora. The priest was silent as Alvis spoke, watching him steadily with the same speculative, appraising expression.

When Alvis had concluded, the priest raised his teacup to him. "My compliments on your unlikely survival, Mr. Stevens," he said. "Strangely enough, I did hear something of your story in the port of Victoria: the unlikely tale of some pale piece of sea trash that washed up on the shore of Espírito Santo, speaking English."

Father Adelir laughed once more. "Of course, at the time," he explained, "I took it for yet another meaningless fragment of the fanciful, incoherent babble those poor people generally are given to, though I admit on rare occasions truth may weave its way precariously into Brazilian port gossip."

When the priest had again mastered his merriment, the talk turned serious as Alvis inquired after the other Confederados Father Adelir had seen. The priest allowed his encounters with Alvis' countrymen had been sporadic, though he estimated, on the basis of river gossip as well as his own observations, that perhaps as many as half a hundred of them had journeyed upriver in the last year. They had settled, he said, on Lake Japaraná, to the north, clinging to each other despite their poor circumstances and seldom frequenting Linhares.

"Yet their plight has surprised me but little," continued Father Adelir, "The word Doce, you see, translates from the Portuguese as 'sweet,' yet the waters proved quite the opposite for the British company that attempted to open the river all the way to Minas Gerais years ago. It remains navigable only so far as Porto de Souza, a hundred miles inland, and the vast stretches in between are savage places, populated by marauding cannibals and given to malarial fevers."

Alvis fidgeted with his chipped teacup and stared at the greasy wooden tabletop, turning over this new information in his mind.

"Your countrymen who remain live in poverty," declared the priest, "but then so do most all who dwell here. Consider what you have seen in the short time following your arrival: a grisly overcrowded graveyard, an unfinished church, a wandering priest with neither flock nor home. These are, I am afraid, but the natural results of the history of a place such as this. You must take care, Confederado, you do not wind up robbed or beaten and left lying in the mud on one of the many lonely, ill-conceived roads."

Alvis thanked Father Adelir for his concern, a grim smile on his lips, and then chose that time to inquire after Lavinia and her family, describing them in detail.

"There was indeed a girl of exceeding beauty who matched the image you gave," recollected the priest. "Yet I remember her departing the place, returning downriver, several months ago with a small group of your countrymen. It was said her parents had perished of fever."

Alvis' countenance did not reveal what effect these words had on him and he let Father Adelir proceed in what appeared to constitute perhaps his favorite pastime: relating the story and circumstances of himself. Yet the gossip proved not devoid of interest as the priest recounted how his predecessor had financed the beginnings of a village church some years ago, but had been killed by Indians during one of his journeys to Rio de Janeiro, after which the villagers briefly converted the partially constructed building into a blacksmith's shop before abandoning it altogether.

"These Brazilian Indians," the priest elaborated, "the Botocudo, are cannibals and continue to be a threat throughout the river region. Indeed, the tribe closest to Linhares, the Nackinhapmás, are counted among the worst and were the instrument of a terrible tragedy in a nearby settlement several years ago. While the manager of that colony, a Dr. Nicolaú Rodrigues da França Leite, was away in Rio de Janeiro, the tribe came through the settlement and purposefully killed the dog of his near relative, a young man named Avelino. After a couple of weeks had elapsed, the tribe returned again and, finding nothing satisfactory to slaughter, burst in upon Avelino as he took his dinner. Stretching him out face down upon his table, they hacked at the back of his neck with a dull axe until finally he perished. Afterward, they cut him into little pieces using their knives and set fire to his hut, roasting his various parts upon the flames of his burning home and consuming them at their leisure. The loathsome devils rested and napped for a time following their blasphemous meal, before retiring back into the forest. It remains a mystery even now why they so despised Avelino, and the fact that he was engaged to a pretty local girl in Linhares made the incident all the more heartbreaking and heinous."

The priest scrutinized Alvis for a reaction but, receiving only his steady gaze, continued. "Even now the Nackinhapmás are known occasionally to steal livestock and abduct women from remote *fazendas*, spiriting them into the forest—sometimes to be ransomed, yet more often never to be heard from again. As with all godless places, this land will know no peace until these awful savages either are converted or purged from the forests."

Father Adelir's gaze had grown distant as he spoke, as if fixed on the prospect of the future purgation he had conjured. But then, suddenly, he seemed to remember Alvis.

"I am afraid a churchless priest such as myself can be of little use or encouragement to you, young foreigner," said the priest, "though I urge you to seek a living most anywhere other than along Lake Japaraná with the handful of your poor countrymen that remain. Yet there are still too many of them for what few primitive dwellings and limited food stores are there. Arriving among them now, you would count merely as one more mouth to feed. Such is the manner, here as elsewhere, of poor, wandering peoples."

"One thing you might tell me," said Alvis, interjecting at last, thinking of how he might secure the means to search for Lavinia. "Where might an able-bodied man go in search of work if he does not wish to add to the burdens of his countrymen?"

At this the priest turned his speculative look upon the gravedigger, visible through the doorway from where he was sitting, and still working steadily.

"To the west," said the priest at last, "there is an old English-speaking man, Evandero he is called, who lives alone on a large, rundown *fazenda*. He is one you might look to for work, if work is to be had in this poor country."

Alvis thanked the priest and when they rose from the table, they shook hands. Yet the naturally jolly demeanor of Father Adelir was grim as he bade Alvis farewell.

"God be with you, Confederado," said the priest. "I believe He does not often frequent the inland reaches of Espírito Santo, but for you I hope he will make an exception."

Following the priest's directions, Alvis wandered along a little-used thoroughfare, really more a trail than a road, the narrow cart ruts packed hard. It was his first incursion into one of the country's inland forests and he marveled at the dark lushness of the deep woods and how periodic wisps of steam or fog clung to the top of the canopy like irregularly-shaped pieces of cotton. It is said in Brazil that God is grand, but the jungle is grander, and to Alvis the shadowy forest seemed an altogether mysterious and alien region—far more so than any he had encountered to the north. Some of the tree trunks were as broad as houses, their massive roots snaking away in all directions. The light of day came and went, splitting the canopy in some places while failing entry everywhere else—blocked, as it were, to the degree that the visibility resembled that of dusk. Alvis felt as though he were venturing into the depths of an old tapestry, in some places faded and in others darkened with age, yet all marvelously rich. The sky, so elusive and rarely visible, served as a comfort whenever he glimpsed it, its precious fragments of sunlight falling through the foliage of the towering upper branches in fluctuating, hazy shafts.

The tired traveler might escape here the heat of the open road, but not the air's omnipresent humidity, which hung about Alvis' head and shoulders like some invisible heavy burden of steam. Yet he felt too a strange sense of comfort amid the variegated stretches, in the rare delicious breezes that periodically swept through, and upon the red clay bluffs which offered rolling variety, gentle climbs and glad descents, to the forested landscape.

By late afternoon Alvis had entered a hilly region and as he ascended a rise not so steep as the others he had traversed, the trail broke out of the forest into rolling fields on either side—overgrown in grasses and weeds, yet conveying the sure signs of prior cultivation. Before him, on a slight rise, the road passed by a small, weather-beaten old homestead, which stood partially obscured by a grove of assorted Brazilian trees. As Alvis neared the place, deep barks rang out and from beneath shady lower branches, bounded toward him two large gray dogs resembling mastiffs.

He stood as still as he might as the big canines barked

vehemently and danced about him. Yet even amid this furious activity, the dogs' tails wagged and their teeth remained unbared. He watched patiently until their onslaught abated before renewing his advance on the homestead. When he moved again, the dogs barked and circled him once more, though their protests now were sporadic and seemingly less vehement. Alvis walked on steadily, avoiding any sudden movements and accounting for the large creatures from the corners of his eyes.

As he neared the main structure, he passed a muddy pen housing an immense white sow with a new litter. The pig peered up at him, squinting and snorting contentedly as its piglets nursed in the gathering evening cool.

When Alvis' gaze returned to the homestead, a tall, stooping old man with disheveled white hair and a ruddy complexion stood watching him from the shaded doorway of the place. The fellow's face was broad, wrinkled, and tough-looking, yet fixed with an expression of kindness. He stepped out into the yard toward Alvis with a slight limp.

The elderly man's eyes having evidently sized up the stranger, he greeted Alvis in English spoken with a curious accent suggesting the unlikely combination of a native Brazilian who had successfully acquired the language and a British country gentleman. Refraining from inquiring after either Alvis' name or why he was there, the old man addressed him simply as traveler and invited him to dinner.

Inside the elderly man's crude, dim place of low rafters, laid out on a rough-hewn table, rested a bowl containing some indeterminate variety of soup. The old man motioned Alvis to a chair before passing him two gourds: one containing the soup and the other brimming with a sweet smelling liquid which Alvis recognized as cachasa, the Brazilian rum made from cocoa.

"I thank you for your hospitality," said Alvis, when he had been served, "but I must first insist on having the honor of my host's name before I consume his food."

"I am called Evandero," said the old man in his fine, venerable English, "and this is my *fazenda*, where it has always been my custom to welcome strangers of the road, however poor and hard put they may appear."

"To Evandero then," said Alvis, toasting the old man with the rum-filled gourd before sipping from it. Then he brought the soup gourd to his lips and commenced to gulp down its contents, choking as he emptied it.

Evandero smiled wryly. "You appear hungry enough to eat my very table," he observed.

Alvis wiped his mouth with the back of his hand and apologized for his bad manners, noting his journey up the Rio Doce had afflicted him with a pervasive, gnawing hunger accompanied by a fever that came and went. The nature of his condition, combined with the rum and his prior lack of regular eating also served to make him light-headed.

"It is of no moment," replied Evandero, assuring Alvis he was genuinely pleased to see him and that hospitality to wanderers was a common and important custom in remote areas since traveling strangers, he related, often brought desired news, good and bad, to such isolated places.

"It is the stuff of food," he continued, refilling Alvis' soup gourd, "for hungry and sometimes idle minds."

To this Evandero added that he had on occasion been called wanderer himself and remained an ardent admirer of chance, which he believed to be much like a woman.

"When she wants us," he observed, "we don't care, and when we do care, she is gone."

The old man's grin was met by an answering smile from Alvis.

"Tell me then," said Evandero, "What drives you along these backcountry paths, young foreigner? What brings you to my remote *fazenda*? And what passes in the world beyond it?"

Evandero's open manner and benevolent demeanor led Alvis to keep nothing from his host as he finished his soup, washed down the rum, and recounted his long tale, including his trials in Virginia, the shipwreck, and even his time with Aletheia Landora.

Evandero smiled when Alvis finished describing his hasty departure from that lonely woman of the sea. "Did she tell you Iemanjá had sent you to her?" he asked.

Alvis' tired nod was followed by an explanation from Evandero. "Since long ago," he said, "the women of the seaside have at once feared and loved the sea goddess Iemanjá, for she takes men for herself as well as bestows them, and she particularly desires brave men and lone travelers. They are her favorites, for they are the strongest of men and are like her."

Taking up his tale again following Evandero's explanation, Alvis concluded with a brief account of the priest he had encountered in Linhares and his hopes of recovering Lavinia before inquiring if there was in fact work to be had on Evandero's farm. Yet the old man merely smiled at this question and, noting Alvis' weariness, said they would speak of it in the morning.

"The word we use for farms such as mine is *fazenda*," said Evandero, showing Alvis to a primitive bed consisting of leaves, straw, and an old bear skin. "In Portugal the *fazenda* is known as the sesmaria, and it is used in reference to land bestowed by the crown. My *fazenda* is called Pallanteo."

"Rest here from your wanderings," said the old man. "May yours be the sleep of the just."

Alvis slept long and well that night, awakened finally by the kindly light of morning and birdsong beneath the eaves. The old man had laid out clothes and sandals for him to replace his rags and Alvis discovered they fit well enough, he and Evandero being of about the same height, though the shirt and pants were snug about the chest and thighs of the muscular young foreigner.

Evandero, seated in the same chair at his table, as if he had chosen to pass the night there, pointed at the small kitchen stove, upon which sat a dented kettle of coffee, and instructed Alvis to help himself. The younger man took up a gourd and poured himself a cup before joining his host at the rough table.

"You spoke last night of work," said Evandero, smiling, when they had established how each had passed the night, "when you were far too spent to perform any."

"Indeed," replied Alvis, "if nothing else, for the generous hospitality you have afforded me. Yesterday I took note of a broken carriage as I approached the house. Using some of its parts, I might build for you a buckboard wagon, a lighter and more maneuverable vehicle than the heavy oxcarts I have seen in these parts since my arrival. Such a wagon might prove some considerable use to you."

Evandero questioned Alvis closely on the nature of the work he proposed, revealing in the process an intellect likely containing enough knowledge to build such a wagon himself if he so desired. Yet, in the end, he accepted the young man's proposal.

"I have long pondered the prospect of cultivating my lands again," he said. "Perhaps a good wagon will serve to make me consider old intentions anew."

Alvis began laboring on the wagon that morning, grateful that Evandero had salvaged the carriage's spoked, iron-bound wheels and stored them inside the ruined passenger compartment. He saw in its skeletal remains the makings of something familiar. Owing to the lack of necessary tools, he proceeded slowly over the course of that week. Often Evandero would come out to the low dusty outbuilding where Alvis was working and watch him silently, occasionally asking a question about a method or technique.

Though it may have appeared Evandero was interested in learning something of North American wagon construction, it was in fact Alvis who desperately required and, in due course, began to receive instruction as to the nature of his surroundings.

When they conversed Evandero began to mix in, rarely at first but then with increasing regularity, Portuguese words and short phrases. And it became habit in the evenings that, when the table was cleared, Alvis would practice his reading by candlelight, using yellowed Portuguese newspapers Evandero had retained. The old man patiently corrected him as Alvis' lips shaped the unfamiliar sounds and sullied the translations. He enjoyed greater success once they moved on to Evandero's heavy Catholic Bible, translated by a Portuguese bishop. The language inside was equally unfamiliar and even more difficult, yet the stories were not and he began slowly to progress.

₧₨

Alvis discovered during those first few days with the old man that Evandero's agreeable and benevolent manner was something more than pretense. One could read his character in his visage, the deep wrinkles in the candlelight reminding Alvis of jagged, worn trail maps, bearing the observer up the face toward the wisdom dwelling within the eyes.

Alvis had become a fair judge of men during the war, and

he suspected that Evandero must have been made privy to some secret understanding of man's condition; and because he had been afforded access to this knowledge, felt pity and compassion for all men alike. Indeed, Alvis likened Evandero to such men as one would hope to fight beside in war. Possessing an understanding of both life and death, he looked upon their inevitabilities with a steady gaze.

When Alvis was not working or learning Portuguese, he took long walks on the *fazenda*, sometimes accompanied by Evandero and his great mastiffs, Atamga and Ubiranan, who bounded ahead of them on narrow game trails and crashed through the thick underbrush. During these excursions, the essence and beauty of the inland Brazilian countryside slowly revealed itself to Alvis. Many of the largest trees were wrapped with the enormous sepoy vine, which grows often to the size of a tree trunk itself, and there seemed everywhere an abundance of wild edible plants which Evandero readily identified: purslane, or hogweed and poke, which could both be eaten like greens; hillside Careh, which Alvis likened to an immense potato plant; and ginger roots, from which Evandero was fond of making preserves. Alvis discovered Evandero had become really more a gatherer than a farmer and marked well the places they visited to collect the countryside's bounty.

Game on the *fazenda*, Alvis discovered, was fruitful as well. Over the course of an afternoon fishing excursion, he learned to identify Evandero's favorite varieties of fish—piáu, piabá, and piabanha—committing to memory their distinct shapes, colors, and markings as they gutted and scaled them on cool water rocks.

Once, as Alvis rested beside a small river during a lone sojourn in the forest, a buff colored Anta burst out of a thicket and struck out into the waters with Atamga and Ubiranan in close pursuit. As they rested in the midst of another woodland jaunt, Evandero informed him of the unlikely fact that the Barbados monkey offered some of the finest meat in the region while they sat watching the little creatures swinging and chattering in the branches above the trail. Yet the eerily human motions and behaviors of the creatures made Alvis loath to test their culinary attributes.

When he informed Evandero of his feelings on the subject, the old man chuckled and recounted to him the tale of an Italian settler who, some years back, new to the region and desperate for meat, had set out to harvest a Barbados for his supper. When the man fired upon the first one he saw, which sat watching him inquisitively on the lower limb of a great tree, the creature fell to the ground much as a person might and lay there wailing, clasping the wound at its side with its little fingers. When approached by his attacker, the little monkey held out a small palm in defense or supplication, soaked though it was in blood. The Italian settler proceeded to slit its throat and cut off its hands and head before demanding of his wife to prepare it for the evening meal.

The woman, horrified but obedient, shoved it into the oven quickly. Then her fear and discomfort conspired to make her leave it in for too long a time, so that when it was withdrawn it looked like some ancient mummy child, deprived of its hands and head yet bearing still some remnant implication of the bodily motion and mechanics that also serve as our own.

Though they harvested no monkeys, Alvis ate well at Evandero's table as he labored on the buckboard wagon. At the hazy conclusion of days, they dined on the things they had gathered and concluded their meals with desserts of tapioca cakes and spiced farinha balls which, like everything else, were served in gourds. The gourds of Brazil, Alvis learned, grow on trees rather than vines and thus appeared odd to him hanging in such a manner, the suggestion of the familiar wrought in peculiar terms—like so many other phenomena in his new country. He would reflect on such things while sitting on a favorite log at the edge of a stream, watching the crawfish drifting along the black, muddy bottom, their pincers and antennae swaying gently on the current.

Having convinced or sufficiently annoyed Evandero that the purchase of a few necessary parts would speed his work on the wagon, Alvis set out early one morning for Linhares, retracing his steps through the deep Brazilian forest. The trip took longer than he had calculated and, indeed, Evandero had warned him the village was farther than Alvis recalled. In the end, however, the old man did nothing to discourage the journey and bade Alvis farewell with the benediction, "May the powers of fortune go with you."

Linhares appeared smaller and quieter to Alvis than the first time he had entered it, and he gathered his parts from the shop appointed by Evandero without incident. Yet the old man's prediction of the errand's distance proved accurate and the return journey spanned into late afternoon and then dusk.

It was amid this gathering time of night that a small, heavily bearded figure clad in filthy rags stepped out from the forest onto the trail ahead of Alvis, speaking loudly and flailing his arms about him. Though Alvis had mastered a fair amount of Portuguese by this time, the man's sentences sounded of gibberish as he came on toward him. Alvis attempted a few words of greeting to no avail when the little man halted before him, eyes wide, arms windmilling in their shoulder sockets, volume of his voice as loud as ever.

"This must be some madman or dire sufferer of jungle fever," Alvis thought. But even as he speculated he heard too late a footfall behind him, a stealthy impression of sound beneath the raised voice of the diminutive man before him, and as he turned a heavy blow connected with the back of his head. He glimpsed the mud of the road rising toward him, the vague imprint of a footprint in a puddle, before all went black and he knew no more.

☙   ❧

He awoke shortly after first light with a terrible head-ache and a growing awareness of a steady scraping noise. At first he believed the methodical sound issued from his ailing skull, yet as he struggled to a sitting position, a richly paint-ed coach drawn by four handsome horses appeared from around the near bend in the forest trail and rolled toward him. Maintaining its speed, the cloaked driver deftly guided his graceful prancing team around Alvis' place in the road. But as the carriage went by him two things happened: a passing wheel splashed mud on him and a pretty female face, ghostly and wide eyed in the pale light of morning, appeared in the vehicle's window, peering down at his wretched form.

Then it was gone and he was left alone with a painful hum in his head. Feeling at his belt, he discovered the pouch containing the small quantity of leftover coins was no lon-ger with him, but looking about in the mud he spotted the pivoting joint he had purchased and the sack containing the custom fitted bolts and rods. Rising stiffly, head pounding with renewed vigor, he staggered down the road, wincing with each footfall.

He traveled very slowly, pausing occasionally to drink and splash water on his face and neck where tiny brooks snaked their way across the trail. He did not reach the *fazenda* until late afternoon, his arrival heralded by the barking of Atamga and Ubiranan, who bounded out to greet him, licking at his hands and nosing the bottom of the sack he bore. Evandero, seated on the porch, watched Alvis without expression as he came to stand before him, haggard-faced and covered in dried mud.

"I have fetched the parts I needed," announced Alvis in a tired voice, setting down the sack and pivot joint, "but I fear the remnant of the funds you lent me did not survive the return journey."

Evandero maintained his silence and lack of expression as he looked Alvis up and down. Then the wrinkled corners of his mouth began to twitch as if some master puppeteer had begun to jerk at the strings which gave the lips expression and life. Suddenly Evandero's head went back and his mouth opened, revealing a set of even white teeth, and from it spilled forth the old man's laughter, loud and hearty in the gathering shadows of late afternoon.

When Evandero had caught his breath he handed to Alvis a gourd filled with cachasa and gestured to the crooked chair beside him.

"Sit and have a rest," said the old man, and as Alvis did so the mastiffs settled themselves on the rough boards between the feet of the two men.

As he surveyed the front yard Alvis noticed Evandero had released Robinho, the little blackish-gray donkey he kept out back of the dwelling, to graze the tall grass. Alvis was fond of the creature's spirit: how he would go to great lengths to shake off his rope halter, after which he would hop about in celebration, braying like some demented circus pony.

A long contemplative silence ensued as the men sipped their cachasa and considered the donkey's grazing amid the arrival of dusk. Every now and then, Alvis would raise a hand to feel the knot on the back his head or pick at the flaking trail of dry blood on his neck.

At last, Evandero spoke. "So now it is time I give you a lesson in earnest," he said, "which lies, after a fashion, behind your own learned lesson today. It is true that this place is a land rich in forests and ruffians, but Brazil, my young friend, is much more than hungry people, poisonous snakes, and lush palm trees. It was founded, you already know, by the seagoing Portuguese who were at once wealthy, terrible, and glorious. When you truly master the language I will have you read Camões' 'Os Lusiadas,' which is the great epic poem of the Portuguese and celebrates their long story, which, though somewhat muted, reverberates within us even now. Why such a great people should happen upon Brazil is an unlooked-for happenstance, as indeed I have found life and history to be, more often than not."

He drank again before continuing, Alvis listening attentively, realizing it was no idle tale Evandero wished to convey. "In brief," he resumed, "the rich old Portuguese gentlemen desired hot Indian spices for their food and sent forth a fleet to determine the shortest route to that part of the world. Yet, to their great surprise, they discovered a body of land where—according to their maps, which were the best known to man at that time—there should have been only water. So they went ashore, not far to the north from here, in what is today southern Bahia, and encountered the natives—a handsome, shiny eyed, stoic people—and made gifts to them. There they planted a great wooden cross on the shore and held mass before departing for India, everyone believing the place they had come upon to be a charming island. In time Vespucci would discover otherwise, but the Portuguese remained more interested in India and its metals and spices.

"When they did eventually resolve to settle the northern coast, the delegation was a motley crew of noblemen, priests, government people, skilled workers, and soldiers. They brought with them no women so, naturally, the development of the Brazilian—part European, part Indian—began to take place, joined later by the African. In fact, some of the first Portuguese to settle in Brazil were Jews who had fled the Inquisition.

"So you see ..." Evandero, glanced over at Alvis with mischievous eyes before draining the last of the cachasa. "We are a curious and complicated—even dangerous—people at our very essence."

⁗⁗⁗

For the next three days Alvis worked on the wagon, but Evandero's history lessons temporarily took the place of his translation exercises and continued almost nightly by firelight as they smoked from old clay pipes and drank cachasa. Among many other things, Alvis learned that he continued to underestimate the sheer immensity of Brazil. In early times its four great sections, called capitanias, each had been administered by a Portuguese fidalgo, but the truly dominant figures of the country's dawning era had been the senhores de engenho—the sugar mill owners— who did as they pleased, invoking civic order or chaos as they saw fit. Many of them, Evandero maintained, were terrible men—cruel overlords. The plantations that fed the mills required workers, even more so as the European demand for sugar escalated, and this arrangement of pressures would lead to the birth of Brazilian slavery and the arrival of the African. Bloody and terrible as it was, the system sustained the country and the senhores de engenho grew richer still, sending their sons to study law at the best places in Portugal, that tiny Iberian realm to which so much Brazilian identity continued to be owed. Often it was only the black-clad missionary priests, albeit usually corrupt in matters of money and flesh, who pled for, or even thought about, the plight of the enslaved Africans and oppressed Indians, though they too had made use of them in earlier times. The mixing of Indians and Africans produced the cafuso, while the merging of Indians and Portuguese resulted in the mamelucos. The old Portuguese language, descended from the venerable Spanish Latin, was broadened in Brazil by the Indian and African dialects with which it vied for utterance and space.

Since their long evening conversations on Brazil's history often appeared meandering and apocryphal to Alvis, he was thus astonished—filled with a new admiration for Evandero's mind and intelligence—when he realized they collectively had led, gradually and indirectly, up to himself in the form of the ongoing Brazilian interest in foreign settlers to help work and develop the country's immense interior.

Colonization, Evandero related, had always been an objective of the Brazilian government, King Joao VI having welcomed the first modern European foreigners, predominantly Germans and Swiss, earlier that century. However the government had argued over whether to try and attract small land-holding farmers or unskilled laborers, and whether or not the venture should come from public or private coffers. In any case, by the 1860s colonization had become attractive for a number of reasons: the establishment of a more representative government, a desire for the development of the Amazon region, and a slow push for the universal emancipation of servants accompanied by the design of a free labor system. In particular, Evandero recalled the Immigration Law of 1860, which allowed for free and self-governing colonies, thus leading directly to the arrival and tenuous existence of Confederado groups.

Here, Alvis at last could contribute something to Evandero's tale and interject what his kinsman Bocock had conveyed to him: that Brazil had established regional immigration offices in New York City, Richmond, Savannah, Mobile, and New Orleans to attract North American settlers.

Evandero, unsurprised, countered that the general reaction to all this among everyday Brazilians ranged from mixed to negative on account of the sorts of immigrants such calls had attracted.

"I have heard tales," said Evandero, "of North American immigrants, those who come from your sad, awful cities, brawling, stealing, mugging, and vandalizing. Most of them have wound up impressed into service against the Paraguayans, begging in the streets, or languishing in our jails."

Alvis shook his head, a little ashamed of his countrymen, yet also not wholly surprised on account of the chaos unleashed by the war.

"Some," Evandero went on, "the worst of them, have been dispatched via firing squad in the wake of their various crimes.

"You must be given to understand," he concluded emphatically, "there are many here who will never look kindly upon your presence, no matter how many wagons you build or fish you prepare."

Notwithstanding Evandero's instruction and warning, Alvis visited Linhares on two more occasions without incident, though it seemed notable new aspects of the culture revealed themselves to him constantly. During one of his sojourns, a strange parade of grotesque figures rolled by in the street, followed by a happy crowd and shrieking children. In the procession were devils with horns, four footed beasts, and mula sem cabeça—the "Headless Mules"—which, he was informed by a fellow onlooker, constituted the legendary forms taken by the elusive mistresses of priests.

During these village excursions, Alvis also was able to favorably employ his growing knowledge of Portuguese, using it to discover, among other things, a little about the background of his host. From the beginning, despite his cultural ignorance as a foreigner, Alvis had recognized Evandero as an atypical Brazilian and the village consensus bore this out, describing him as a poor but honorable hermit given to drink and curious ways. His father long ago had been a legendary messenger in the Emperor's court and a friend of the village eponym, Count Linhares. Evandero, strong and handsome in his youth, had married a beautiful woman who perished along with a daughter during an outbreak of fever. He eventually married again but lost his second wife as well. He vanished altogether from village life shortly thereafter and more than one person, when Alvis inquired after him, asked incredulously if he was still alive.

As Alvis mastered the proper expressions and motions to accompany his growing knowledge of the language, the locals began to speak to him more comfortably and openly. On the second of his village trips he was alerted, via his conversations with a number of storekeepers and loafers, to a momentous impending event described by locals as a great hunt in which representatives of all the local farms were expected to participate. There had been, he was informed, for some months now a great serpent, a prodigious anaconda, plaguing a number of the *fazendas* near Linhares. The creature's eyes, it was said, glowed in the night with bloodshot yellow fire and there were those who claimed that when it hissed, a kind of lightning came forth from its mouth, scorching nearby leaves and grass by virtue of its poison. It had collected livestock from two dozen *fazendas* along the Doce—everything from laying hens to half-grown calves—

and it crushed the young shoots of growing crops, cutting short their ripeness, as its mighty form, seven men in length and as big around as the neck of a mammoth steer, came and went. The village market had come to await its promised harvest in vain, on account of the serpent's great appetite. No herdsman or dog, nor even the fiercest of bulls, had succeeded in defending the livestock. And even many of the people had become fearful, lying awake at night, besieged within their own walls by a creature said to have a maw that might consume them and their children whole.

When Alvis reported this news to Evandero and offered to represent the *fazenda* in the hunt on his behalf, the old man was pleased and brought out from a dusty chest an antique single shot pistol for Alvis to bear with him. Then he offered steady words of warning to accompany the bestowed sidearm.

"This creature," he said, "is not so devilish as it is described, but it is every bit as large and can crush the life even from a man as strong as you if you allow its coils to encircle you."

"If you encounter it, aim carefully and shoot for the head," counseled Evandero. "May the powers of fortune go with you."

❧❧

Early on the morning of the appointed day of the hunt there gathered on the village green the representatives of all the local *fazendas*, many of them handsomely attired and longing for glory, and all of them carrying spears or pistols or both. A mixed pack of hunting dogs barked at the assemblage and each other from beneath the shade tree where an impromptu corral had been thrown together to hold them. Notable among these virile men of the region were the Avila twins, one of them famous on the river for boxing, the other for his graceful horsemanship; Mathias and Maximino, young and unproven with their weapons but renowned for their good fellowship and courage; Atilio and Thiago, the dexterous sons of Henriques; steady Lino and swift Jeronimo, the pride of Ida; mighty Emilio, the petulant and prideful bastard adopted by the wealthy Ferreira family; and other young men, large and small, remote and renowned.

Notable among the assembly, for she was no man, was tall Camilla, the great huntress who had once been a servant but had purchased her freedom by degrees through the meat and pelts she harvested from the forest. A polished brooch hung from her neck and she wore her black hair simply, caught in a single knot. A leather quiver hung from her left shoulder, containing arrows which rattled as she sauntered among the men, frankly appraising their faces and arms. Her bow hung across her chest and in her right hand she clutched a thin, razor-tipped spear which matched her in height.

It was rumored Camilla had killed her husband, a riverman legendary for his good singing voice and terrible cruelty, but this did nothing to inhibit the desire of many a fellow who gazed upon her. Yet most of them feared and resented her, even as they loved her, as a result of the implicit threat she presented in embodying much of that which made them men.

"O happy the man whom she might find worthy!" announced friendly Mathias to his circle of companions, as he watched her skirt the edge of their company.

However time did not allow Mathias and his companions further appreciation or words, as the task at hand took precedence and the assemblage of hunters was organized into pairs. Alvis, standing off to the side in the rough old clothes of Evandero, pistol shoved down into a cracked, weatherbeaten belt, came forward to receive his companion.

Either by chance or careful determination—the fear among the others at having to hunt alongside a woman or foreigner—Alvis was paired with Camilla. Yet as he went to greet her he was met by a face of stone, which considered him with dark, expressionless eyes. They held neither malice in them nor warmth, but rather the simple look of disinterest in the proximity of matters of far greater import.

Their organization complete, the hunting party proceeded as a group west of the village and into an old stand of forest thick with mighty trees which had never been cut. When they reached a clearing they all wished each other luck and broke off into their teams, those who had brought dogs loosing them from their leashes, while others speedily struck out in different directions along various trails, keen to discover their quarry.

Deep in the forest was a place where the trees gave way to a valley that collected streams of rainwater. Along its rocky floor grew smooth sedges and marsh grasses, and osiers and tall bulrushes, which swayed on the breezes above the lowly reeds. It was in this valley that four of the dogs found the serpent and roused it from its rest.

When the first men arrived, having followed the sound of the frenzied canine chorus, they could not see the serpent, its body obscured by the thick bushes and underbrush. Yet as they peered closely at the area where the dogs danced and barked, the flora suddenly erupted into agitation in a pattern suggesting something large advancing rapidly along the valley floor toward the place where they stood. In this way, completely invisible, as if guided by some malicious intellect, the anaconda charged into the midst of its enemies like lightning forced from colliding clouds. The woods crashed and echoed as it drove into them, thrashing its massive body in all directions and knocking men to the ground.

When it had passed among them once, it turned and charged again, scattering the dogs, putting the now-baying pack to flight with sidelong swipes of its tail. The first spear, delivered by Maximino's arm, proved ineffectual, and gave the trunk but a glancing blow. The next, hurled by Emilio, was aimed at the creature's back—and certainly would have stuck there had it connected—but the throw was too long.

Then Thiago cried out amid the fray: "Lord God, I have worshipped you long! Grant what I ask! Let my spear strike true!"

Thiago flung his weapon and his prayer was answered. The mighty serpent was hit, but the impact failed to penetrate the scales and thus left no wound. Now the beast's anger was aroused, and blazed out no more gently than lightning. Yellow cinders seemed to burn in its eyes, and its great flickering tongue was as a flame breathed from deep within its chest. With dangerous and unerring momentum, it launched itself among the young men as a heavy stone flies forth from a taut catapult aimed at walls or battlements full of soldiers. Maximino and Mathias, brothers in peace as well as in the hunt, were laid out upon their backs, stunned by the impact of the thrashing tail. The creature then recoiled and struck at Atilio, who knelt on the ground loading his pistol. Seizing him about the neck with its enormous maw as a dog might a rat, the serpent shook Atilio violently in its jaws before flinging his body, its spirit departed, against the trunk of a mighty tree.

Now the creature turned its attention back to Mathias and Maximino, the former of whom was attempting to drag his unconscious sibling into the underbrush. Yet it was then that Camilla, followed by Alvis, burst forth from the woods. The huntress paused to string a swift arrow and sent it speeding from her curved bow. The razor-sharp shaft lodged near the top of the serpent's back and the creature convulsed. Then, as if understanding this new threat of projectiles hurled from afar, the anaconda turned and vanished into the dense woods as quickly as it had struck, disturbed bushes and limbs marking its progress as it slithered away along the forest floor at great speed.

Camilla and Alvis followed, the foreigner hard pressed to keep pace with the long-legged huntress, who deftly sidestepped branches that would have struck him full in the face and leapt over roots that stubbed his sandaled toes.

The hunters, pursuing some distance back, marveled at their speed. And it was Emilio among their number who was first to discern the trail of blood on the ground.

Pointing out the crimson traces to his companions, he lamented, "Camilla will be honored for drawing first blood and now speeds ahead to the kill, while we have nothing to show for our efforts!"

The men flushed with shame and redoubled their efforts, urging each other on with harsh words and, as is often the case with men who are afraid, working up their courage with the sound of their collective racket.

Up ahead Camilla paused to survey a flat area of forest where no foliage moved. The serpent either had lost them or paused there, motionless, hoping perhaps to elude its pursuers by going to ground. Alvis leaned forward, hands braced on his knees, gasping for breath.

Having listened carefully for some time, Camilla knelt, picked up a rock, and cast it out into the underbrush. She listened carefully, but all was silent.

The next sound the unlikely hunting tandem discerned was the loud approach of their companions as they crashed through the forest behind them, shouting and clashing their arms.

Joining the woman and the foreigner, the men established the status of the hunt and resolved to spread out systematically so as to canvass the area and thus force the creature out from wherever it hid, if in fact it still lurked in the vicinity.

A slow search ensued with the hunters poking among the thickets with sticks and spears. After a time some in their number began to despair and conclude the creature had eluded them.

Yet, it was the more powerful of the Avila twins, Atlaseo, whose fists had been likened to thunder, who spotted the creature at last where it lay motionless beneath some bushes, next to a great rotted log matching it in color.

Never one for subtlety or much forethought, Atlaseo sprang toward the anaconda, exclaiming loudly, "Learn now, beast, how a man strikes more powerfully than a girl!"

Swollen with pride at his boastful words and the apparent obliviousness of his quarry, Atlaseo raised the axe he bore and, standing on tiptoe, poised himself for a mighty downward blow. But even as he did, the anaconda rose suddenly, faster than human motion, and whipped its body so that it struck Atlaseo hard between the legs, laying him out in agony.

Then the fight was on anew. Hot-headed Emilio, hungry for glory, raised his pistol and fired. Though well-aimed, the bullet was deflected from its trajectory by a low-hanging leafy branch. Then Giraldo, a notorious drunkard who had been sipping cachasa all morning in an effort to strengthen his resolve and calm his nerves, cast his spear, but the throw was fatally awry, flying well beyond its intended target and lodging itself in the chest of steady Lino, who stood preparing to attack on the other side of the serpent. Uttering a despairing groan, Lino dropped to one knee, his arms hanging uselessly at his sides. So it is in life that the good and reliable too often perish at the hands of the weak and foolhardy.

Even as the men cried out at the awful fate which had befallen Lino, Camilla cast her slender, sharp-bladed spear, which fixed itself in the middle of the serpent's long back. The creature raged and twisted its prodigious body round, hissing, before plunging into the brush and fleeing once more. The hunters took up the pursuit again, Camilla at the head—all except Jeronimo, who knelt wailing at his brother's side, cradling his lifeless head.

The anaconda fled now in the direction of the river, its preferred haven and home, slithering down a narrow ravine, loosening earth and rocks as it went. Men slid and fell as the hunters came after it, following their prey downward into the flood plain. As a body they rushed on, fueled by righteous determination or prehistoric blood lust—who could say which?—the serpent's bloody trail across the bottom land palpable and slippery beneath their muddy-soled sandals and boots.

It appeared they would be too late, for even as Camilla arrived, first among them, at the Doce's riverbank, she spied the creature already in the water, the downstream current pink and cloudy with its blood. She strung her bow and fired at it twice, both of the shots sailing awry on account of her heavy breathing, then lifted her face to the sky and howled in despair, deprived as she was of her quarry. Arriving beside her, Alvis fixed his eyes on the snake, and placing Evandero's old pistol between his teeth, shed his faded garments. Entirely naked, he waded out into the river and began swimming toward the beast.

There being no swimmers among them, the party of hunters watched mutely as the foreigner's steady strokes carried him closer to the creature, which continued making its way slowly to the opposite side. Alvis nearly had come even with its tail by the time its great reptilian head made landfall and began nosing its way up the muddy red bank.

When he reached the shallows where he could stand, Alvis grasped the serpent's tail and pulled on it, attempting to tumble the beast back into the waters of the Doce. Yet the creature proved far too heavy to impede, much less move. Giving up this plan, Alvis splashed toward the river's edge and clambered up the bank. Locating the serpent's head in the tall grass, he removed the old pistol from his mouth and took careful aim. When he pulled the trigger, however, there ensued only a dry, metallic click.

Alvis let the pistol drop to his side as he looked about him. The creature, its wounds foaming and oozing blood, was making limited progress in the tall grass, as it extracted the hind end of its great injured body from the river. His gaze shifted from the creature to the bank and there spied in the mud a great rock. Running to it, Alvis jerked and pulled at the object to no avail. Then, remembering his dysfunctional sidearm, he retrieved it and thrust the barrel of the pistol into the mud beside the heavy piece of stone, digging and prying at it. Working fast, he wiggled the rock on all its sides, until at last the mud relinquished the small boulder with a loud sucking sound.

Grunting, the scar on his forehead flushed hot, Alvis lifted the large rock to waist level and staggered toward the anaconda. Tracing the outline of its body, he located the creature's head in the grass swaying this way and that, searching out its next move, tongue aflicker. With another grunt, he threw down the rock upon the head of the mighty serpent, striking a terrible blow to the side of its skull. The creature's prodigious body writhed into motion, the undulating torso knocking Alvis to the ground as if he were a child's plaything. As he lay there, attempting to recover his wind, the body, sensing the position of its attacker, began coiling itself about his thighs—once, twice—tightening with unbelievable force, cutting off the circulation to his feet.

Alvis desperately felt about himself in the grass for something, anything as the creature's bloodied head rose, swaying, before him. His right hand cut itself on fragmented rocks, pebbles, and then it seized onto something larger. As the snake's head came toward his own, Alvis brought up a fist sized rock in his hand, swinging it in a wide arc—roundhouse style—so that when it struck the serpent it did so on the side of its head, connecting with a harsh wet thud.

The anaconda's visage shook and listed to one side as its grip on Alvis' lower body relaxed. Lunging forward from the stunned coils, he again struck the mighty serpent hard upon the head. Now the creature was on the defensive and sought protection by hiding its bloodied skull beneath one of its coils. Yet Alvis was quick to renew the onslaught and, kneeling again beside the great rock, lifted it once more before bringing it down upon the serpent's body and head, mashing and pinning them to the ground with a sickening crunch.

Though the creature's head lay crushed, the skin of its hinter parts continued to ripple and flex for some time, the reptilian body's instinctual attempt to extricate itself from its predicament continuing, even when the brain could no longer dictate its course of action.

The great serpent had ceased moving by the time the hunting party arrived, having found a rocky place upstream to ford the river. They marveled for a moment at the nude foreigner who rested near his kill and then gave proof of their joy and admiration, shouting, and crowding about him to grasp his hand in theirs. Afterward, one by one or in pairs, the men gazed wonderingly at the huge creature which covered so much of the earth where it lay, some of them loath to touch it, others attracted by the spasmodic rippling of its skin.

The hunting party, having gathered its dead and wounded, returned to Linhares, sad for the families of Atilio and Lino yet proud at having collectively rid the countryside of its menace. Following an impromptu celebration in the central local tavern, a brief ceremony ensued on the village green, during which the mayor of Linhares presented to Alvis a purse of gold. Yet even as he stood with the official, Alvis called for Camilla, still disappointed at not having killed the beast herself, to join him and requested to have the purse split between them since her wounding of the creature had resulted in his own opportunity to kill it. To this all agreed, though some of the men, Emilio the loudest, still mumbled in sore protest at the woman's involvement in the hunt.

"Destilado!" exclaimed Evandero that night when Alvis arrived back at the *fazenda*, not a little drunk with celebratory spirits, and recounted the day's events. "You are master of the hunt!"

Next morning Alvis, late in rising, awoke to find his limbs sore—his legs and thighs bruised—but nonetheless spent the remainder of that day completing his work on the buckboard wagon. He had some money now, though not enough to resume his search for Lavinia, and felt he had little time to waste. It troubled his mind to think that if she was still in Brazil—and he had secured no news of her, despite offering her description to travelers in Linhares—then it was possible she was moving farther from him with each passing day. Perhaps she had boarded a northbound ship already and returned to the land he could never visit again. He recalled how the thought of her had kept him going during the war—how his love-driven fixidity of purpose afforded the daily events of the conflict, however terrible they sometimes were, a certain measure of surreal detachment, as if they were happening to someone else. He would remember a saying of his father's at such times: "We are but horsemen passing by, the hooves carrying us away from here, into an uncertain future, as we cast a cold eye on life and death alike."

In quiet moments, when a prolonged measure of calm was lent to the war, Alvis would think of the things he and Lavinia would do together when the hostilities at last concluded: how next Christmas they would dance the "Virginia Reel," after which he would lead her beneath the mistletoe and kiss her there in front of everyone. In entertaining himself with such fancies, he realized he was no different from many other men who sought strength to bear the immense burden of their sufferings through the image of a beautiful woman and the ghostly life they might share in some hazy future time. War, he discovered, is rich in time; it demands a habit of deferring and postponing. So why not dwell upon a beautiful face and the prospect of elaborate future plans? By hook or by crook, he had determined to last it out—to beat it—and he had, barely. Now the same face, the same hope—faint though it was—guided him in his labors and lent them speed.

Prior to the hunt, Alvis had been working with Robinho, having the little donkey drag his reins and then graduating him to a crudely constructed sled which he pulled about the yard, leaving grooved lines in the grass. Now Alvis brought Robinho out from his lot in back of the homestead and hooked him to the wagon. Speaking to him softly, he urged the small animal forward and the wagon rolled after him, its wheels smooth and quiet in their turning. Watching from the porch, Evandero clapped when Robinho had steadily pulled the wagon about the yard in a complete circle. Alvis motioned to him and the old man climbed aboard. Together they took a long, slow ride about the *fazenda*, not returning until mid-afternoon.

ဆာ

Now Alvis' mind, molded and forced by the events of his life to be ever canny and forward-thinking—and propelled by the long-held yearnings in his heart—fixed itself upon the pursuits that might allow him to resume his search. He had observed closely the main crops in the area—sugar cane, tobacco, coffee, cotton, and mandioca—as well as the nature of the market in Linhares, and had come to believe watermelon, pumpkins and other North American vegetables might perform well in the *fazenda*'s rich loamy ground. These were unusual crops for Brazil and he was forced to great lengths to special-order the exotic seeds by post from Rio de Janeiro. With these and other crops in mind he proposed to Evandero the cultivation of the *fazenda*'s long-fallow fields. In this venture Alvis pledged to invest the sum of his reward from the hunt so that the old man stood to lose nothing, but would receive a full half of any profits. To this Evandero agreed, smiling indulgently and expecting nothing, but curious to see how the young foreigner would fare in this new endeavor.

That spring Alvis planned the organization of crops, learning from Evandero what had worked well on the *fazenda* before and questioning local farmers in detail whenever he encountered them along the roads or in Linhares. His foremost problem, he understood, was labor: men to plant, maintain, and harvest the ranging fields. Though servitude as an institution still existed in Brazil, only a very few of the largest and most wealthy *fazendas* along the river enjoyed the luxury of owning their field workers. The more common method of securing farm labor, Evandero informed him, lay in hiring out enxadeiros, the unskilled field hands or hoers of the earth, who roamed the region lending their services with the changing of the seasons and the rotating of crops.

The services of the enxadeiros had to be competed for and Alvis, despite his still substantial local fame as the destroyer of the great serpent, initially lost out in his bid for workers, largely on account of his foreignness and the peculiar quality of the crops he proposed to raise. The enxandeiros, after all, did not desire the reputation for having planted and cultivated something that did not perform well. Confident in their handling of familiar Brazilian crops they balked at the Confederado's talk of curious vined plants and sweet-tasting orange globes.

It was Evandero who eventually brought about the involvement of a certain renowned party of enxandeiros through his connection to one of its leaders: an infamous local man named Santos Bezerra. Evandero had sheltered Santos for a time during his youth, following the death of his alcoholic father on the Doce. His mother, a whore in Victoria, had never wanted the child and, indeed, remained unknown to him altogether. A bastard by circumstance, Santos had come to the *fazenda* in a manner not unlike Alvis and there worked for his keep while receiving a measure of education from Evandero. The time soon arrived when he departed to seek his fortune, which would lead him into a realm of hard work and rough men. But even in his maturity, he remained ever in Evandero's debt.

"Santos is renowned in the region for his cruelty," Evandero noted to Alvis matter-of-factly. "Yet he is more loyal to me than even the most devoted of dogs."

When pressed by Alvis as to the nature of the man he would deal with in recovering the *fazenda*, Evandero turned cryptic. "There are many devices," he said, "in every danger by which to avoid death if a man is willing to perform or do anything. Santos is one of life's survivors and honors that quality in those with whom he conducts his business."

Then the old man's voice turned speculative. "Santos," he said, "recounted to me how he once went late one night to the hut of a man who had crossed him terribly—given him false information in fact, so as to be caught by enemies who desired to kill him. Without bothering to wake the man, Santos threw him from his bed onto the floor and beat him severely before dragging him over to a great heavy chest. Then he made the fellow strip, face the chest on his knees, and place his nuts inside it. Santos proceeded to shut the lid as gently as he might and lock it. When he exited the hut he took the key with him but left the man a sharp knife. Then he set fire to the hut and turned his back on it, abandoning the fellow to his terrible decision: to be burned to death or to cut off his own balls."

Evandero smiled gently at Alvis' expression of disbelief. "Yet for all this barbarity," he concluded, "I have never known Santos to be untrue to his heart or to his friends. And he is a hard and honest worker."

When the enxadeiros finally arrived, the planting time having grown very late indeed, Alvis took note of them as an earthy sort, roughly shaped by their toil and given to drinking and brawling amongst themselves if no common enemy presented itself. Wife beaters and murderers many of them were, accustomed to using their powerful hands to break skin and bone not unlike the manner in which they tore open the ground. Though lacking in education, each vaguely sensed a tide of circumstances that would one day result in a violent doom, and so each was a lonely man fearing in every stranger a potential enemy and in each shadow or sound some new danger. A malignant, perpetual watchfulness marked many of their faces, accompanying their scars and bad teeth.

Santos, dark-eyed, taller and wider than the rest, kept

them at their work by way of fear and forcefulness, cracking a head when the pace flagged or a hoer grew surly in his speech.

"Back to work, dogs!" he would exclaim, brandishing his heavy grubbing hoe in one hand, its blade-end notched but sharp all the same. Then he would grin wolfishly at Alvis and move on to inspect how the work went in the next field.

Alvis stayed out of their way for the most part, though he succeeded in speeding the enxandeiros' groundbreaking by way of a small moldboard plow he designed which he trained Robinho to draw behind him. Even with good training, the little donkey was too inexperienced to hold a line and make a straight row, but the plow, pulled back and forth, aided in loosening the long-fallow topsoil—the massapé, the enxandeiros called it—and breaking up the shallow root systems of shrubs and saplings that had nudged their way steadily inward from the edges of the fields.

The enxadeiros, even Santos, marveled at the plow but Alvis was careful not to boast of its attributes. People, he had discovered, regardless of their places and ways, have pride in the things and habits they have developed, and usually it is a pride well-earned. He answered questions about the plow and allowed those who asked to use it to do so, but otherwise spoke of it not at all.

The breaking of the fields into long, dark stretches of loose soil was followed by the planting of Brazilian corn, followed by sugar cane, pumpkins, squash, Irish potatoes, cornfield peas, snap beans, butter beans, okra, tomatoes, watermelon and even tobacco—all modest in volume compared to other *fazendas*, but set out skillfully in good ground and in such a way that all might remain well-tended and healthy while requiring the least labor.

The rains that season conspired with the hard work of

Alvis and the periodic hoeings by the enxadeiros to create bountiful fields. Beans grew alongside corn, each enriching the soil in a way that benefited the other, while thick vines of squash, watermelon, and pumpkins climbed the corn stalks in scattered fields so that their fruit hung at chest level or eventually bent the stalks over and snapped them altogether with their bountiful weight.

When harvest time arrived, Atamga and Ubiranon rushed among the narrow and grown-over rows flushing cavies and rats, their barks mingling with the working songs of the enxadeiros and the swish of swinging scythes. Later the corn and cane were sorted, the vegetables dried or boiled and sealed in jars.

Alvis did well enough at the market that season not only to resume his search for Lavinia but to secure materials for a new palm-covered, Mexican-style hut. On a knoll some two hundred yards from Evandero's homestead, the enxadeiros, under the direction of Santos, drove poles into the ground for posts and began working their way up. It took little time. The rafters for the roof were made of poles tied together with strong vines. The daubing began once the roof of palmetto was on and the lathing securely tied inside and out from post to post. The mortar used in the daubing—a mixture of clay and water—was then dumped onto the floor and beaten with heavy wooden pestles. When the first layer dried, another was added and then several more, until the floor was level, hard, and smooth and cool to the touch.

It had been Alvis' plan to offer this new house to Evandero as a gift and symbol of his appreciation, but the old man proved unwilling to leave his venerable, cramped homestead, and so it was Alvis who took up residence there. On the evening he finished redaubing a number of places in the walls where the mortar had not previously held, he returned to the old homestead to discover Evandero had fallen asleep in his customary chair at the table. He watched the old man for a moment, noting how old he looked, how tired, before quietly stirring the fire in the stove, its cast iron door grinding as he lightly swung it shut. Then he cast a blanket over his friend as gently as he could. Yet Evandero stirred and, opening his eyes, regarded him steadily, alertly.

"More than a century ago," he said in a bleary voice, "northwest of here, in Minas Gerais, there lived a little crippled man with no hands whom people called 'The Aleijadinho.' He was a renowned sculptor, his hammer and chisel tied about his blunted wrists with rope or ribbon which allowed him to work steadily, albeit in constant pain. In this way he released angels and saints from the stones, often leaving on their faces the expression of his own suffering."

Alvis sometimes smiled indulgently or laughed outright at Evandero's random tales and curious sayings. Yet he discovered that when he reflected upon them later, in the midst of some task out on the *fazenda*, he nearly always found a use for them. The meanings rang true.

He watched, silent as Evandero rose a little awkwardly, sighed, and shuffled off to bed.

ഇൽ

With autumn came heavy rains, thwarting Alvis' plans for departure. The leaves which came to litter the forest floor fell during the downpours, pressing themselves to the ground and rotting rather than rustling beneath one's feet as they had the fall previous. In the central tavern of Linhares, Alvis heard tales of various Confederado colonies in different areas of Brazil consolidating, while still other groups and families had resolved to give up Brazil entirely and return to North America. Still no news came of Lavinia, but amid these scattered reports there arrived an invitation from a member of the Confederado colony north of Linhares, a Mr. Henderson, requesting that Alvis join his family for dinner Sunday after next. Though Alvis remained wary as to the nature of this sudden overture of fellowship from one of his countrymen in the region, he was curious to learn how they fared, and if they recalled Lavinia and might even provide some clue. And he was hungry to converse in English with someone other than Evandero, charming as the old man was.

Sunday next was a clear fall day, the sky piercingly blue and the air crisp and dry on the hills and rich and succulent in the bottom areas. Robinho had to be held in check as the invigorating weather urged him to run at a full gallop. Alvis held the reigns tightly, Evandero at his side, as the buckboard wagon swayed and rumbled through the forest, dust rising from the spoked wooden wheels.

At Linhares they turned north, following a trail which ran alongside the Rio Japaraná, a swift-running channel some fifty feet across which fed into the Doce. The Japaraná was fed in turn by Lagôa Juparanõa, a lake along the northern reaches of which the Confederado colony rested. When the forest broke open on a rise to reveal Juparanõa, Alvis was surprised by its size, which melted into the horizon in length, and in some places looked as much as four miles wide. It lay bordered mostly by wooded bluffs and the water shone a light, milky color beneath the afternoon's golden autumnal light. With the exception of some sporadic coffee fields, the shores of the lake gave way to the secretive shadows of deep forest.

When they came upon the meager Confederado settlement, pressed against the shore of the lake's far end like some wreckage that had washed up on it, Alvis' mind flashed back to what the priest had described to him months ago in Linhares. As a village, it reminded him of Povoacao, though not so large: muddy paths lying between a dozen thatched huts, many of them fallen in and others apparently incomplete. The domiciles appeared abandoned, except for an old woman who sat knitting on a stump outside the door of one of the far structures.

Up the bluff from the lake, Alvis noted a larger adobe dwelling and from it a heavyset man emerged and waved, motioning for them to ascend the steep trail leading up to the abode.

As the wagon neared the domicile, Robinho's flanks damp with sweat, a boy emerged from the dwelling and conversed briefly with the larger figure before running to meet the wagon. Seizing Robinho's halter, he led them to a makeshift water trough and hitching post braced by two great shady trees.

Evandero spoke to the young boy as he and Alvis dismounted the wagon, but the youth afforded him merely a short glance and sharp grin, the haughty, arrogant smile which youth often gives to age. Despite this reception, Evandero smiled back, kindly but also a little sadly, as age so often smiles at youth.

Before Alvis could speak to the boy, they were joined by the heavyset man, who, ignoring Evandero, came forward to shake Alvis' hand.

"George Henderson," said the fellow when Alvis received his fleshy grip. "Welcome to our humble settlement."

Alvis gave his name and thanked his host before introducing Evandero, who received only a nod and word of greeting from Mr. Henderson.

"David there will see to your little burro," said Henderson, motioning at the boy. "Shall we go inside?"

Alvis considered Henderson in profile as the obese host led them toward his dwelling. He would have been a handsome man if not for his obvious sloth, the double chins concealing the lines of his jaw and neck. His cheek bones were large and thick, as were his lips, which had conspired to form his words of greeting clumsily, as though in flaccid contempt. His voice was oily but conversational. The boy, David, who now raced ahead of them and through the doorway, resembled the man, who must have been his father. Though not so fat, he possessed the same short neck and thick facial physiognomy.

Inside the adobe home, Alvis took in a number of fine pieces of furniture and implements from North America, a great, green corner-cupboard among them, as he and Evandero were introduced to Mrs. Henderson—a plump, wide-faced woman with a high-pitched voice and animated manner—before they were invited to take their seats at a long table covered in a white cloth and strewn with various dishes.

Mr. Henderson remained standing and delivered a perfunctory grace before seating himself and passing the nearest plate—an oblong platter of baked potatoes—to Alvis. Henderson appeared about to speak but his son was quicker, bluntly inquiring of Alvis if he had fought in the war.

When Alvis owned that he had, the boy peppered him excitedly with additional questions, his pleasure particularly obvious when he learned the veteran guest had served with John Mosby.

"I wish I could have ridden with Mosby or Forrest!" exclaimed the boy, at which point Alvis felt compelled to hastily close the subject.

"War remains terrible, young man," he replied, "no matter who you ride into it with."

Alvis then asked Mr. Henderson about the establishment and apparent dissolution of his colony. George Henderson briefly and uneasily met his wife's eyes before embarking upon his tale.

"It is a sad story, Mr. Stevens," he began, "but one you deserve to know."

Families such as theirs, Henderson noted, had formed companies or associations after the war, sending agents ahead of them to scout, purchase, and secure land in Brazil. In such a way, he explained, they acquired their land along the lake. However, they were forced to move quickly in their plans since the military governor of their home state, "Lil' Phil" Sheridan, was in the process of issuing orders prohibiting emigration. In the end, however, despite various obstructions, they effected their departure, sailing out of New Orleans on a ship which bore a number of other families.

Henderson's eyes grew distant as he recalled their arrival in Rio de Janeiro: the friendly welcome from local officials and interpreters and the band that serenaded them with "Dixie." It was a time, Henderson maintained, of many hopes, the government having pledged, among other things, to connect the various Confederado colonies to the country's railroad system through the construction of new wagon roads. As he recounted this, however, Henderson smiled bitterly.

That promise and others, he explained, would all come to naught and he grew more agitated as his account dissolved into a series of acerbic complaints about Brazil—its government and people—and the slow failure of the colony as settlers, dissatisfied with their standard of living along the lake, forsook it to join other settlements or return to North America. He particularly lamented that the Confederados had brought no servants with them and that Brazilian chattels proved too expensive, thus reducing the once proud colonists to a sad, odious toil of subsistence.

"Yet, for all this, we—this family—shall never return to North America," concluded Henderson, smiling at what he took to be the courage of his words, face beaming with misbegotten joy.

"What of those who left this colony?" countered Alvis, seeking to steer the conversation in a direction that might prove useful.

"Most have boarded ships," Henderson replied, "though a few relocated."

Alvis inquired then after Lavinia and her family, Henderson's eyebrows rising at the mention of their names.

"Good people, well liked in the colony, and the girl so beautiful." Henderson's sigh sounded genuine. "It was a deep tragedy among many when fever took them and left her parentless here. She was an industrious girl, uncommonly clever for her sex, and made herself useful about the village until she departed back downriver. It was said she was to take ship from Rio."

Alvis' heart sank as he heard these words.

As if sensing Alvis' silent distress, Mr. Henderson shifted his attention to Alvis himself, his oily voice suddenly rife with compliments.

"But you have fared much better here than those who departed," he said, "and in a very short time, I understand. It is said in the village that as a result of your labors you have gold in your hands but that over you gold has no dominion."

"They flatter me unduly," Alvis quietly replied.

"And whatever our divergent lots here," Henderson continued, "we share a common legacy. So, come, for David's sake and ours, let us hear a tale of your time in that patriotic war. For though it ended in defeat, it remains both a source of pride and the very thing, after all, that brings us to this place, regardless of our circumstances."

Alvis paused and glanced down at the table briefly before replying. "I am obliged to you for your hospitality, Mr. Henderson," he said, "but whatever prosperity I have enjoyed in this land I account to this good man beside me."

Evandero was silent and impassive when Alvis said these words.

"As for the war," Alvis continued, "what more can be said of it? My friends are in their graves and I cannot summon them with words. For my part, I am loath to dwell much on those times, but as you are my host and have asked for a tale, I will honor your request as best I can."

Alvis looked around at his hosts, speculating from their attentive expressions they had been deprived of any new stories for some time.

"Man was made for joy and woe," Alvis began. "Life is hard and sad happenings surround us at all times. Yet I have come to believe the Lord likes a jest, even in the worst of circumstances.

"During the earliest days of the Rangers there was a man I rode with whose life's vocation was to do nothing or, at worst, as little as possible. An amiable lout, altogether devoid of intelligence, his mind generally was incapable of tension or even attention. A bumbling, red-headed fellow he was—stupid, good humored, with a pot belly that jiggled whenever he rode or laughed, which is to say it jiggled often.

"He always donned his uniform with the flourishing, gaudy tactlessness of a provincial on holiday in the city. Yet he always favored and haunted the tail end of the outfit, except when we entered an unoccupied town. On those occasions, without fail, he managed to be at our front, sitting tall in his saddle and bowing to the admiring ladies and children while flourishing his hat. I hesitate to call any man a coward without first acknowledging my own mortal fears, yet this fellow took great pains to strategically place himself far out of harm's way on every occasion of imminent danger.

"'Stay at home or fight all day,' he would say, grinning at his own self-styled wisdom, 'and you get only equal pay.

Death is coming if you shirk, and he is coming if you work.'

"Despite all this, however, and to the wonderment and instruction of all in our outfit, he was the first man in the company to die, felled from his horse by a stray shot in the dark—all his elaborate measures and preparations having come to naught."

Alvis paused and glanced around the table. "That," he said, "in essence, brief though it may be, is a fitting enough tale for conveying my thoughts on war, any war: that it is, like life, unknowable and that it will treat its participants in the ways it so chooses, regardless of all their well laid plans and intentions."

Silence followed in the room for a moment before Mr. Henderson hastily broke in with questions, "But what of the glory of the cause? Surely there were not many men such as this cowardly dandy? And how could a soldier fight so long and give so much while entertaining such a view of the over-all contest? Was there not a higher aim which compelled men to suffer such circumstances?"

Henderson's voice had come to resume its bitter quality and, indeed, had taken on an almost contemptuous tone, the bitterness cultivated by his fruitless months in Brazil boiling to the surface. "Did your service," he pressed, "teach you nothing?"

"It taught me this," Alvis replied emphatically. "That everyone has their appointed time. That life's day is short and can never be won back. But to attempt to extend it with courage and generosity is the task set before every man whose heart is good."

To these words Mr. Henderson made no reply—indeed, it seemed suddenly as if all substance had been deflated from him—and Alvis and Evandero took their leave shortly thereafter, as gracefully as they might.

Alvis played over the evening's events in his mind as their wagon jolted and rolled through the forested night on the return journey to Evandero's *fazenda*. Like Alvis, the Hendersons had fixed their futures upon Brazil, yet were reluctant to bid farewell either to their North American pre-war days or the cataclysm that followed them. This backward-looking gaze, fixed on the prospect of their luxuries before the war, was ill-suited for the life they had found and slowly grown to loathe in Espirito Santo. Alvis tried to sympathize, but the manner in which they were oblivious to most of their surroundings and contemptuous of that which they did perceive disgusted him.

"I may be the only man on this continent," he muttered to himself, "who will try to live in the best of the old ways of my land, think the best of the old thoughts."

Sadness and loneliness were in his heart as he made this silent declaration, but also a sense of resignation and something akin to pride. He had made little effort to choose enemies or friends in this new land. He was content to earn them by virtue of who he was. He was not afraid to die—that fear had been purged from him long ago, far to the north—and so he would live on as he believed a man should. He held out little hope of seeing Lavinia again—even less after hearing the words of Mr. Henderson—but try and confirm her departure he would do. He had grown sleepy but the thought of Lavinia made him adjust himself and sit a little straighter next to his old companion as the wagon jostled on through the Brazilian night.

LOVE AND DEPARTURE:
War of the Triple Alliance

Whether man die in his bed or the rifle knocks him dead,
a parting from those dear is the worst man has to fear.
—W.B. Yeats

THE tale of Alvis' skill with strange crops and in making Evandero's *fazenda* bountiful again quickly spread beyond Linhares and throughout much of the Doce region, and as a result he began to receive invitations to work on or consult in other farming operations. Among them arrived a lucrative request to direct the spring planting at the Ferreira *fazenda*, some forty miles distant and one of the largest estates in all Espírito Santo.

Accepting this work as a final necessary labor before taking up his search for Lavinia in earnest, he plunged into it with a ferocious dedication. Whereas earlier he had enacted the placement of crops with some tentativeness and trepidation, he now directed the work decisively, moving swiftly about the fields on the mount which also constituted a portion of his payment and which he knew would prove necessary to his own purposes: a majestic Andalusian palomino with large, intelligent eyes, lines sleek as subtle river currents, and a long, graceful stride. Heliodoro, he called him, which means "gift of the sun."

Though Alvis fared well enough in his duties, there remained one on the Ferreira *fazenda* who did not look kindly upon his arrival and brooded with mounting jealousy upon the position of significance it afforded him. This was Emilio, the strong, hotheaded bastard from Curitiba whom Mr. Ferreira—desirous of raising a son, yet having been unsuccessful in siring any children—had adopted from an orphanage when the boy was but six.

Whereas Emilio held no legal claim to the *fazenda* and was treated by Mr. Ferreira more as a servant than a family member, he nonetheless fancied himself a son in all capacities, even though he secretly entertained designs to marry the wealthy man's recently adopted daughter, despite the fact they lived beneath the same roof. The arrival of the Confederado, whom Emilio recalled with acute annoyance and bitter envy from the anaconda hunt, had seemed a natural affront to his status and place, and thus something he inwardly vowed to thwart at every opportunity.

"What do we need with this poor, stupid foreigner?" he demanded of Mr. Ferreira.

"Can you grow these strange, exotic crops people clamor for in the Rio markets?" the elder man had countered, immediately severing the conversation and deepening Emilio's resentment all the more.

The passionate young man had no choice but to respect his master's decree, but when he returned to his chamber he seized an unlucky wine glass and dashed it upon the floor. He then proceeded to place his displeasure on display by sulking about the immense *fazenda*, cantering about with his two hulking body servants and refusing to lend any measure of aid in the planting and cultivating. Alvis occasionally glimpsed Emilio riding along the edges of the fields, attendants in tow, and heard vague accounts of his displeasure from the servants, as well as rumors of the beauty of Mr. Ferreira's mysterious adopted daughter, but otherwise he took little notice, absorbing himself instead in the labors before him.

In order to monitor all of the work occurring simultaneously on the immense Ferreira *fazenda*, Alvis galloped Heliodoro from place to place following the narrow, uneven forest paths up and down the rough gullies which lay between the long open fields. The horse loved these intense excursions as much as or perhaps more than his master and would stamp and snort, eager to move on, when Alvis tarried too long in one of the cultivated stretches.

Late one afternoon, air cool in the wake of one of those brief intense showers that move swiftly along the Doce river valley—Alvis mounted Heliodoro and cantered off in the direction of the last field he wished to inspect that day, a remote expanse of rocky ground sitting atop a plateau surrounded by thick jungle. Their journey soon carried them into deep forest, its aspect made darker by the approach of evening and the lingering patches of cloud which persisted in the wake of the river storm, like a loose procession of bridesmaids trailing behind the one who is to be wed.

As the trail widened and Alvis prepared to give Heliodoro his head, affording the animal his long-awaited, breakneck gallop, a dark mounted figure emerged from the dense leafy trailside, blocking the path. The Andalusian whinnied as Alvis reined him in anew. The unidentified horse was all black, a sleek, moderate-sized thoroughbred with lines as fine as Heliodoro's, its muscled neck and legs appearing sculpted in minute detail. Alvis initially suspected this lone figure must be Emilio, yet the Ferreira bastard owned no such horse and the rider, wanting in stature, did not match Emilio in size. Atop his magnificent creature the mysterious figure sat, completely concealed by a tightly fastened, black hooded cloak which obscured his features and glistened in places where lingering crystal droplets of rain clung to it.

The rider leaned forward to whisper into his horse's ear and the stunning thoroughbred reared up suddenly and snorted, pawing the air with its sharp hooves. The rider then turned his mount so that he—for the horse's sex was revealed in his rearing—faced away from Alvis and Heliodoro, and proceeded to back the creature up, stopping when the mysterious pair came level with the Confederado and his Andalusian.

"What can I do for you, stranger?" Alvis asked, peering closely at the hood but unable to discern the visage resting deep inside its folds.

In response, the thoroughbred lunged back and forth in two short bursts before prancing, tail high, in a circle around Alvis and Heliodoro until horse and rider again came to a stop in the place they had started.

Alvis' laugh echoed loudly off the trailside trees for he divined the rider's voiceless purpose.

"Very well, silent one," said Alvis, smiling grimly, "but shall we not sweeten the contest with a wager? If you are fastest in reaching the field that lies ahead on the plateau I shall give you my gloves. They are of fine leather and only just arrived from Rio. On the other hand, if God smiles upon my cause and Heliodoro here is swiftest in gaining that high lonely place, then you shall cast back your hood and reveal the face of him who rides voiceless and cloaked along lonely jungle paths."

The hooded rider seemed to consider Alvis' proposal momentarily before signing his agreement with a slow nod. Then, without further signal or warning, the mysterious figure shook the reins and his dark mount lunged forward down the trail, leaving Alvis to hastily adjust his grip on the reins as Heliodoro, having intuitively sensed the nature of the contest at hand, immediately plunged after them in pursuit.

As the steeds galloped furiously along the level—albeit debris-strewn—path, it quickly became apparent that the black horse was both surer of foot and slightly swifter, its quick feet dancing over logs and adroitly missing stumps. Heliodoro, by contrast—stronger and longer in his strides, yet less agile—negotiated the littered terrain in a different manner. Lacking altogether the dexterity to evade such obstacles at full gallop, he shattered rotten stumps beneath his hooves and snapped bodily the dead, brittle branches reaching into the trail.

Out of the woods and down a bare gully-side they went, rocks sliding and pebbles flying out from beneath them. At the bottom they crossed a rocky stream, the black stallion so fleet its hooves barely disrupted the surface and, indeed, appeared almost to glide upon it. Heliodoro's powerful legs, on the other hand, violently parted the waters, dispatching cool spray high into the air along his flanks. Then it was up the longer, steeper opposite side of the gully and here Heliodoro, being the stronger of the two, began slowly to gain, his mighty legs churning, hooves cleaving in twain the brittle trail rocks while sending the smallest of them flying far out behind. Alvis bent forward in the saddle, head nearly pressed against Heliodoro's neck, as the trail steepened and gravity pushed against them.

Alvis hoped to pass and then cut off his opponent here on the hillside, for he feared the black would prove impossible to catch once they gained the level ground at its crest. Vigorously then he urged on Heliodoro, who in truth required no urging, his hooves gouging out chunks of hillside, his bright burning will as bent upon victory as his master's.

They achieved a small triumph when Heliodoro's head pulled alongside the dark horse's rump. Then, a greater victory, when they drew neck and neck, Alvis stealing an appraising glance at the mystery rider as he drew alongside him. The man rode expertly, in perfect harmony with his animal, his body a fluid complement to the powerful jolting form beneath him. A draw string must have held his hood in place or it otherwise would have long since fallen back. Indeed, Alvis concluded with appreciation, it was a master horseman with whom he dueled, though there remained something curious in the way the man's body sat and moved beneath his cloak which Alvis could not place specifically yet gnawed at him with a vague familiarity.

It was at that moment the race was decided. Alvis' eyes, having lingered too long in considering the mystery of his opponent, returning to the trail not in time to react to the tree bough which lay across it. As Heliodoro leapt, Alvis' foot came loose from the stirrup and he next found himself airborne and apart from his horse.

He landed heavily on his back in the rocky trail, the impact knocking the wind from him. Supine and gasping for air, he heard the horses' hooves slow and then become a confused jumble of sound as they paused and turned.

A moment later, hoofbeats having drawn nigh, the black rider appeared above him, still mounted and holding Heliodoro's reins in an extended hand. The Andalusian nickered as he came to stand over his master and the rider released hold of the reins so that the horse might lower his head to nibble first at Alvis' chin before moving down to a shirt pocket containing sugar. Gently and deftly, the equine lips worked and nudged the fabric until the white lumps tumbled forth and quickly consumed.

As Heliodoro collected the sugar from his prostrate master's shirt, a high, musical sound erupted from the rider which Alvis recognized as laughter—feminine laughter. And as the figure's laughing head fell back with the weight of its merriment so, at last, did its hood, revealing a countenance of singular beauty. She was a young woman still, her black hair matching that of her steed and hanging low around the nape of her neck. Her smiling mouth was wide and sensual and her eyes likewise were wide apart, revealing their charcoal color when their owner, perhaps wearying of her merriment, fixed her gaze candidly upon Alvis. Her expression was a curious one which did not often cross her face. Mingled in it were the last vestiges of humor mixed with the gathering hint of something far more powerful.

"I will have those gloves, sir ... when you are able," said Lavinia, with a measured degree of the affected mockery Alvis recognized from long ago.

Tentatively, Alvis rose to a sitting position and absently patted the nearest leg of Heliodoro, who had near exhausted what sugar grains he could find. Truly he was stunned more by this sudden appearance of the love he thought lost than his tumble.

"My gloves are yours for the taking," he said at last, his voice a little shaky, "though I believe they will not fit your hands to your liking."

"Indeed, your gloves certainly will not serve me in any useful fashion," said Lavinia, matter-of-factly in the sassy tone he remembered, "but I will have them nonetheless to remind me of my victory on this day and our reunion a thousand miles from where we first knew each other."

Stiffly dragging himself up by Heliodoro's halter, Alvis removed the gloves and silently handed them up to her. Yet as she bent to take them he grasped her hand and offered his lips as well. The long-parted lovers kissed long in this way until tears streamed from both sets of eyes. When at last their lips parted, she slid gently from her horse and into his waiting arms.

⊰⊱

So it was that Alvis Stevens' lost love unexpectedly was discovered—or rather recognized and revealed herself to him—in a manner foreseen by none, least of all by him. She had been taken in by the Ferreira family over a year before, following her parents' passing, on account of Mrs. Ferreira's desire for accomplished and stylish feminine company on the isolated *fazenda*—what the English termed "a companion." Following an initial period spent at convent school for girls of means, Lavinia quickly won over the Ferreira household: Mrs. Ferreira on account of her grace and wit; Mr. Ferreira for the potential he saw in her as an ornament and hostess for his business functions; and Emilio as an object of desire that might also serve to legitimize his place in life.

Lavinia had been careful to project an air of indifference when she heard Alvis' name mentioned in the Ferreira home and later confirmed his identity peering out a window as he rode away from the house after conducting some business with the overseer. Following their happy reunion, each of them was filled both with an overpowering joy and a strong temptation to immediately announce publicly their past history and unwavering love, yet each knew complications would ensue from doing so. Alvis had a large job to complete; Lavinia owed a measure of loyalty to this family that had taken her in.

Then there was Emilio who was determined to have her, stoked already by a bitter jealousy of Alvis and encouraged by his role as Lavinia's frequent riding escort. It was, in fact, Emilio who had first placed her astride Mr. Ferreira's finest stallion, using the lack of proper feminine riding tack on the isolated *fazenda* as an excuse to answer their foster mother's protests. Lavinia knew how Emilio felt about her, but tolerated his presence since it afforded her the pleasure of riding.

Moreover a kind word here and there sometimes resulted in his releasing her to ride alone. Such precious intervals were treasured ones indeed.

Since, for the moment at least, each had a part to play and tasks to perform in their separate spheres, their association remained secret, though far from an easy one to maintain.

Just how hard would become obvious the next day when Alvis' heart was sorely plagued at not seeing her. When he did finally catch sight of her again the following afternoon it was at a distance. High above a field they were planting, on a bare rocky hill, Lavinia sat atop the swift black thorough-bred. She was far enough away that Alvis could not divine where her eyes fell, though horse and rider stood with their heads pointed in his direction. Required to return to the task at hand, he found them vanished when his glance next took in the hill. When he discovered their departure, he felt as though a piece of him had departed as well.

For two more days this routine persisted. Lavinia and the black—whose name, he had learned, was Meainoite and who belonged to Mr. Ferreira—appearing along the far edge of a field or a nearby hill only to disappear after an interval. It has been noted that little is stranger in life than the bond between two people who observe each other daily with powerful interest and yet are compelled to keep up the pose of anonymous indifference. There exists between them curiosity, attraction, and frustration—all unexpressed save in the lingering gaze of the eyes, watching as each desired individual withdraws from sight once more.

It was through one of the servants, an old man named Soriano who had been confined to house duties on account of a lingering limp, that Alvis eventually succeeded in communicating with Lavinia, reaching her with a note requesting a late afternoon meeting atop the hill where he had first glimpsed her watching him. As his patience was nigh at an end and Emilio had been summoned to Rio by Mr. Ferreira, it seemed his best—perhaps only—chance.

He received no reply, but the next day, not long into the early evening hour he had proposed for their meeting, he heard the deep sound of approaching hoofbeats. Lavinia galloped onto the summit undisguised, her beauty on full display, cambric skirt aflutter and fine, rebellious strands of hair swirling in the air and curling round her flushed face as she deftly reined in Meainoite. Alvis suggested they sit upon a large rock and take in the sunset, but the saddle, it seemed, had become as much a home to her as it had been for any Ranger of Alvis' acquaintance, and she insisted they go for a ride instead.

"I have thought only of you since the day you found me," he said to her, giving the reins a gentle shake. With a slow, thoughtful nod, she trotted after him.

Though they had many questions to ask of each other and much to share, they spoke but little on that initial excursion. However a brief ride about the *fazenda* became a daily ritual for them, Lavinia explaining it was the one way in which they might interact without arousing much suspicion due to the fact that Emilio had joined her father and she was in need of a riding escort. A mere glance at them after all confirmed they were foreigners of similar stock and likely would have much to discuss of their former land in their own tongue. Alvis' appearance was a godsend for Lavinia in many ways, not least of which were these rides which offered her a precious escape from the tiresome world of the *fazenda* and allowed the lovers to fill in the awful yawning gaps of their lonely parted years at last.

Usually they would ride and talk for a time, after which Lavinia would softly sing to him a Brazilian song. When the tune concluded, a description followed of what it meant and when she had learned it. These songs delighted Alvis since they reminded him of those pre-war days when she told him stories during their long walks on her family's farm. Most of her Brazilian tales, he learned, stretched back to her time at the convent school where she had been sent by Mr. Ferreira upon her arrival. One of the nuns there, Sister Josephine, had come from a village that was home to a singing master and had taken to Lavinia on account of her prior musical training and rare gift for sensing and learning the spirit of a composition as well as its technical aspects.

As in riding, Lavinia established in music another manner of expressing herself both exhilarating and heretofore unknown. She excelled in particular at the organ, improvising upon the work of the celebrated composer and priest José Maurício Nunes Garcia, himself a gifted improviser. Divining what this musician had meant as well as what he had written, she often would redirect his passages in fluid, alternate directions, not unlike the manner in which she gracefully guided Meainoite down unexplored forest paths. Sometimes she would giggle at the close of these pieces, delighted at her own playful cleverness, and such occasions were the only times she was scolded by the sisters.

Though possessed of a natural and sometimes mischievous ironic wit which bit Alvis periodically, Lavinia remained at heart a genuinely humble girl. She had forgotten altogether how beautiful she was until she departed the convent school, for there were no mirrors in the bare, whitewashed cells and all the girls dressed alike in their smocks. Another building near the school functioned as an orphanage for poor girls, affording them some small education and training them in various domestic labors. These girls came from all manner of backgrounds and places in Brazil: little, furtive African

girls, rough girls from squalid, city families; and strange, stoic country girls with Indian features, for whom the reserved
otherworldly manner of the sisters came effortless and natural. The sole man about the convent and orphanage was an
old, half-blind Indian charged with keeping the gardens. He
wore a small bell on his belt so that by its tinkling the girls
might be warned of the approach of a man and vanish before
he appeared, like fawns before the huntsman. And certainly
any sisterly affection among the girls that ripened into light
kisses or caresses—tentative little butterflies of desire—was
purged immediately by the watchful nuns whose virginal
hands nonetheless aptly wielded strong sticks.

Lavinia related to Alvis that her lone bosom friend and
confidante at the convent was a girl named Glória who always
wore a locket pin with two frames. On one side was the smiling
picture of a young girl; on the other, a dark-haired man with
large, sad eyes. They were portraits of the dead, for Glória, like
Lavinia, had been orphaned and the pictures were of her parents. Her mother had died in childbirth at sixteen, without
having really encountered the joys of the world, though she
perished in full knowledge of its sufferings. Her father, solemn yet tender of heart, had raised her with an attentiveness
that was neither doting nor overbearing. He had been all her
world, to the point that she alternately called him Mama and
Papa until she was four years old.

At night, when the sisters were all asleep, Lavinia would
crawl into bed with Glória and, opening the locket, peer
closely at the portrait of the girl's dead father, fascinated that
her friend loved still this sad-looking man so long deceased,
even as she longed for her own dead father and lamented
how she owned no portraits of her parents. After a while,
Glória would close the picture and smile at Lavinia sadly,
fingering the locket pin as she did so.

These were tragic intimations of fate since Glória was destined to die young in childbirth, and possibly because she felt ordained to some predestined conclusion, she marveled all the more and took joy in Lavinia's independence and tales of roaming about the countryside—how when on the *fazenda* she would gallop the rutted back roads terrorizing the cart masters and poor people traveling on foot.

The one occasion on which Glória accompanied Lavinia to the Ferreira home, she refused to ride herself but watched and clapped with delight as Lavinia galloped back and forth across the great field in front of the house, jumping fences and sending up into the air great wet clods of grassy earth.

One day during her visit, while the girls were out touring the countryside in Mr. Ferreira's carriage, Lavinia having at last forsaken her beloved saddle for her friend's close company, they came upon an old wooden crucifix standing alone on a hilltop where it had been erected long ago by some forgotten missionary. With a sudden, uncharacteristic shout, Glória ordered the driver to stop and, taking Lavinia's hand, flung open the carriage door. Together they ran and scrambled up to the foot of the cross, where Glória, face flushed and gasping for breath, dropped to her knees and looked up at its splintered, weatherbeaten visage in adoration as though it were the very face of God.

In relating these tales Lavinia gave something new of her heart, expressing sympathy for a fervor in her friend she did not share. As Alvis received them, he invisibly returned to her some portion of his, gazing upon her and listening with the same intensity as in those days of long ago. For the first time since he had lost her, it seemed to him as though he could hear faintly the echo of himself in another's mind.

"Do you remember the last letter you wrote me during the war?" he asked.

"Was it about the wounded men at the Institute?"

He nodded slowly and then, gazing out over the fields, proceeded to recite it:

There was a dance at the Institute, organized in part, I believe, to cheer the wounded soldiers from this section. The tables glowed with candlelight and were very beautiful, to the point one might almost have forgotten there even was a war, if not for the wounded gentlemen hobbling about or the absence of an arm or a finger on their persons.

These poor unfortunate men, ashamed of their wounds and appearance, were loath to dance at first, but then a bearded gentleman on crutches, significantly older than the others, put one of his supports aside and addressed one of the younger girls, saying if she would kindly stand in for one of his crutches he would dance with her as best he could. This exchange served as a relief to all and afterwards nearly everyone began to dance, both the men and the girls appearing to enjoy themselves, though a light breeze of melancholy, the constant stirring of the war, accompanied the gay time.

Oh Alvis, what small moments of happiness we are reduced to, and all of them so thoroughly blunted for me by the absence of you.

"I knew I would lose the letter eventually," he said by way of explanation, "so I committed it to memory. It was the last bit of you I had, made all the more precious by the rumor your family had departed the country."

Drawing Meainoite close, Lavinia kissed him. Soft and barely discernible, a love far deeper than that which they had known to the north had stolen in upon them here, so that when at last its close presence was recognized, not even the fastest of steeds could have borne either of them away from it. Indeed it felt almost as if the love that existed between them had taken on a disguise over the years in order to deceive them as it grew, only to spurn that disguise at last, revealing itself suddenly, startling them in its grandeur: the sheer blinding power and essence of love.

Their rides were never long, but sometimes they dismounted in a dark shady stretch of forest or next to a murmuring creek. When Lavinia lay on the grass or leaves next to him Alvis would remark how her hair had the appearance of a folded flower. Or perhaps it was he who would lie in the grass, his head in her lap, as she gently hummed "A Linda Rosa Juvenil" until he dozed off, at which point she would tickle his nose with a leaf and thus deliver him back, snorting into wakefulness.

"We must go," she would say then.

She knew she loved him more than before, yet she recognized too something different about him. He could be quiet for long periods of time, and he smiled but rarely. She was drawn to him as before and yet a little frightened by him now. She recalled how, during those dark years of separation, even in times of apparent peace and stillness, the war had ever stirred and moved invisibly among them all, spreading its destruction both in ways that were expected and those completely invisible and unlooked for. It was clear its hand had fallen upon Alvis, fallen upon him most heavily, yet the burden he so clearly bore from those trials made her love him all the more even as she grieved for the loss of the young man he had once been—who had been destroyed by it.

And how odd it felt to Alvis Stevens to laugh at all, to be in love. Yet for all his laughter and for having known and loved her before, Lavinia remained a powerful mystery to him, just as all women remain mysteries to the men who fall in love with them. Deeper he sank into that riddle, caring neither for answer nor conclusion, yet ever marveling at the nature of the question.

It happened that the *fazenda's coronelismo*, Lavinia's father, Mr. Ferreira, usually was away from home, conducting his extensive business affairs in Rio de Janeiro and so remained entirely oblivious of his adopted charge's activities. When he did, however, eventually return to the *fazenda* to hear tales of Lavinia's evening rides with the foreigner—their details fancifully deepened and expounded upon by Emilio's loose, vitriolic tongue —he grew ill-pleased to the point that his outrage simmered.

The *coronelismo* said nothing of these accounts to Lavinia, but embraced and doted upon her warmly, as was his custom. Yet he took the first opportunity when she was away from the house to summon the Confederado to him.

Alvis had accepted his agricultural post on the *fazenda* via correspondence with the overseer and never had met the farm's oft-absent master. When he was shown into the *coronelismo*'s study, he beheld a tall, dry, close man, standing straight and rigid before a desk, awaiting him.

Mr. Ferreira had risen from very humble beginnings to earn his magnificent house and splendid equipage, and he stood amid them now erect, silent, and proud—but also alone. Indeed, it seemed that whenever he was at home in the country, Mr. Ferreira found himself anxiously searching in vain for something, anything, to bear out the ever-nagging dogma of his lonely material importance. He was known and often ridiculed among his business associates and economic equals in Rio as an iron-hard man and a miser. He received his social invitations out of a certain fear and respect, but it was of no matter since he rarely attended such functions unless some business was to be conducted in that sphere. On the odd occasion his name arose in social company, it was usually in the context of finance.

In fact the only personal story people related about him

centered around his unwillingness to forgive a rival business-man his modest debt, choosing instead to unleash ruthless creditors upon him, who seized the unfortunate man's lands and made his family homeless. A few months later, the ru-ined businessman committed suicide. A shudder often ran through the on-hand assemblage whenever this grim tale was recounted.

So it was that well past the age of retirement, Mr. Ferreira usually was away conducting his beloved business, and now a lowly foreigner charged with working his fields and making them more profitable had ostentatiously taken advantage of his absence in an attempt to deprive him of one of his prized possessions.

"So you dwell on poor old Evandero's rundown tapera," the *coronelismo* sarcastically announced by way of greeting.

"For the moment," Alvis replied, matching his employ-er's Portuguese, "I have the good fortune of dwelling as his guest."

"Then I take it you own no land," said Mr. Ferreira.

"Apart from my horse, what I own is what you see before you," Alvis answered simply.

The *coronelismo* considered Alvis for a moment and then walked behind his desk. He looked down at the bills of re-ceipt lying there and sighed before his expressionless eyes re-turned to Alvis and he spoke again.

"I am told I am a very hard man," he said, "and, indeed, I have always been so and would not have it otherwise. I have a distaste for the things of the body, which has grown more pronounced with age. I do not like the sight of blood. Sweat is offensive to me, tears disgust me. In such things a man's bones are dissolved, as they are in his relationships with peo-ple: those with whom he enters into the bonds of fellowship and love. I once destroyed a man, a business associate, because I would not allow him to dissolve my bones. But gold, my young friend from the South that is far to the north, gold is hard. It is proof against dissolution."

He paused for a moment before continuing. "For all you may have experienced in your short life, I see you still have about you youth's yearning for those things that dissolve people. But I assure you I shall not be dissolved, and neither shall the young lady I have in my charge."

This last point was delivered with emphasis, yet Alvis was quick to respond. "I am honored to know your thoughts, sir, and your knowledge of business and gold certainly far outweighs mine. Yet I have seen myself laid upon and forged by hard matter as well: the miniball, the bayonet, the shot of grape. I have learned too well how soft and fragile man is, torn to bits by things just as he may be bought and sold by a rich man's gold. However, in my own short life, it has been the weaknesses of which you speak, the old human verities, that have accounted for whatever faith and survival have been my good fortune. I do not dispute that the best weapons eventually triumph on the battlefield, just as the most gold wins the best possessions, yet I would gladly give up either for fellowship and love."

Their divergent philosophies delivered to one another, the conversation between the Confederado and the *coronelismo* promised no hope for a resolution grounded in understanding and quickly degenerated. Alvis declared he loved Lavinia, that he would not be separated from her again, and Mr. Ferreira pledged he would protect her from any doubtful prospects that threatened her—particularly foreigners with no land or prospects. When Alvis left the *coronelismo's* office, he did so jobless and charged with vacating the *fazenda* immediately. If he was not gone by nightfall, he was informed, he would be seized and shot. As much as

Alvis might have wished to justify his love for Lavinia with the claim that he had been a man of means at one time and would surely be so again, the substance of their exchange convinced him such assertions would be wasted on this man.

It remains, however, that one does not sever love as one concludes a business transaction and that evening Alvis managed to see Lavinia briefly on the hilltop that had become their regular meeting place. Side by side they sat on the large rock that looked out westward toward the day's end. Behind them, to the east, the hills were sunset-flushed and a stillness hung about them of that peculiar quality which sometimes foretells the twilight. The dying day's mysterious solemnity reflected their mood. Together they sat until the sun vanished and the crickets and other nocturnal insects commenced their overture. When at last Alvis rose and departed, he left Lavinia weeping amid the dew of evening, but not without the promise they would be reunited yet again.

Alvis meditated night and day on the best course of action to take. For two weeks they communicated via Old Soriano, attempting to establish a passable degree of anonymity in the dispatches by employing coded messages and false names, Alvis taking the shepherd's name of Dirceu and Lavinia signing her letters Marília. Yet these exchanges were halted when Emilio discovered Soriano bearing one of Alvis' correspondences. Of narrow mind and imperfect education, Emilio was subject to violent and hasty passions, as if some serpent dwelt within his bosom, ever coiled and ready to strike. And now he recognized an object for his vengeance in the form of the old crippled man. Seizing Soriano by his shoulders, he threw him to the floor and proceeded to kick him as he would some hunting dog that displeased him.

Having administered a thorough beating to the old servant, one which would leave the elderly fellow unable to rise from his bed for a week, Emilio addressed Lavinia later that afternoon with a lubricious air.

"I am going to see to it there are no more scribblings borne about this place," he said, smiling at her grimly before quitting the house.

Following his declaration, Emilio remained true to its implied purpose and, accompanied by his servants, took to riding the roads in the vicinity of Evandero's *fazenda*. His hope and aim, it was not difficult to gather, was an encounter with Alvis on some secluded stretch of trail. Folk who frequented the roads reported to Evandero the trio of horsemen they sometimes met riding here and there. Thus, Alvis learned he was a hunted man once more.

"The world, it seems, has become too small for you and Emilio to live in together," observed Evandero as they sat on his porch one evening sipping cachasa, "but an encounter between you will not bring any good to the world or anyone. You have accomplished much here and there is hope yet. See that you do not forfeit it all on account of this worthless bastard."

"It may be he will make the choice for me," Alvis replied, shaking his head.

"Remember that in death," Evandero continued, "there are no great loves. There is no cachasa, no fine food, no good horses, no sunshine or cool breezes. Victory and success last a very short time, my friend, but death is for always."

Alvis' intuition concurred with Evandero's wise words and he did his best to avoid his nemesis, keeping to circuitous, obscure routes on his infrequent journeys to Linhares, where he made inquiries of ships bound for other parts of South America—a vessel that might bear Lavinia and him away. Yet, try as he might, the day eventually arrived—a sweltering late-summer evening—when the paths of the hunted foreigner and hotheaded bastard finally crossed.

Having learned of Alvis' presence in Linhares earlier in the day, Emilio at last guessed correctly the Confederado's obscure return route and, bidding his servants wait, rode forth from the roadside trees when he glimpsed the tall Andalusian advancing slowly down the narrow muddy trail.

Alvis, for his part, wary and unarmed, considered briefly the prospect of galloping away, but instead—as he had done so often across hemispheres—embraced the element of chance and rode forward to greet his enemy.

"I hear you have sought me long, Emilio," he said, "and now you discover me at last, unarmed and without cause for conflict. I no longer frequent the Ferreira *fazenda*. Let us, therefore, ride our separate ways from here and out of each other's lives."

"The words of a coward!" spat Emilio, who drew forth a pistol from his saddlebag and, cocking it, leveled the weapon at Alvis.

"Cowards should be shot like dogs," he growled between clenched teeth, his forefinger tightening.

Yet as he uttered these words, Alvis wheeled Helidoro and exclaimed, "If you gun me down like a dog it will be in the back, and then it shall be Emilio who is known everywhere as a murdering coward!"

Emilio cursed and shouted for his servant, Baranga. Stealing a glance over his shoulder, Alvis beheld the big henchman hastily ride forward and receive Emilio's pistol.

"You think you are bala e onça," remarked Emilio dismounting his horse and throwing the reins up to Baranga, "but I will teach you otherwise."

Alvis did not immediately answer but instead got down off Heliodoro and tied him to a roadside tree before delivering his response. "Your tongue is such a little thing, Ferreira bastard, to deliver such large boasts."

It was almost dark by then and when Emilio rapidly approached his hated rival and cast a wild punch, Alvis sensed the swing as much as saw it and ducked so that the blow only grazed the top of his skull. He hit Emilio twice solidly in the jaw between two more of the bastard's wide swings. When Emilio did not go down after the second blow, Alvis grimly marked his toughness and knew he was in for a fight, recalling how in Linhares it was said Emilio never had been bested by blows.

The bastard hit Alvis in the body, then beside his eye, blows that did not connect solidly but behind which lay formidable strength. Alvis landed another fist to Emilio's jaw, but as the bastard staggered, he grabbed onto Alvis' shirt and ripped the right sleeve. Then they were toe to toe, slugging viciously. Both men were cut, both bleeding. Their breaths came in haggard gasps as their feet slid in the mud of the road.

When Alvis jerked himself free of Emilio in an effort to regroup and establish some space, his nemesis slipped to one knee. When he came back up he held in his right hand a knife, deftly drawn from a boot. Fatigued but fueled onward by his fermented rage, Emilio swung the blade in a wicked slice that would have opened Alvis' belly had it connected.

For all his bulk and height, Emilio was exceedingly quick and when next his knife flicked out like a snake's tongue, Alvis felt its sting on his forearm. Another swing penetrated his shirt and the skin burned where the blade's tip sliced it. Emilio smiled malignantly as Alvis realized his opponent's strategy. Many knife fighters, he recalled, employ flicking slashes with only the point of the blade, never getting too close, so that in a matter of minutes a man may be bleeding from a half dozen small wounds and growing steadily weaker.

Knowing he could not last long at such a disadvantage and banking on Emilio's arrogance, Alvis played to his opponent's style, feigning weakness and holding his bleeding forearm to his body.

"Now I am going to kill you, foreign trash," declared the bastard, stepping in. Sensing an easy triumph Emilio swung wildly, Alvis evading the blow yet stumbling as he did so to give the impression of exhausted clumsiness. But at Emilio's next wild swing, Alvis powerfully lunged forward, closing with him. The bastard proved nearly as strong as Alvis but not so well coordinated or conditioned, and as he shifted his feet a boot slipped in the mud. Alvis took advantage of the opportunity to seize Emilio's wrist and twist it with all his two-handed might. The men swayed, almost tumbling to the ground. Then, with a strangled cry of pain, Emilio's weapon tumbled into the roadside weeds.

They grappled and tottered anew until Emilio again exposed himself when his grasp slipped on Alvis' bare sweaty arm. His hands freed briefly, Alvis boxed Emilio twice behind the ears and then smashed him with his fist as he pushed him away. When Emilio hit the ground his head hit first, striking a rock.

"Baranga!" cried the bastard, rolling to and fro in the mud, craddling his head in his arms.

Before Alvis could turn to account for Emilio's henchman, the swift-moving, burly servant had slipped his forearms beneath Alvis' armpits and grasped his neck with his powerful fingers, suppressing him in an iron hold. Winded from his struggle with Emilio, Alvis did not possess the energy to combat this new, stronger menace. In vain he struggled against the crushing grip.

Upon collecting himself and rising, Emilio instructed his

henchman to hold Alvis securely. His quarry now trapped and helpless, Emilio proceeded to deliver a series of punches and kicks to Alvis' defenseless form, cursing as he did so. The blows landed especially around Alvis' head and the portion of his chest where blood issued forth from the knife wound.

When Emilio had exhausted himself, he ordered his accomplice to let Alvis' battered body drop. Then, having caught his breath, he kicked the prone form several more times in the head and the gut before instructing both his servants to drag the unconscious body to a deep rut in the trail and to dump it there. Emilio crowned the deed by spitting twice upon the discarded body before he and his servants mounted and rode off into the night.

The Confederado awoke in agony sometime around the middle of the following morning, consciousness trickling back into his brain as water slowly finds its way through rocks. The bursts of jabbing pain that accompanied the swaying and bumping beneath him told him he was in a cart. His head burned and each breath was a new torture. Strange birds cawed somewhere off in the distance. His futile attempt at speech emerged as a barely audible gasp. Then the cart struck something, a rock perhaps, jolting his body, and the overpowering pain plunged him back into unconsciousness.

When next he was conscious, the pain was still present but less, and he was aware of a terrible stiffness throughout his limbs. He recognized Evandero's thatched ceiling above him and then the old man's wrinkled face appeared before it, its crooked lines drawn into an expression of concern.

He slept again but when he awoke he was in agony once more, the rattling beneath him informing him his body was again borne by wagon. Evandero sat above him to his right, swaying with the shifting contours of the road.

The old man noticed Alvis' open eyes and his look turned grave. "Santos and I are taking you to the healing woman Pomona, who dwells among the Botocudo," he said, leaning forward and speaking softly. "I fear it will require savage medicine to combat your savage maladies."

As he drifted in and out of consciousness, Alvis noted the sun scarcely shone over the course of that day, though the air remained thick and warm. A smoky mist, resembling that of Virginia's Indian summer, seemed to envelop all things.

When next he awoke, he discovered the sun was below the horizon and the summer twilight had begun to deepen across the land. Cold hopelessness overtook his mind. Had he ever been hurt this badly before? The thought brought to mind the war wound that had nearly killed him—that had left the jagged scar. One does not remember pain, but perhaps that had been as bad, and he summoned those circumstances now, concentrating upon them—forcing them to coalesce in his mind—as a salve against the awful jolting agonies of the present.

During the war there had come upon him on occasion a devil-may-care recklessness which his companions took for courage, but in reality signaled some dark desire for his own annihilation. The worst such manifestation occurred while leading a countercharge against overextended enemy cavalry that had driven the Rangers from the field. With sudden resolve, he jerked Tamerlane's reins, brought him about hard, and fired his pistol into the nearest pursuing enemy horseman, knocking him backward from his saddle. As the Partisans around him wheeled their mounts in answer, there arose from Alvis' throat a high pitched cry, joined almost simultaneously by the voices of his companions, creating a primal, spine-tingling chorus: the terrible sound of the Rebel Yell.

As the enemy hesitated, Alvis leaned forward and spoke to Tamerlane, and man and horse charged toward them, hair and mane a tumult in the headlong air. He fired his pistol into a man fruitlessly seeking to turn his mount, and then moved past the rearing, riderless horse to fire upon another. Bodies tumbled from their saddles until steel clicked against steel and Alvis circled behind his fellows to reload. Then, in the dim twilight of that dying day, he raged again, pistol blazing, shining anew, like the harvest star, whose rays are always brightest on murky nights. Orion's Dog that star has been called for more than two thousand years, but for all his brilliance he has ever been a sign of impending fevers and troubles among men. All over the field galloped Alvis Stevens in his wrath, pausing only to reload his spent pistol. Tamerlane's coat and mane stiffened with splattered enemy blood. And everywhere they rode, men fell.

But the madness of war is a madness that blinds, and so it was that the Rangers lingered too long, collecting spoils from the enemy in the wake of their counterattack, so that they themselves suddenly were accosted once more by a re-inforcement cavalry company armed with Spenser repeating rifles. As the Rangers abandoned the field in haste and disorder, a bullet struck Alvis in the upper arm, its impact jerking him sideways and sending his body plunging headlong from the saddle.

He regained consciousness to the sound of the enemy wandering across the field finishing off the wounded with bayonet and pistol, the wet penetrating thud of the former and the sharp report of the latter preceded now and then by a faint cry of defiance or supplication. Though he found he could not move, he was lying on his back, which allowed him to gaze upward into a star-strewn, twilight sky as he listened to the advancing sounds of death. At last a figure with a low forehead and heavy-lidded eyes appeared above him. Alvis fixed his gaze upon the face slowly while the man looked down on him, the rising moon highlighting his grim, expressionless manner. As the soldier bent forward, rifle held at waist level, Alvis was struck by the odd notion that the whole upper half of the man's face appeared to retreat below the lower. The soldier's thick features and veiled eyes afforded him an air of primitive melancholy devoid of any trace of brutality as he pulled his rifle back along his right hip preparing to plunge it downward. There was, too, behind all this, the miscellaneous sounds of the enemy elsewhere in the field beginning to stack arms.

Then a sudden accompaniment joined the relaxed tune of the enemy's repose: the heavy rumbling of many hooves and the crack of pistol fire—the approach of yet another attack to answer the enemy's counterattack. The man above Alvis looked up in the direction of the growing tumult, his expression changed to one of stupid amazement. Then a heavy wet thud and a mist filled the air as a ball entered the upper part of his chest. Alvis felt the warm dewy droplets of the man's blood cascading down upon his face as he lost consciousness again amid the rising din of battle. It remained, however, that though he realized himself unconscious to the outside world, he experienced the peculiar sensation that his mind was alert and watching itself even as his body slumbered; and that, in inhabiting this unusual place, the mind was made privy to impressions that evaded it at other times. He fancied, for instance, he could hear Death murmuring his song somewhere close by on the field, though it seemed to him as if the tune entered through his bodily flesh rather than his ears. The song went on for some time, heavy and plodding, inevitable and unavoidable, before growing fainter and abandoning his body to a pervading and overpowering sense of fatigue. Such was Death, he thought, as his comrades galloped past his still form, rolling up the enemy on the seemingly endlessly-contested field. To die, to be taken by Death, was ultimately only to sleep, to rest.

Yet on this occasion too, Alvis Stevens proved discontent to die and awoke in the pale light of daybreak to discover his arms could move. He lifted his right hand gingerly, tentatively, to touch the dried blood on his face and then raised it higher to his hair, knotted with dried gore. He was desperately thirsty, his throat so parched that it was some time before his comrades who lingered nearby heard his soft entreaties for aid.

Discovered at last, he was given water and carefully loaded upon a wagon with a half dozen other wounded men. In a croaking voice he inquired after Tamerlane, but none had seen or heard anything of him, though more than one Ranger departed to make inquiries on Alvis' behalf. It was as if the mighty horse, having been relieved of his master and ever partial to his own counsel when free to enact it, had resolved to depart suddenly and forever on misty wings, and had done so successfully and unseen amid the chaos of the field.

The bodies of the wounded jostled and knocked against each other as the wagon bore them over uneven roads, the blood from their bodies intermingling as it ran and pooled along the wagon's rough boards or dripped in congealing droplets down onto the muddy ruts. When they at last arrived in Charlottesville, two of the men were dead and Alvis' face wore a leaden hue, his eyes utterly lusterless.

The town's university campus had been converted into a hospital, for its students and faculty had all gone to the war and many would never attend a lecture or inhabit a classroom again. Surgeons entered and left the Rotunda, perpetually anxious at the pitiable quantity of available medical supplies. In the small student chambers on the Ranges and here and there in the faculty homes lay the wounded, nurses and a few grief-stricken family members moving among them on their regrettable errands.

A stretcher bore Alvis to Room 13 of the West Range, the previous occupant of which had succumbed to a sucking chest wound only just that morning and whose soiled uniform and effects had yet to be removed. The sheets however had been changed and, transferred from a stretcher to the bed, Alvis was relieved of his uniform and washed by a servant who announced himself as Ailstock.

Alvis must have lost consciousness soon thereafter, but when he awoke discovered an outlandish figure inspecting him. Ageless, tall, thin, and stooped, the man prodded Alvis' body with long emaciated fingers. His studious face was bloodless, the forehead low and brooding. His mouth, which perpetually worked, forming inaudible comments to itself, looked unnaturally large and flexible, and was home to a wild collection of uneven teeth. Perhaps noticing its patient's wakefulness, the mouth ceased its working inner dialogue to offer Alvis something apparently meant to resemble a reassuring smile.

"A clean wound," Alvis heard the strange man mutter to someone he could not see.

In and out of consciousness Alvis went over the course of that night amid the perpetual sensations of pain, liquid slipperiness, and the powerful odors of chemicals and blood.

Next morning Alvis was greeted and fed by Ailstock before receiving a visit from the outlandish surgeon, who introduced himself as Augustus Bedloe. By the light of day Dr. Bedloe's features appeared less exotic, though still peculiar—the unusual mouth fixed in a melancholy smile above which large, round eyes looked down upon Alvis with a dull and expressionless luster only barely more animated, Alvis thought, than the open-eyed stares of the battlefield dead. He learned in time that Bedloe's appearance owed itself to an old and very odd illness, which had led him to undergo extreme experimental treatments under the care of an elderly Charlottesville doctor named Templeton. This physician would later take him on as an apprentice and educate him in the application of various French theories of magnetic rehabilitation as well as M. Ernest Valdemar's concepts of Mesmerism.

It had become Dr. Bedloe's custom, in addition to his routine medical duties, to keep a separate journal on his patients' accounts of and opinions on the war in the wake of their wounds and other maladies. Often he conducted these interviews not long after the patient had been administered a heavy dose of laudanum so as to garner, or so he maintained, the most truthful and accurate responses to his queries.

So the time came when, having administered to Alvis a significant volume of the narcotic by legerdemain, he drew up a chair to converse with and observe his patient.

"When any strange, violent, or necromatic adventure has occurred to a human being," the odd physician began, "that being, however desirous he may be to conceal the same, feels at certain periods torn up as it were by a mental earthquake, which may only be assuaged in baring the inner depths of his spirit to another. Thus, I would have you share the depths of your recent experiences for the benefit of your brother soldiers and the advancement of the scientific arts."

Bedloe's expression was curious—expectant, yet apprehensive—as if he were entreating for some special favor that it might yet grieve him to obtain.

"Well," answered Alvis sleepily, "on those occasions I was thrown in with the army for a major battle, I couldn't help but think the event was somehow larger than any of its reasons and, indeed, any of us. And it felt to me sometimes—especially during those long winter nights at Fredericksburg when the heavens were all lit up with color—that there was nothing new about any of it, as if we were simply repeating the tired, brutal motions of all the wars that had come before us on this continent. It seemed to me at such times, strange as the notion may appear now, that the man who fell before me might as well have been a Redcoat, or a Redman for that matter, for all the difference it might make. I gather you know the old army legend, that when the moon is up the restless souls of dead fighting men drift up out of the earth on moonbeams and wander the land. I never glimpsed such specters, though I knew there were far older bones beneath those of the dead we would bury the next day."

Bedloe had ceased his note-taking and regarded Alvis intently, a curious light hovering beneath the surface of his dark, expressionless eyes. Yet when he spoke, his voice was whimsical: "You have a very interesting imagination for a mere Ranger, Mr. Stevens."

Dr. Bedloe visited Alvis often over the next few days. As Alvis' health and perceptions improved, it became plain to him that part of Bedloe's strangeness likely stemmed from the fact that he regularly imbibed prodigious amounts of the medicine he was so fond of administering to his patients. When the dosage the doctor had taken was particularly large, Alvis would note the sweat on his face and the hollow, grating peals of laughter that sometimes would arrive suddenly and unexpectedly from that fantastic mouth, almost compelling one's hair to stand on end.

As a result of his interest in Alvis, Bedloe usually interviewed him at night in the wake of his rounds, and when he departed Alvis would fall into a narcotic slumber almost immediately, his dreams mingling with his waking reality so that his life became less like a road along which one marks one's time and progress, and more like a great endless meadow or prairie upon which distance is dubious and days run together. He dreamed vividly of dead companions and saw their faces buried beneath the ground.

One rainy night the darkness of his room shaped itself into fearful forms resembling people. When they had departed, he listened silently to the tapping of drops against the window panes and then followed the water as it worked its way jaggedly down the outside walls of his room and seeped into the ground, continuing its descent until at last it reached a place where lay the dead–their arms, their feet, their eyes. He saw in his mind the tiny scavengers of the earth stripping their bones, gnawing at their tongues, and burrowing through their decaying bellies. Toward dawn he awoke sweating, with the powerful odors of rotting flesh and gunpowder in his nostrils.

Though Alvis daily grew stronger in body, his self felt foreign to him, the luminous eyes and long stringy hair of a stranger greeting him when Ailstock brought a mirror before his face—a stranger young in years but old in experience, grown ancient in his suffering. His wounds, it seemed, and the manner in which he had received them, had changed forever his philosophy of war and life; had changed him.

"The science of the mind," Dr. Bedloe said on the morning of Alvis' discharge from the hospital, "will one day reveal that a man may die, for all intents and purposes, while alive. If and when he comes to live again, he is, in effect, a different man."

§⊃Q℞

He must have slept very long, for when next he knew consciousness, his eyes focused on an old woman bending over him. She appeared short in stature and thin, her posture was rigid and its slightness concealed a certain strength and wiriness of body suggested in the small lumps of muscle between her gnarled thumbs and forefingers. Her outer garments were faded, ragged, and streaked with dirt. There were deep wrinkles about her eyes, forming large pockets beneath, but the animated look in her gaze, when she at last turned it upon him, was so alive that it added to the unease of his feverish state.

She did not speak but forced a series of bitter concoctions into his mouth, the last of which caused him to gag. A small, green-eyed charcoal cat considered him expectantly at the woman's feet and licked at the spilt soup with its pink tongue. By virtue of the cobwebs lining the rock walls and ceiling and the echoes that accompanied all sound, including the faint distant drip of water, he fancied he must be in a cave.

As he watched the woman, his fever summoned vague recollections of frightening tales from his boyhood about Grace Sherwood, the witch of Gisburne in Princess Anne County, who, it was said, lived beneath the ground and possessed webbing in her armpits so as to frolic with the devil on moonlit nights in the inlets of the Chesapeake Bay. And, indeed, more than one old fisherman claimed to have witnessed them dancing on the ice in the predawn during the winter Caucus Bay froze over.

When these musings had vanished so, he discovered, had the old woman, and he suddenly fancied the cave shrunk and grown darker as though seeking to enclose his body and become its tomb. His sweaty skin clung to the rough furs that surrounded it as strange conceits and whimsicalities gnawed steadily at his brain like worms. Bizarre faraway voices whispered in an unknown tongue. And was it dream or reality that in that dark, shrinking cave a young woman came to him, joining him beneath the animal skins? He could not discern her face clearly as she writhed and moved against him. But then, as she twisted and pressed, her body appeared to change, to ceaselessly transform, in the dimness so that it resembled, by turns, a lioness, then a serpent, and then a great bird. At last she was gone and there remained only his exhaustion, the blackness of the chamber, and the far-off echo of slow, dripping water.

Alvis slept then, but in his slumber he inexplicably heard his father's voice. The words were a confused murmuring jumble but fragments of comprehension emerged here and there. Death was near, his father informed him, but not yet fully present. It held back, he said, somewhere round the edges. Alvis gradually became aware of a terrible aching cold, followed, after an interval, by a gentle reassuring warmth as though his father, the essence of him, was all around him, holding him in his arms as if he were a child once more. Then, at last, he could hear his father clearly and distinctly, almost as if his lips were at his ear.

"Do not watch for Death now, my son," his father murmured in a voice devoid of age; otherworldly, yet warm and gentle. "Watch instead where you put your feet. And when at last he is before you, return his look, face-to-face, eye-to-eye, as the man I knew you would live to be."

When Alvis at last knew himself again wholly, he could discern it was day by the light which worked its way around a heavy dark curtain hanging in the cave's small opening. His body felt utterly spent but he could move his head now, and he peered about the cave, noting that it was really a kind of small cavern—a hollow place in a wall of rock with a hardened clay floor. Across from where he lay among the animal skins was another bed made of ox hide. A triangle of soot-stained bricks supported a great cauldron near the cave's entrance.

He lay there for some time, watching the opening's curtain sway slightly as the outside breezes struck it, the occasional odor of deep forest borne to him on the swirling air. After a while, the old woman who had tended him returned, suddenly thrusting the curtain aside and entering, a canvas sack slung over her shoulder.

She ignored his hoarse-voiced questions and instead moved methodically about the dim chamber, depositing in various places the roots and plants she pulled forth from her sack. Then she piled dry wood beneath the cauldron and struck up a fire, the flames illuminating the cave and highlighting the old woman's deep wrinkles and facial lines, which together conspired to promise a singular history in a voiceless tongue.

Alvis watched her silently, recalling how Evandero once had mentioned in passing a woman rumored to have left her husband long ago and set out to live among the cannibals. She had been raised and educated, it was said, in a remote Jesuit monastery but eventually fled it with a man she was to marry: a wild local fellow who earned a precarious living as a hunter and fisherman. Yet never having established that matrimonial bond, she had taken to the forest where she was rumored to have matched her Jesuit knowledge with the savage wisdom of the Botocudo and become in time a powerful healer. Whether or not this was that woman, Alvis could not establish. Her features certainly were not Indian, but her stubborn silence afforded him no clues. Silently, methodically, she fed him some variety of mashed vegetable which she had boiled in the cauldron, her gnarled wrinkled fingers dropping the hot cooked fragments into his mouth. The food warmed his body and filled his head with a heavy drowsiness so that slumber nearly took him ere the last swallow.

Next day Alvis was able to rise and totter weakly about the cave. He did so clad in a raggedy, threadbare woman's dress, which was the only garment of civilization he could find about the place, his own clothes having vanished. He ate from a bowl left out for him and at the cave's entrance pushed aside the curtain flap to look upon a large, open grassy area, sun of full day forcing him to squint. On the other side, perhaps fifty yards distant, lounged a number of men and women he recognized as Botocudo. He stood there watching them as they sat and moved about casually. Though wanting in stature, the males were notably broad-chested, which allowed them to bend their signature taut bows made from springy Ayri or Brijaubá wood. The hands of the men and the women alike were small and their legs lean and muscular. Two elder members of the tribe, who sat off to one side in a patch of shade, wore curious circular wooden mouth ornaments which looked to have been inserted into a cut opening in the bottom lip. He wished to consider them longer but a bout of dizziness sent him stumbling back to the furs.

When he woke again, it was night. The fire beneath the caldron flickered, its smoke wafting slowly through the cave's opening, and the old woman sat next to him on a stool, scrutinizing him closely, the green-eyed, charcoal cat purring in her lap.

Then she startled Alvis by speaking. "You are altogether yourself once more," she announced in English, her voice raspy and distorted by the cave's echo.

Incredulous both at her voice and its use of his native tongue, Alvis could manage only the question, "English?"

"I could not speak to you earlier," she continued, watching him steadily, "for it was paramount that you find your way back to yourself, by yourself. But, yes, I learned to speak English long ago, though I have had little use for it here."

So this, Alvis realized, was indeed the woman Evandero had spoken of, the medicine woman Pomona, who had lived among the Jesuits and the Botocudo and intimately mastered the ways of both. Having established the old woman's identity, Alvis asked her a number of questions regarding the nature of his malady. His bruised ribs and lacerations, he discovered, were little cause for concern compared to infected knife wounds and malarial fever he had contracted from lying so long in the mud of the pathway. It was that, she informed him, which nearly had killed him.

"But you are ill no longer," she concluded, "save for the wound on your heart. And in that you are as marked by love as the moon."

Noting Alvis' expression of incomprehension, she continued, "Let me elaborate by way of a brief tale, for it is not often I speak in English. But then there shall be no more questions and you shall sleep again, for tomorrow you will find you can sit a horse and so resume your place next to old Evandero, to whom I have long owed a favor which I now have repaid in full."

She bade Alvis drink one of her bitter draughts before adjusting herself on the stool, her knees creaking softly, and continuing. "It is said among the Botocudo there was once a very handsome warrior who often was visited during the dark of the moon in secret by a girl who loved him ardently. Because she came to him in such darkness he could never see her face, yet longed to know her identity. On the day the next dark of the moon was at hand, he decided to cover his face with the black resin of a jungle plant so that her face might be stained when she set it against his that evening. Next day he would know which of the village girls loved him with such great desire. She came that night and they lay together as was their custom, but in the early morning light, as she made her way back to her hut, she saw the black marks on her face while kneeling at her favorite brook to drink. Terrified, she scrubbed at her face with water and leaves, but the marks would not disappear.

"Now though her skill remained unknown to any but herself and her father who had trained her, the girl was a great archer—better, in fact, than any man in her village. And taking up her supple bow, she began firing arrows into the sky, which collectively formed a ladder ascending into the air which allowed her to climb heavenward, away from her village and fearful situation. As she climbed, Tupan, the god of gods, spied the beautiful fleeing figure and, cupping his great hands beneath her, gently raised her up further, her countenance lightening and brightening as it moved upward.

"That is how, according to the Botocudo, the moon's white face came to have dark spots upon it. They are marks of love. And that is why the Queen of Night, who was once as mortal as you and I, never tires of gazing down into the watery mirrors of seas, brooks, and rivers—to glimpse and dwell upon those marks of love, forever branded upon her face."

Alvis drowsily mumbled something inarticulate, his voice hoarse and heavy with sleep.

The old woman sighed wearily and the cat looked up at her before leaping down from the nest it had made for itself in her lap. "I recount such tales to lighten myself for death," she continued. "Just as there are books that cannot be read, so it remains there are stories that cannot be told. That is a truth for Jesuits and Botocudo alike. But often it is a great detriment to the would-be teller, who dies with her heart in convulsions of despair on account of those mysteries which did not suffer themselves to be revealed. The burden of horror is too great for her to shrug off in life and so lends weight to her body when it is cast into the grave."

She eyed him evenly. "Rest now, Confederado," she said, "but know there will yet be more war for you before you rest truly. Yield not to disasters, therefore, but press onward the more bravely."

Alvis, heavy-lidded now, thanked her both for his life and her good words. "Your counsel would be mine even had you not uttered it," he murmured, finding his voice. "For I have been close to death enough times to learn that each man's path is revealed to him when death draws near."

Next morning Alvis, though still suffering from stiffness in his joints and an aching about the ribs, found he could rise and walk about well enough. Once again, food had been laid out for him but the old woman, Pomona, and her familiar were gone.

When he had eaten, he pushed aside the curtain and to his surprise glimpsed Heliodoro in full tack grazing in the meadow below the cave. A strange figure Alvis likely made to any watchful Botocudo as he staggered down the slope in his ill-fitting, threadbare dress. Heliodoro's head jerked up from the ground's bounty to appraise the curiously-attired, slow-moving figure and, catching Alvis' scent on the wind, whinnied suddenly in recognition and walked, head bobbing, to meet him.

After Alvis had rubbed his friend about the ears and flanks, he mounted slowly with no small expense of pain. Once in the saddle, his sore body forbade him from attempting even a slow canter, but a deep sense of joy accompanied the discomfort as he reined Heliodoro homeward.

Upon arriving at the *fazenda*, he embraced Evandero warmly, the old man having slowly looked him up and down while squeezing his arm. Alvis wasted no time—save in changing his clothes—before inquiring after Lavinia. They had taken up their customary places on the porch in their old manner, Alvis wincing as he descended into his seat.

"She was," Evandero recounted, looking out across the fields and shrugging, "naturally most distressed when Emilio boasted of having beaten you to death, yet we succeeded at last in getting word to her through one of the servants that you were in fact alive and recovering safely.

"This, however, regrettably was not the end of the matter. Mr. Ferreira, it seems, unaware of Emilio's designs, had made plans of his own to separate the two of you. He has removed her to a finishing school in Minas Gerais. Moreover, he has seen to it that you, I am very sad to say, have been officially drafted into the Brazilian army."

Evandero grimly took in Alvis' stunned expression.

"These are very dark, serious matters," continued Evandero, his visage grown uncharacteristically stern, "and they have not been allowed to go unanswered. Emilio's cowardly thug, Baranga, never shall serve as an instrument of discord again for Santos and the enxadeiros took it upon themselves to administer the law. Emilio, I could have told them, is too careful and protected for them to have conveniently reached and secured, yet Baranga was not so fortunate.

"I do not know how they came upon him but I know how they left him. Crippled, his legs in a tangle, they dragged him to a small ravine in the foothills into which the carcasses of dead calves and other animals have been cast for as far back as the oldest of locals can recall. Perhaps a dozen buzzards, used to feeding at the place, always sit watching from the bare upper branches of the larger trees which rise up out of the ravine.

"One can imagine how their eyes must have followed Baranga as they pushed him over the edge. How he must have rolled and slid over the loose dirt and rocks until he came to rest at the bottom upon the bed of indeterminate bones that cover the ravine's floor.

"This being all that had been required of the enxadeiros, they would have then turned their backs on the ravine, leaving Baranga there at the bottom, able only to drag himself in great pain, as the great carrion birds, likely already gliding down from above, alighted awkwardly among all those scattered, sun-bleached bones and begin shuffling toward him. Santos and I have viewed these birds at work before. It is something to behold how they tear at the flesh, jostling for position and pecking at one another. Baranga's will not be the first human skeleton to lie picked and scattered along the floor of that ravine."

Alvis was silent when Evandero recounted all this. He reached down for the jug that sat between them and filled his gourd. Then he proceeded to drain the vessel in a series of quick gulps and choking slightly.

Evandero smiled. "It may interest you to know," he said, "that in the city of Curitiba there is a graveyard solely designated for drunkards. If you were to die now, I could carry you there in that fine wagon you built for me and dump you among your fellows."

Alvis wiped his mouth with the back of his hand and grinned at his old friend, then laughed and toasted him, the cachasa sloshing noisily in the gourds as the vessels met with a dry, hollow click.

"I have something I wish to relate to you," Evandero said, serious once more, "which may hearten you somewhat in the wake of these dark developments and new trials. And, if not, perhaps it will at least allow you to better understand this aged hermit who knows so intimately strange savage healers and valleys of death.

"I am an old man," Evandero began simply. "I have lived in this world longer and more deeply than most. I have learned that whatever you cling to will only hurt and disappoint you in the end. Apart from my parents, they who raised me, I have loved only three people in my life: my two wives and my daughter. They are all dead.

"My first wife I met on an excursion with a party of lighthearted young people who, like me, are all now faded, crooked, and deaf—if they are even alive. In any event, the particular girl in their number who would come to be my wife was audacious in a manner that was intimidating, for she was very beautiful and much admired. The old men of that long-ago time said that her mother had been a great beauty as well, projecting a pleasing appearance that was as much a result of her manner, her grace of movement and expression, as of her fine features. I remember how the old men standing about would tamp their pipes and remark that this girl's mother had worn a jeweled necklace as naturally as a country girl might don a garland of flowers. Her daughter was the same way.

"On two separate social occasions I attempted to approach her but was struck dumb, for I was very young myself and could not even bring myself to believe she was real. To those young eyes she appeared to walk in overpowering beauty everywhere she went. Indeed, so fair and fine she seemed that at times even the very air about her appeared to shine and quiver as she moved.

"Finally, I secured her for a walk and away we went, in the cool of an evening, over an old stone bridge. We neither of us spoke ten words. That stroll, simple as it may have been, made my heart fuller and more happy than it had ever been before. I distinctly remember lying awake late into the night dwelling upon her. Already you know that a young man in love almost inevitably is overwhelmed by the presence of that emotion as it burns and swells inside him. In middle age, however, you will come to find that you are visited by humility, and you give up the belief that some benevolent power is watching and guiding you apart from other human beings. When you begin to conceive of yourself along with other people, that is when your youth is really over and you begin to grow old.

Alvis nodded slowly in silent agreement.

"But young as we were then, she reminded me of some indistinct figure out of one of the old tales. Even on our wedding night her smile was a mystery and a secret. I undressed her slowly and clumsily, with these hands."

Smiling, Evandero held up his gnarled, spotted fingers, marveling at them in the dim moonlight. Only the hum of insects steady in the deep evening and the occasional pouring of cachasa filled the quiet.

Evandero took up his account again. "The second woman I fell in love with," he continued, "I met in a brothel in Rio some years after the death of my first wife. I had gone there with a group of old friends. It was not the most glamorous place—the type frequented by the best political and church officials—nor was it the kind of dank, queer establishment visited by artists, criminals, and the like. It was clean, despite the curious assortment of smells that greeted you in the narrow street outside. The girl who entertained me that evening was that rare sort of beauty who seems almost self-luminous—one of those precious creatures who shines in the dark of her own accord.

"When I awoke early the next day in my quarters, I was altogether doubtful of what I had experienced. Perhaps I had drunk too much rum. But then I thought to myself,

'How could I have invented such a strange and arresting image, even under the effects of drink?' This question troubled me to the point that I returned to the brothel and bribed a house boy to give me the girl's home address. When I arrived there I found her at breakfast with her family, and she looked just as stunning as she had the night before. She had only to give me one glance and I felt as though I were in heaven.'

"I married her later that week in the city and brought her back here. She turned out to be a good woman behind the comely illusion that surrounded her, pushing me up as a strong breeze or current drives on a reluctant old barnacled ship. She was not particularly fond of the country but worked hard and remained grateful to me for delivering her from a whore's existence. It was she who gave me the daughter she would later perish alongside of. When you are married you will discover it is most difficult even for a very attentive husband to know whether he makes his wife truly happy or not, but I reflected long upon that question when she was no longer with me, and at last concluded that, indeed, she had been. Her name was Consuelo."

Evandero stood slowly, stepped to the edge of the porch, and proceeded to blow his nose in the country fashion, pressing his thumb first to one nostril and then to the other. Then he turned to face Alvis and bade him rise.

"The only thing wanting," he said, "is the necessary thing. Come, I have something else to share that will serve you better than the tired tales of an old man."

Evandero led Alvis out into the fields, which appeared ghostly in the pale moonlight, as if an improbable light coat of new snow lay upon their subequatorial expanse. The two friends walked slowly, one of them crippled by age, the other by his injuries. At last they came to a hilltop where they could survey all the surrounding fields. The soft light of stars afforded Alvis a vague prospect of both the house he had built and the grove far below them where stood Evandero's. Grasping Alvis' arm tightly, Evandero spread out his other and let it drift across the fine line where cultivated field met moonlit horizon.

"You are the son who was never born to me," he said, turning to Alvis. "Tonight, I name you Fazendeiro of this land, of which my father once named me. When you return from the war you shall dwell here and the powers of fortune will smile upon you and your children, who shall be Capixabas!"

‰)Ч

Alvis rose early the morning after next to hitch up Robinho and prepare the wagon for the journey to Linhares. His joints continued to plague him with tightness and his ribs ached when he stooped, but otherwise he felt almost himself in body. From Linhares he planned to float to the mouth of the Doce and there board a schooner bound for Rio with a shipment of jacaranda. A part of him wished to march boldly into Mina Gerais—to seize Lavinia and spirit her away—but he knew they would not be able to live in Brazil if he did so and he had no reliable plan for settling elsewhere, where the trials they encountered might prove just as formidable—perhaps worse.

Thus even though he was not required to officially report for duty until the end of the week, he hoped in leaving early to familiarize himself with Rio and the latest news of this new war that had reached out to clutch him. He had gleaned enough information from Evandero and others to know that it would not have required much inquiry or arrangement for a man of Mr. Ferreira's wealth and influence to have an upstart immigrant such as himself drafted into the Brazilian army. Nearly four years of war had made the new recruit a precious commodity to the Brazilian government—to the point that individual circumstances and all other considerations might easily go overlooked or ignored altogether.

Early in the war, the Brazilian navy had crushed Paraguay's sea forces and blockaded the Paraná River—its only water route to the outside world—yet Paraguay's extensive land defenses and modern army ensured the blockade alone would not decide the struggle and a bitter, costly land war ensued. It was Duque de Caxias who had begun actively recruiting any man he could find into the Brazilian army, and the Emperor's son-in-law, Count d'Eu, had continued the practice when he assumed supreme command of Brazil's military forces.

Alvis' suspicion that he constituted merely one more faceless, meaningless body in one more ceaseless, meaningless struggle was lent credence by Evandero's perspective on the conflict. "They march and fight for the same reasons men have always quarreled," he said with a dismissive gesture, "land and borders."

Of course, it remained that Alvis might flee the assignment, and perhaps Ferreira hoped that he would, but that would mean departing Brazil, losing face, and forfeiting all hope of ever seeing Lavinia again. It was something he simply could not do.

On the old, leaning dock at Linhares Alvis embraced Evandero, who required he take an earnest pledge of safe return. The previous evening, Alvis had set upon the mantle above the old man's hearth a rear tooth loosened when Emilio had beat him that eventually had worked its way out during his convalescence. This *dente* of Virginia, he informed his friend, was the only object he possessed from his homeland outside his own body, and would await his return with Evandero there at the *fazenda*.

This parting accomplished, Alvis stepped from the dock into a wide canoe manned by two rivermen. But as they pushed away from the dock and dipped their oars into the current, Evandero called after them, his precious blessing floating across the water: "May the powers of fortune go with you."

∎

So Alvis Stevens reluctantly embarked to serve in a second American war, four years and five thousand miles removed from the previous struggle. His trip down the Doce and ensuing southward voyage along the coastline were uneventful, the weather and sea languorous beneath the heavy sun, and he spent much of his time reading old newspapers and learning what he could of the war from the ship's crew, who owned they occasionally transported supplies to the army as well as contraband for themselves.

Gazing upon the sea, Alvis's thoughts naturally drifted back to the former war, searching his mind for anything that might serve him now. Seated upon the transom, his eyes took in the seemingly limitless expanse of water, and as he did so, strange, isolated moments recounted themselves to him from the early days of his time in the Rangers—his brutal initiation into a brand of war unlike any other.

It was Thomas Bocock who had urged and helped Alvis to depart the misery of the main army and join a proposed outfit led by a man named John Mosby that would come to be known variously as Rangers, Partisans, scouts, or bushwhackers. The Partisan Ranger Act passed the Confederate Congress in April 1862, but its ramifications and the personages that arose from it were not limited to the war in Virginia, and in May of that same year there appeared in the Memphis Appeal a stunning notice from a Tennessee officer named Nathan Bedford Forrest:

200 RECRUITS WANTED!

I will receive 200 able-bodied men if they will present themselves at my headquarters by the first of June with good horse and gun. I wish none but those who desire to be actively engaged.–Come on, boys, if you want a heap of fun and to kill some Yankees.

N.B. Forrest

Colonel, Commanding

Forrest's Regiment

Such postings appeared glamorous and liberating to men who had come to deride the long, stinking drudgery of army life. Moreover, Section III of the Partisan Ranger Act dictated that men could retain certain captured arms, munitions, and other items. Indeed, it seemed to some as if the Confederacy sought to spawn some special variety of swashbuckling land-pirate to hound the enemy across all the oceanic leagues of Southern forests and fields. It was not surprising then that soon the attraction of the Partisan Ranger Corps became so great the Confederate authorities were forced to prohibit altogether transfer from the line.

That first summer of 1862 was one of the hottest old-timers in Virginia could remember, though not a dry one; the pasture grass grown tall and blooming eventually into a purple cloud with specks of gold here and there where goldenrod peeked out amid the fescue. During those long days of hard riding, the stench of the body beneath one's garments sweetened into something else when joined by the more powerful odor of the horse's lather. Come night, Alvis slept in his stiff uniform, serenaded into slumber by the songs of whippoorwills, cicadas, and crickets.

There was the firm, gentle quiet with which Old Mose— for that was what they came to call him—would wake them, oft-times exactly at that tenuous point just before daybreak, an hour when the uneasiness of the air affects trees and animals and often makes men turn silently in their sleep for no apparent reason.

And there was too, on the opposite end of the mind's spectrum, in the midst of battle, the feverish reloading upon which life so often depended: removing the cylinder; tearing the covering on the cartridge and separating the bullet; then trying to be deliberate, slight tremble in the black-stained fingers, as he poured the powder into each chamber, before ramming the bullet into the powder. Finally, placing a brass percussion cap in a notch at the rear of each chamber–all life reduced in that brief span to a process Alvis might perform blindfolded, with the dexterous practiced fingerwork of a master musician.

Mostly, beyond all other things, there remained with Alvis the feeling of the closeness of the fighting—of looking the enemy full in the face before firing into it—and the nature of the inevitable death that accompanied it. He could recall clearly a wounded man he had come upon still on his knees, head and shoulders slumped, one arm a hanging weight, the left hand of the other resting someplace inside a gaping stomach wound, a terrible odor rising from the aperture like a curse. The fellow's right hand had taken a bullet, the ball having passed through clean. Alvis knew the shot had occurred at close range for the skin about the wound was burnt. He assessed all this even as he gently urged Tamerlane on with the accompanying thought that a wound affords a strange dignity to him who bears it.

Ever, it seemed, did they ride on across battlefields, from life and death alike—from one field toward the next—in a blind, sleepy haze of madness: loading and reloading, charging and wheeling. On went Alvis among the others, so many of whom were ordained to fall, the hooves of their horses wet with mud and the blood of the dead, as a devouring fire fed by high winds rages down a bone-dry mountainside, consuming all that has life in it.

But there were the times too, usually revolving around major battles, when groups of them were collapsed back into the main army. It was true the Rangers viewed regular service with disdain, identifying assignment to it as a sentence to "Botany Bay," yet it was from those occasions in the main army—perhaps partially on account of the sheer immensity of its actions and milieus—that some of Alvis' most curious experiences arose.

He marked how the long, seemingly endless column of men would move forth hour after hour—slow, voiceless, dreamlike—but then once they had stopped for the night laughter ensued, half-audible jokes, and the ringing of axes, bringing down trees from whence a hundred bivouac fires would spring up, illuminating the countryside.

Or stranger nocturnal light: the curious flickering of color in the night sky, the oddities of weather during the Fredericksburg Campaign. Those bitter cold nights had come so swiftly and suddenly that they might have been running ahead of themselves. Men looked to each other as if posing the same question. It seemed to Alvis that they all wondered at the strange nights come before their appointed times and, thinking of them, shivered in the dark. The expressions of the men betrayed their uneasiness and they stacked arms closer to the fires.

In the wake of the enemy's attack on the heights, as terrible a procession of slaughter and futility as Alvis ever had seen, there arose on the night's breeze from the abandoned sloping battlefield a peculiar chorus of groans from a maimed, reluctant choir, pierced by an occasional scream.

High above the frozen field, far against the dim horizon, the Northern Lights restlessly shifted and moved, the great undulating shapes of color swaying east and west and upward toward the stars; while below, on the dark hillside, the moans and occasional delirious laughter of the abandoned enemy wounded, lying where they had fallen, serenaded the gray soldiers on the heights, sporadic galloping hooves behind the line echoing loudly on the hard, cold ground.

Alvis, bundled and huddled as close to his fire as he dared get, listened and watched, trying without much success to remember Lavinia's face or even her words from the letters which seldom reached him anymore. The stranger laid out on the other side of the fire—a figure with a sharp-featured, wind-gnawed face joined him in considering the distant lights with bleak, sleepy eyes. Perhaps the stranger was seeking to arrange in his mind the features of a wife, a lover, a child.

"It is queer," the man muttered drowsily, his voice misty in the frigid air, "that God would show us such a thing on this particular night. It troubles the heart: such beauty overhead and all the moaning down yonder. It almost makes a body believe the Lord might next hurl all the stars from the sky."

"If He did," Alvis replied after a thoughtful silence, "there might not be enough of them for all the lives this war has claimed."

The other man closed his eyes and shifted from his back to his side soon thereafter. Alvis remained wakeful for a long time, peering up at the curious, shifting heavens as the cries on the battlefield became less frequent and the fire gave way to cold.

Bleak nights followed, though none quite so strange, the day's winter sun a mere ghost of itself as the men sought groves and bottom areas for their camps, safe from the biting winds. Most of the boys from places like Mississippi and Alabama had never seen snow and ran about trying to catch flakes on their tongues or, failing that, rolling in it like playful puppies, rubbing their faces with melting handfuls. Watching them proved one of the few times Alvis laughed during the war—perhaps the only time genuine mirth, the joy of honest good humor, rose from his belly.

Alvis thought Rio's harbor picturesque as the schooner entered it on an overcast midmorning, wisps of low sea clouds drifting slowly overhead. The bay, its sheltered expanse of gently lapping water, lay framed by irregular hills, including an unusual one resembling the foretopsail of a vessel, dotted by little palm-clad islands. As they neared the docks, the wind shifted, and with the land breezes came the rich odor of earth and something resembling flowers. Along the hilly coast, white-walled buildings with red-tiled roofs stood out from the terrain's lush greenery.

On the docks, servants, sent out by their masters to earn money as dock footmen, rushed forward to seize the chests of the two more prominent-looking passengers. Lifting each a piece of heavy luggage, they balanced it upon their heads between raised arms before walking swiftly in the direction of their appointed destinations. Alvis possessed no luggage and waited for the crowd of passengers and servants to disperse before sauntering along the edge of a wide street, away from the docks.

In the Palace Square, he drank from the great fountain, while about him barefoot servants, men and women alike, some clad in bright outfits, filled their containers and bore them away upon their heads. He took in the market with its lush tables of fresh fish, fruits, and vegetables accompanied by the fragrance of the bright bouquets. One of the woman peddlers smiled at him as he selected a mammoon from her assortment and placed a few milreis into her hand. From her, he also obtained the names of some likely lodging prospects, while a parrot screeched at him from the confines of a nearby shop.

He familiarized himself with the city over the next two days. During the intervening night a fine, misty rain swirled beyond his window, pavement glistening beneath the street lamps, but strolling down the Rua Dereita in the light of day he was witness, on more than one occasion, to a very strange sight: a troop of servants dressed only in pantaloons, jogging in a loose formation with great sacks upon their heads. One hand steadied the burden while the other held a strange rattle-box which kept time with their heavy strides. Attuned to the presence of lawmen as a result of his fugitive interval in Virginia, Alvis also took special note of the police, whom he found infrequently positioned at fountains and corners. Bored and self-important, they stood handsomely clad in their dark blue military uniforms with undress caps upon their heads and sabre and brace of pistols at their sides.

He found Rio's overall organization sprawling, its suburbs spanning perhaps four miles from its center. The streets, with the exception of the Rua Dereita, were very narrow and confined in comparison to the open thoroughfares and cobbled lanes of Richmond. At last he grew restless amid the closed streets and endless domiciles, and resolved to set out for Mount Corcovado, the hill from which, he had been told, one could take in a magnificent view of the entire region.

Walking in the company of workers and errand boys along the road to Botafogo, he entered the Larangeiras, the "Valley of the Orange Groves," where during the time of harvest the fruit hangs reddish yellow and oblong in shape. In a deep ravine, lavandeiras, the washerwomen of the city, stood in a rushing mountain stream beating their garments against rocks or bleaching them in the sun along the stony banks. Here and there, an infant hung strapped to the back of its working mother. Near the mineral springs known as Agoa Ferrea, Alvis departed the road and took up the eroded trail that ascends Corcovado. He proceeded slowly, the foliage altering significantly as he climbed, the largest trees giving way to thick stands of bamboo and fern. At the rocky summit, iron posts and railings had been erected to protect the traveler from the dangerous edge and its sheer drop. The city and its outlying areas lay below him, everything from Saint Christovno to Botafogo. He could see the sun-sparkled harbor with its dotted islands, and even the forts. The pride of Brazil, its mightiest city, stretched out before him, dispatching the power of the Emperor in all directions.

The quarters Alvis obtained were situated agreeably on the second floor of a long gray stone building, the bedroom window large enough for him to sit in. It quickly became his favorite site of repose as it allowed him to read comfortably while also keeping the street beneath his gaze. When his eyes grew tired of the Portuguese print before them, they would drift down into the street, noting the faces of the merchants, the servants, the policemen—seeing some trace of Lavinia in the graceful turn or gesture of each attractive woman.

The next morning he peered out to find flags hanging from balconies and posts, even a Confederate standard, fluttering softly in the bright air as if summoned by some unexplained fancy. The folk who emerged into the street were dressed in elaborate clothes of many colors and fine fabrics—silks, velvets, laces. The sides of the avenue continued to fill with people until it became evident that a spectacle of consequence was expected to unfold soon.

Slowly a crowd assembled below, bodies pouring in from

buildings and other thoroughfares like water flowing through the open lock of a canal. Trumpets blared somewhere far off and with the sound came palpable, felt more than seen, that celebratory predilection for festival which slumbers in the heart of each human animal. After some time, a shout went up from the crowd and a great throng approached up the street. In its midst four or five men supported two poles, on the top of which a board covered in blue represented the sea and supported a tiny ship. Another arrangement followed, depicting Neptune riding a fish. He was followed, naturally enough, by sailors who bore a banner portraying a ship in a storm. Then came a fellow rendering a convincing Bacchus, wreath of grapes about his head and a cup of wine sloshing in his hand, as he leered at the young women in the crowd. The final procession was extraordinarily dark and macabre. It included a hearse drawn by six horses with great emerald green plumes upon their heads. In the hearse was a dark-clad figure of Death bearing a scythe in one hand and an hour-glass in the other. His mask was a skeleton's face. Behind him came white-clad ghosts and angry cannibals howling to have their appetites appeased by the flesh of children. As this savage assembly passed, the young boys and girls among the onlookers shrieked and covered their eyes, clinging to their mothers. Following this spectacle occured a number of fireworks explosions. Then lastly came a series of marching bands and, as they stomped and played, the mass of onlookers began to undulate and dance to the music as one, as if collectively constituting a single great wave upon the sea. All the air was filled with such mingled sounds and sights as these as Alvis quietly rose from his window and drew in the shutters.

Upon reporting for duty on his appointed day at one of the forts along the bay, Alvis underwent, perhaps on account of his foreignness, an extensive examination by a squat, bureaucratic lieutenant who carefully recorded each of his answers in cramped shorthand. However Alvis' confession that he had served in the American war to the north made the interviewing officer hesitate in his recording as though uncertain how to proceed. Likely none of his beloved rubrics had informed him of the appropriate manner in which to process a veteran of a foreign war. At last Alvis answered the final query and was dismissed, abandoning the room to the little bureaucrat, who continued to write.

When his orders arrived the following day, Alvis discovered it was a cavalry regiment to which he had been assigned. His papers, the orders stated, had been sent ahead of him and he was to join a camp of cavalry replacements south of the city preparing to ride west to the main army. So he found himself trading in his pleasing city quarters for a tent of rough canvas, and at the edge of camp the bored ordnance officer issued him a new uniform, which chafed his skin, a cheap sabre, and a pistol with workings as worn as the old nag he was given to ride.

For all this, despite the wanting state of his equipment and stale army food, the ensuing return to military life generally constituted a peaceful development for Alvis, as it is to many men who have served before at lengthy intervals under dire circumstances. Gone is all indecisiveness and responsibility which accompany living one's own life; one rises in the morning to follow the orders of the day and falls asleep in the dark, the day's duty done. Occasionally, he was visited during the night by the image of Lavinia and moved restlessly in his sleep. Yet always there lay the next day and the next task—the endless store of time and duties which is the luxury of every army.

More than once he thought of his first days among the Rangers and the education that comes with living among other men while adopting a new way of life. He recalled the secretiveness of his arrival: how when he and his companions reached the Partisan assembly area, a crossroads in southern Loudoun County, they found themselves met and escorted by a contingent of horsemen for some miles along game trails through rolling thick forest, until at last, nightfall nearly upon them, they came to a camp that stood in a draw at the foot of the Blue Ridge Mountains.

Alvis did not see Colonel Mosby that evening nor the next morning, for he learned the colonel was out overnight and likely would not rise until after the midday meal. And when he finally did report to his new commander, he was somewhat disappointed by the encounter.

John Mosby, the man they would in time all come to speak of in veneration as Old Mose, was slight of body and exuded a very quiet demeanor. He had not any of the magnetism or charisma that Alvis had expected in one who had been called upon to command an elite collection of soldiers. Indeed, Mosby's personal manner, as he took in Alvis' salute and welcomed him, was altogether flat—what someone other than Alvis might have considered downright cold. His hair, which was sandy colored, lay uncombed atop a hatchet face from which protruded a hawk nose. The only interesting aspect about him, Alvis thought, was his eyes—blue, luminous, and piercing, as if something violently passionate behind them was seeking a way out into the world. Alvis had heard him described as a tireless man who could sit in a saddle for three days straight if necessary. Such feats, he knew, were manifestations of sheer will and what Alvis eventually would come to divine, having observed Mosby for a period of weeks, was that not only the man's will, but his whole being—the entirety of his essence as a creature—seemed bent upon his military function: intellect, body, and purpose all forged and focused upon the art of war.

Long irregular hours of duty and a perpetually sore bottom constituted Alvis' trial-by-fire initiation into the Rangers, quickly demonstrating to him the enormity of the duty he had undertaken. Indeed, the work and hours were at first so exhausting that he longed for the regular army with all its drab discomfort and woe.

Mosby lacked any real headquarters—save in the saddle—and the unpredictable and far-between places they dismounted and rested were nearly always isolated, forlorn stretches of nowhere.

"My corps," Alvis would hear him boast more than once, "is made as much of hemlock and beech and dogwood as it is of men."

It was then a strange and sometimes eerily peaceful variety of military life that Alvis found himself embracing beside placid streams or on silent, lonesome country roads where the sun shone lightly on wind-fluttered leaves and the war's sweeping roar remained but a faraway murmured rumor.

Yet they grew expert in their art, and the enemy felt their presence often and with significant loss, so that Mosby's name became an oath and a word of fear among the soldiers they did battle with. The youthfulness of the Rangers and the prestige—what in time would come to be near celebrity—they enjoyed fueled their vanity, many of them choosing to sport the choicest items of their plunder: uniform coats with buff trimming, hats with gold braids and ostrich plumes, red capes. Yet Mosby knew his men and cared not for their foppishness off the battlefield, so long as they continued to garner distinction upon it. To secure that end, he told them almost nothing of his plans so that they were forced to follow him in blind trust. Rarely did they know what operation they were partaking of until sometime after their final rendezvous point, the men having usually arrived in pairs at some minute crossroad. Then they would ride off as a force in a given direction, perhaps changing course and taking up new roads once or twice, before Mosby actually revealed to them the true object of their bellicose errand.

Now Alvis found himself on another continent with strange horsemen, riding to war again, yet the feel of it all proved very familiar to him, and whatever inherent exoticism may have provoked some initial measure of wariness among his fellows quickly was balanced and then overcome by his instinctual, exemplary soldiering: his quick attention to the routine military tasks at hand and enviable horsemanship and stamina in the saddle. By the time they arrived, following long days of unremarkable riding in the rain, at the camp of the main army in the southern portion of the immense state of Mato Grosso—the countryside swarming with assembled horses and soldiers—he had earned the respect of the men alongside him. Warm and reluctant farewells ensued as comrades trickled away to their various companies, most of them too young and green to have yet realized that military life is a life of constant departure and dispatch—by order, by chance, by death.

As if exercising the element of chance in their dispensation, Alvis' new orders upon his arrival contained an unexpected twist. Rather than joining his regiment as previously intimated in Rio, he was to report first to the headquarters of Count D'Eu, the peculiarity of this directive readily reflected in the response of the indignant adjutant who examined the papers outside the Count's tent. A narrow-eyed, bearded fellow, the officer looked up from the orders to study Alvis' face

suspiciously. And when the foreigner shrugged at the adjutant's inquiry regarding his business with the Count, the wariness waxed into annoyance, and he turned to vanish behind
the white tent flap with a barked command for Alvis to wait.

When the officer returned after a few moments, all traces
of irritation and, indeed, color were erased from his face and
he stiffly instructed Alvis to follow him inside. The interior
of the Count's tent was dark, cool, and Spartan in aspect.
A military bed of canvas stood in a corner surrounded by
mosquito-netting and a great, map-covered table occupied
the center of the chamber, over which bent a tall, comely
figure, sharply dressed in a dark uniform, head crowned by
close-cut blonde hair and a short beard. When the Count's
eyes rose from the table to appraise the Confederado, Alvis
noted they were blue enough to have been his own. Count
D'Eu looked to be in his middle twenties, the same age as
Alvis, though the foreigner would have appeared significantly his senior to the impartial observer on account of his
weatherbeaten skin and jagged forehead scar.

Alvis and the adjutant stopped and saluted as the Count
came round the table, appraising the foreigner with a frank
expression. Alvis knew little of the nobleman other than he
was French royalty by birth and son-in-law to the Emperor.
He had been afforded command of the army in March of that
year and his lack of military experience and poor pronuncia-
tion of Portuguese had elicited jokes in the ranks, though it
was reluctantly conceded that he commanded with a firm
hand and daily pursued his goal of ending the war quickly
with irreproachable ardor. His father-in-law must have seen
something in him which gave him hope, for the Emperor
knew, as Alvis did, that forfeiting a major campaign would
present a significant threat both to the Brazilian war effort
and himself.

"I have heard of Mosby's Rangers," said the Count in a level Portuguese tinged with what Alvis took to be a French accent as he came to stand before Alvis and gestured for the pair of subordinates to be at their ease. "Of horsemen who could materialize out of the earth as stealthily as deep-jungle Indians and as lawless and benevolent as good-hearted pirates."

Alvis met the Count's ensuing smile with a cautious one of his own.

"I have need of such horsemen," said the Count, "to accurately inform me of the enemy's movements and plague them where possible."

The Count's smile waned then and was replaced by the frank, penetrating expression which appeared customary to his countenance. "I have studied your war in some detail," he continued, "and it troubles me—indeed, seems to me very nearly impossible—that your Confederacy lasted so long as it did in light of your opponent's virtually unlimited material resources and willingness, especially in those last years, to wage war on the populace of your country. Indeed, this troubles me greatly, for though we significantly outnumber the Paraguayans, enjoy better health, and possess superior equipment, the example of your struggle lingers. Is it not true that Lee's army was starved and worn-out rather than defeated militarily? And is it not said everywhere that your Lee is the greatest soldier to direct an army since that frightful little Corsican made all Europe tremble?"

Again the smile appeared, a soldier's smile—rueful and ready yet quickly drawn in, clipped when necessary, by the business at hand. Alvis stood mutely, uncertain whether or not the questions the Count posed were offered with the expectation of receiving answers or if their answers already were understood. But then the Count gracefully held out an open hand in inquiry and Alvis realized he was meant to respond.

"I must own I know very little of far-ranging strategies," Alvis began, "but I have fought in enough engagements to have learned a few of the unremarkable secrets of war. That war is treachery and hatred. That it is torture and killing and sickness and tiredness, until at last it grinds to a halt and the lone soldier, as if waking from some fanciful nightmare, finds, in reality, that nothing much has changed. I am afraid, sir, that is the nearest I can explain my general understanding of it, wanting though the explanation may be."

The count regarded him levelly, arms crossed on his chest.

"I understand too well what troubles you regarding that war to the north and, indeed, can verify that material advantage worked in some ways to the detriment of our enemy. His superiority in supply and manpower were truly vast, yet he generally was clumsy in his administration and deployment of them, which led to many a costly defeat on the battlefield. And, of course, it always boosted our morale to prevail against such overwhelming odds. It led many, in fact, to believe and trust that God favored our side, directing the hands of our leaders."

At this point, the adjutant, who had been watching Alvis distrustfully, interjected. "But this is foolishness, sir," he appealed to the Count. "What use to us are foreign tales from one who has no business in our war?"

"Don't be a fool, Amaro," snapped the Count. "And be careful of your insults. Bear in mind your war currently is waged by a French nobleman. I think you had better leave us now."

As the chastened officer departed, the Count apologized to Alvis for the adjutant's remark before idly lapsing into an anecdote on rudeness, perhaps for the purpose of recovering the air of ease with which their conversation had begun. "Before the war," he said, "the American representative to the Emperor was a gentleman from your homeland of Virginia named Richard Meade—a likable, humble fellow who enjoyed the court's favor. He was replaced in time by an arrogant man named James Watson Webb, who not only lectured the Emperor on what he considered the negative aspects of Brazilian culture, but sought to enrich himself by placing his son at the head of a company that would manage a steamer line between Rio de Janeiro and New York. Needless to say, the Emperor gradually and gracefully, as is ever his magnanimous custom, pushed this man to the periphery of the court.

"But I am afraid I digress too much," said the Count with a sigh. "It is my way of escaping, if only for a matter of moments, the immense charge before me. But tell me, you have spoken of your war only in generalities. How would you relate the personal experience of it as opposed to what you have encountered here?"

"As I have yet to see any action here," replied Alvis, "I am reluctant to speculate much upon the nature of these hostilities, but I would be surprised if they differed overly much in degree or kind. In the war to the north it seemed as though engagements and events remained more or less the same in their nature, despite the vast stretches of time and geography one marched across between them. For me the experience of it came to resemble a kind of dream in which sad, lone men followed the same orders again and again, like a great mindless mob driven by some single and erroneous impulse. As is the case in most fantasies of the night, it is difficult to recall specific events or your own particular actions once they have passed—the battles you took part in, the men you killed. As I say, you remember it as you would a dream—some great, dim dream—in which the faces and places remain familiar yet ultimately faceless and placeless. You wake from it and wonder if it ever really occurred."

Alvis shook his head before continuing. "But I fear that is of little use to you, sir," he said, "though I believe the manner of war I conducted in the Rangers likely would be applicable to most any engagement, and, indeed, likely as not will remain so far into the future. 'Ol Mose,' that is Colonel Mosby, had learned that using small forces to threaten many points upon the enemy, especially a rearmost supply line, might neutralize more than a hundred times its own number. The enemy, you see, is forced to expend his numbers watching for possible attack at out-of-the way-places rather than throwing those resources into his own defenses and the points where he needs them most. Fear is the phantom ally of the smaller force, for the enemy's concern occupies his focus and forces him to design unnecessary elaborate contingencies, wasting time and resources."

The Count had brought his fist to his bearded chin as Alvis talked and his eyes had fallen to the collection of maps on the large table. His aspect was one of deep thought. Then, suddenly, he looked up at Alvis and smiled.

When Alvis departed the Count's tent, he did so as a captain bearing two Colt revolvers, a gaudy stipend for the purchase of new uniforms and a fast horse, and a packet of orders directing him to train a detachment of fifty handpicked men for the purpose of reconnoitering Marshal President Lopez's Paraguayan army and disrupting its movements.

Time passed quickly for Alvis in the camp of the Brazilian army on account of his new duties. By the beginning of July, he had selected his men from the general cavalry based on recommendations from their officers. Competition was fierce and he knew he was getting the best the Brazilian army could offer. The appeal, he knew, was the promised nature of the duty and he recalled the excitement he felt during his journey northward to join Mosby's outfit accompanied by two men: a burly, silent man from Bath County and a loquacious little fellow from Emporia who rode like a jockey and boasted of the money he had won racing against cavalrymen while in winter camp.

"I aim to fight my own way," the rodent-like vagabond had announced, "not set like a toy soldier on some line with somebody in my ear telling me what to do and when. They say Mosby wants men who can ride fast and long. And it ain't no secret the horsemen that strike quick don't never lose many."

Alvis and the man from Bath County rode on silently as the small horseman continued to hold forth, peppering his stories with humorous lies and half-truths, until the big man from southwest Virginia pressed in next to him, stirrup to stirrup, and instructed the fellow he'd best rein in his mouth for a spell or risk losing use of it.

There was similar excitement among the recruits here and Alvis was grateful for it, spending no small amount of time contemplating how best to maintain that high morale. He knew they would need it.

Count d'Eu, meanwhile, was equally active, reorganizing his entire army of twenty-six thousand into two corps commanded by the experienced generals Polidoro and Osório the Legendary. Alvis was awakened from an afternoon nap when the latter general, Osório, rode into camp, the thunderous ovation of his men growing in volume as the celebrated commander neared the vicinity of the Count's tent. It was said the jaw wound Osório suffered at Avay was not fully healed, but that he had returned nonetheless to lead his veterans, injury or no, toward what he hoped would constitute their final campaign and long-sought-after victory. Such was the nature of The Legend's dedication to his men and the loyalty it sparked among them in return.

Though spirits waxed high, all was not ideal in the army. Based on the cynical complaints and cursing he heard from other officers, Alvis counted himself fortunate to have had the luxury of selecting veteran horsemen, for there were tales of new infantry having to be flogged in order to form up properly. Often he heard an officer cry out in frustration on the drilling fields, "These *tabaréos* are no soldiers!" What he did not initially realize, but would later discover, was the fact that many of the new men were conscripts or former servants who had been granted freedom by enlisting in the army. Backgrounds and circumstances notwithstanding, their mantras were the same as his: "One struggle more and I am free." And the hope of freedom and happiness for him, as it had in the prior war, again rested in the image of a beautiful woman.

Though Alvis found the Brazilian army's discipline wanting compared to what he favored, his exploradors—what his handpicked contingent of scouts came to be called—were skilled riders and generally satisfactory in their comportment. Alvis' second-in-command, a subtle man called Vergara, helped to sustain the discipline and breach the matter of the Confederado's foreignness for those who doubted him. Vergara was of medium height and wiry, and though his visage usually gave the impression of drowsiness, he remained ever wary and watchful, his black eyes twinkling behind drooping, lazy lids. Stoic in his grim resignation, he answered when spoken to but rarely volunteered a word of his own volition. He was a man who prudently expected the worst and was prepared for it—a good and valuable soldier.

The exploradors moved out a week-and-a-half before the army broke camp, riding cautiously along trails, often at night, in the general direction of Lopez's army. They scraped meager meals from brittle wooden bowls at the edges of impoverished villages and slept beneath great, vine-clad trees or in old, abandoned places. The people they encountered, dazed and jaded by their sufferings, regarded them with little interest, save one notable old woman who, laying a hand upon her heart, called out to them from the doorway of her hut as they rode by.

"Poor young boys!" she cried, "to be mown down like grass in a meadow!"

Alvis had hoped early on to burn a railway bridge or crossties behind Paraguayan lines so as to reward the Count's decision to finance the unit of scouts, but in these endeavors he proved unsuccessful. Operating in country unfamiliar to him or his men, Alvis found himself ever a step slow when promising information presented itself. They would learn, for instance, of an unguarded bridge and ride hard overnight only to discover the enemy in force upon their arrival. Or there would be news of straggling wagons, yet when they sought to locate them they would find themselves wandering indefinitely through lonely stretches of forest. Slowly and gravely it dawned on Alvis that much of his prior experience was inapplicable here since his force in truth possessed more in common with the enemy from his prior war than the Confederate Rangers he had served alongside. Aggressors and occupiers in a land not theirs, the work of the exploradors remained arduous and unfruitful.

So it was that on those rare occasions when the bullets flew, it was the exploradors who most often found themselves at a pronounced disadvantage, fleeing like flushed birds, or leaping from their horses to seek cover like farmers driven from their summer fields by hailstones. The forests they rode through were uncharted and so dense that even the local guides they paid to lead them often paused in confusion while navigating their depths. And then there was that overarching heavy and perpetual feel of hostility, like an invisible pressure directed upon them, wearing upon their nerves, spoiling their slumber.

"*Macacos*! Little Monkeys!" anonymous Paraguayan voices taunted from the confines of barricaded huts or deep underbrush.

"*Caboclos*!" the exploradors would curse them in return, perhaps firing a few stray rounds in the direction of the hecklers.

"Easy men," Alvis counseled, when it was all said and done, thinking of Virginia. "Remember they didn't invite us here."

The limited action they saw during those first few weeks was, in total, very light. Yet that would all change in August when, while reconnoitering the hillside village of Piribebuy— a collection of small thatched structures set along four rough streets—they discovered, by the weak light of a crescent moon, the Marshal President's small army dug in just outside of town. Moreover, early the next morning they learned from a drunken fisherman that the Paraguayan state treasury and archives were said to accompany the army as well.

Alvis wasted no time dispatching two riders by separate routes to bear this precious intelligence to the Count before establishing a fireless camp amid the dense underbrush of a neighboring hillside from whence he might view the general movements of both the army and the townspeople. The stream for which the hillside village was named ran along the base of the slope and the villagers bathed in it daily, the children splashing each other and the women demurely descending to the warm waters only after nightfall, the exploradors cursing softly as they squinted in the dark and prayed for cloudless moonlit nights. The meager Paraguayan force, Alvis discovered, was but a thousand and a half in number and consisted mostly of old men, young boys, wounded or otherwise crippled army regulars, and a few women. Many of them were without guns and instead toted sharp stones and broken bottles as they moved along the lines.

Alvis had learned long ago how to wait and watch—how to wait and watch with patience for an animal he hunted or for some subtle change in the force he reconnoitered. And as he did so here, he jotted down notes, periodically sending a rider to update the Count of any significant alterations in movement among the Paraguayans.

When, after several days, the Count's army finally arrived, Alvis' little band grimly watched the ensuing contest unfold from their high place. Those who have never seen two armies drawn up for battle, regardless of their size and relative conditions, have no idea of the beauty and brilliance on display, the brightly colored flags and implements of steel catching the light of the sun. Yet it is a prospect that quickly dissolves into ugliness and disorder as pomp and plumage give way to the base carnage that necessarily must determine all battles.

The Brazilians having been thoroughly briefed by Alvis on the organization and condition of their opponent, it did not take long, once the order for attack was given, for them to break through the limited and ill-equipped defenses of the Paraguayans, though the enemy soldiers abdicated nothing and fought with stubborn ferocity at close quarters.

In the midst of this initial assault, the commander of the Brazilian offensive, General João Manoel Mena Barreto, accompanying the offensive as it surged forward, was struck by two bullets in the stomach, condemning him to a slow, agonizing death. As news of this development passed through the ranks, it kindled among the enlisted men and officers alike a vengeful fury. On the Caacupé road, cavalry overtook a line of war refugees that had struck out from the village, riding down fleeing women, hacking at them with their sabres, and setting fire to carts. Closer to the battlefield, the Paraguayan hospital, nothing more in essence than a collection of rags and drooping tents, caught fire as well and burned quickly, the wild cries and screams of the wounded lying within rising from the field. Indeed, in a matter of moments the entire scene below the exploradors quickly turned to one of utter chaos.

Tiny figures, who Alvis later would learn consisted of Colonel Pablo Caballero and his staff, were separated from a group of prisoners and executed, their throats hacked open with bayonets. Riderless horses ran in all directions along the roads and lanes of the village, and smoke drifted across the battlefield in slow, lazy puffs and curls, obscuring in places the nature of the mayhem which continued to rise to their ears.

At last the vengeance of the Brazilians began to diminish and Alvis led the exploradors, eager for their portion of spoil, down into the village. Entering its outskirts, they were greeted by unlikely melodic tones of music and, cutting his men loose to partake of the looting, Alvis followed the sound to a roofless residence where he discovered the Count's adjutant seated at an antique grand piano—a decapitated Paraguayan soldier leaning against one of its polished legs—playing graceful long runs of classical fare. The cascade of notes was joined in short order by the clanging of bottles, which emerged from a newly-discovered wine cellar nearby.

The officers, Alvis moving to join them, toasted each other and the Count and embarked upon an impromptu soirée while not twenty yards from them, in a pile of rubble, a wounded elderly man crawled slowly and quietly—only the muffled grating of stones—dragging the bloody stumps of his legs behind him. These grisly events, coupled with the stubborn Paraguyan defense, later would come to be remembered as "Scenes from Saragossa" in reference to that passionate, albeit hopeless, defensive stand made by the Spanish against the French during the Peninsular Wars of long ago.

For the intelligence they delivered and the ensuing success at Piribebuy, the exploradors received a congratulatory address from the Count, four dozen bottles of rum, and promotions all around. Yet the month of August promised more surprises and atrocities, though the scouts, riding along the edges of the action, more often than not encountered only the vestiges, the light peripheral brush strokes, of the horror rather than the terrifying entity itself.

Alvis gave his life over to the Brazilian men in his charge, learning the stories of their lives and families and straining his mind to remember how Mosby had led, struggling to recall the best lessons of that war now so distant in geography and years. The chief principle was that all men must ride light. In Virginia they generally had depended upon the goodwill of the populace for food—a few ears of corn or some biscuits wrapped in a rag when they passed a village or friendly house—but they could not do so here and so were forced to burden their saddle bags.

Horses and pistols were the essential items, the real livelihood of this kind of war. The mounts of the Rangers had been drawn from enemy stock or the horse-rich counties of Fauquier or Loudoun. They were fine animals, the best that could be collected, for so much of their success depended on the speed and endurance of the creatures that bore them. More than once he had shucked a lone ear of corn for Ta-

merlane and gone hungry himself, so crucial was the health
of the animal. Often he marveled the black had not been
shot out from under him, while many a veteran he served
with had been through a half dozen or so mounts.

Yet the quality of horses they were issued served as yet
another impediment in the war at hand, the animals having
already seen a good deal of use. Pistols had been coveted by
Mosby since he had contemptuously rejected sabres as out-
moded, useless weapons. "They might as well charge us with
corn stalks," Alvis heard him sneer. And in this regard the
Brazilian contingent was fortunate, the Count having seen
to it that each man was issued a pair of pistols.

The overall success Old Mose had enjoyed in harassing
the enemy, Alvis concluded, had less to do with weapons
and stemmed more from the general fact that he came to
recognize his opponent as bureaucratic and overly time-
minded—enamored of structure and technology—hurrying toward his destiny as if he could not realize it quickly
enough. The enemy's predictability and sheer scale of his
endeavor made for a situation that invited disaster, the slow-
moving and lightly-defended Union sutlers' wagons, laden
with their supplies, more or less constituting fully-stocked
stores on wheels. The situation here was the opposite—the
Paraguayans were disorganized, down to their last supplies,
and, in some cases, starving.

Owing to the Rangers' small numbers and dependence
on the element of surprise, their engagements were very sudden and occurred seemingly away from everything: a desperate intelligence followed by a feverish deployment to
a remote place where lay the enemy's vulnerability. When
they attacked, they rode in swiftly with little organization,
pistols drawn, howling like bandits. It is little wonder the
enemy derisively named them bushwhackers.

Mostly they hit unprotected wagons but occasionally

they encountered mounted units mustered solely for the purpose of countering them. The toughest of these were Lowell's Californians, rugged westerners who neither scared nor broke so readily as the northeasterners, and typically gave as well as they got. Rarely did anyone claim a field in victory; it was instead the spontaneous site of a quick, unexpected clash, the dead and dying often left unattended: the jerking in the body, the shuddering once and for all, observed by no one. Then the wild dogs and the buzzards invariably played their parts. Alvis had glimpsed the latter feeding upon dead horses, though never a man. The war made them bold to the point it seemed to Alvis as if the large creatures' strange avian intelligence had come to expect carrion laid out for them on almost every field. They did not circle long, as he had watched them glide in his youth, but rather landed near their feast quickly and awkwardly with little short hops and leaps, the wings wide open and the great long beaks wheezing. They ate pinch by pinch, by jerks. One would drag a sliver a short distance from the main carcass and its fellows, and then tilt back its ungainly head to swallow.

More maddening to the enemy's leadership than the Rangers' attacks was the fact that in the wake of the mayhem and slaughter ensued complete silence and absence—the apparent utter disappearance of the Partisans from the vicinity. In reality the Rangers merely dispersed and boarded individually with remotely located families, retiring to crude shelters in the woods—shebangs, they called them—if the enemy ventured close. So it was that the forces which sought to engage and capture the Rangers met mostly with failure and frustration. Their foe took the form of something elusive, yet somehow everywhere, and the Partisans they occasionally did kill or collect did not offset their own losses, as they suffered repeated harassment and attacks in the forlorn places they roamed.

Alvis eventually recognized the lessons learned in his North American war had their limitations here and it troubled his heart not a little that the Paraguayans they found themselves shooting at, and occasionally fleeing from, were not unlike the soldiers he had marched beside toward the end of the contest to the north: old men, grizzled and gaunt, accompanied by bright-eyed, sharp-voiced beardless boys, stubbornly courageous and naive despite the hopeless nightmare unfolding about them.

Nowhere would the tragedy of Paraguayan circumstances prove more evident than at the Battle of Campo Grande, in which their forces, outnumbered better than three to one, were composed largely of children. On account of the exploradors' instructions to remain in reserve for the contest, Alvis would not realize this fact until he glimpsed a number of the enemy wounded borne back though the lines en route to the hospital. Some of the boys looked to be as young as ten or eleven and wore fake beards so as to fool their enemies into believing they grappled with veterans. Yet the disguise was betrayed at close quarters by their undeveloped forms and high pitched voices, which cried out shrilly for their mothers or wept in soft, muffled tones into the arm or hand which covered their expressions of anguish.

When Brazilian regiments from the front cycled back to the rear, the looks on the faces of the men were haunted and hollow. Former servants in the ranks chattered animatedly and wild-eyed to one another, claiming they had glimpsed the god Oshosse, the great hunter and hurler of stones, treading amongst them while the battle raged at its most furious pitch. It was he, they maintained, who held steady the fading gazes of the dying and encircled the souls of perished children in his mighty arms.

If it is possible for success on a battlefield to serve as a demoralizing instrument, then Campo Grande was such an occasion. The victory was tempered with vast regret throughout the ranks, for as many a veteran lamented, there can be no honor or pleasure in the slaughtering of children. And only following the battle's conclusion was the extent of the pitiable state of Paraguayan arms discovered, some of the guns, flintlocks and others, appearing as though they might have been salvaged from museums or archaeological sites. Yet to the surprise of the Count's staff, one of Wilhelm Wagener's modern Congréve rocket launchers presented itself among the spoils as well. Officers sipped their celebratory rum and speculated at length as to how the Paraguayans had acquired such a weapon even as they crowded about it and began breaking it down for study. So the soldier's mind moves ever onward, past the brutality of the recent lived moment, in contemplation of war's next unlikely mystery.

Echoes of the last days of the other war haunted Alvis as the exploradors witnessed the final devastation, the utter unraveling, of Paraguay. They rode past shanties and decaying homesteads where starving women—their husbands, sons, and fathers all dead—worked small plots of ground with old wooden plows, or ox yokes, or their bare hands. For years they had fed the army in which their menfolk fought while retaining almost nothing for themselves. Yet each year they grew weaker and produced less. Some had taken to eating their mules and horses. It was worse than anything Alvis had seen in Virginia, and here he was conqueror—rather than kin—to family after family of dispossessed victims. Yet he felt a terrible sympathy for them, a kinship nonetheless. He gave them rations when he could and forbade his men from looting their wanting hovels, all the while knowing such actions accomplished little.

Amid this annihilation, he recalled one of the few instances of genuine human generosity he had encountered near the end of the other war. How a fat, bluish grey pigeon lit upon the stage road, hurrying to drink from a puddle beside a rock wall, as he and a wounded Partisan galloped away from an engagement gone plum sour until their spent horses could endure no more and they set them free in the gathering shadows of evening, taking refuge in a roadside farmhouse. Once inside they were directed to an upstairs room by a girl who was perhaps eleven or twelve years old. There Alvis lowered his comrade onto a low-lying trundle bed and attempted to stop his bleeding as best he could, the welling intensifying slightly with each beat of the man's heart.

When hooves were heard on the road, the same young girl stuck her head in the room and gestured at the thick low ceiling planks above Alvis. A few moments later she returned, lantern in hand, accompanied by a tall enemy soldier. Alvis lay motionless, belly down, atop a plank almost directly above his injured comrade. As the enemy soldier's eyes shifted from the wounded man to take in the rest of the room Alvis noticed the girl subtly casting the shadow of the lantern in such a way as to allow almost no light to direct itself toward the ceiling. To an untrained eye it might seem she aided the soldier as she held out the lantern wherever he turned his gaze, though in reality she carefully cloaked that which she did not wish him to see.

Tentatively and gently, not unlike a surgeon probing with his instrument, the solider raised his boot and touched the Partisan's chest wound ever so lightly. A ragged cry rang out from the wounded man's unconscious feverish face and, though he did not come around, he began to moan and move his wet head slowly from side to side.

Again the soldier pressed the toe of his boot to the

wound and again the Ranger cried out, the light of the room wavering as the girl's lantern hand trembled.

Alvis' grip on the ceiling beam tightened and the muscles in his back bunched. Though he had been at war for years, rarely had he felt hatred for the enemy. It flared only on isolated occasions, and always very briefly. One exception was the episode near Dranesville during which the Prussian Partisan, Baron von Massow, captured the commanding officer of the 2nd Massachusetts Cavalry, a Captain Reed. Viewed as something of an exotic character among the men on account of his foreign voice and appearance, the Baron had not been long with them and perhaps still entertained an overly idealistic view of chivalry, for he honorably allowed the enemy captain to retain his personal sidearm in the wake of his capture. Yet as the Baron galloped off in pursuit of other enemy cavalrymen, Reed raised the pistol and shot the Prussian in the back. This treachery resulted in Reed's quick, subsequent death at the hands of Captain Chapman who, aiming from the hip, gut-shot his counterpart in rank before proceeding to finish the officer with a bullet to the temple. Baron von Massow would pull through in time, but the Rangers, Alvis among them, never forgot Reed's heinous deed, though it remained, in the end, but one of many episodes that increased by steady gradual degrees Alvis' wariness and cynicism as the war ground on.

But at that present moment, peering down from the dark rafters on the soldier below torturing his wounded comrade, Alvis did feel the bitter pull of hatred, and he shifted his arms and upper body, preparing to leap down. Yet his plan was interrupted by the sudden entry into the room of an enemy officer, who, striding purposefully toward the enlisted man, pistol whipped him on the shoulder and barked for his immediate departure.

The lieutenant looked round the room himself, offering a nod to the trembling lantern bearer, as if to calm and reassure her. He then knelt beside the injured Partisan and considered his wound without expression. Having assessed the man's condition, he brought his face almost level with that of Alvis' comrade who, perhaps sensing the nearness of the officer's presence, demonstrated a tenuous flicker of consciousness.

"You look as though you are going to die," the lieutenant said in a slow, clear voice. "I do not believe there is any miracle a doctor could perform for you."

Alvis discerned no reply from his comrade, but the officer bent forward silently as though listening carefully to a response.

When the lieutenant spoke again his voice was very soft. "There is nothing that can be done," he said, "but I am a Christian and I will pray for you."

With that the Lieutenant took the wounded man's hand and, remaining on his knees, bowed his head. The Partisan's moans became fainter and his breathing more relaxed. A strange quiet filled the room. In life, Alvis thought then, there are men whom we regret but are proud to have for our enemies; this lieutenant was one of them.

The officer remained kneeling in prayer for perhaps a full quarter of an hour. At last no sound or motion came forth from the wounded man and Alvis sensed a faint stirring of air brush his cheek. Dizzy with his own weariness, he wondered if he might have just felt his comrade's last breath, or perhaps his spirit, passing heavenward. The lieutenant rose stiffly, his duty done, and exited, gesturing for the girl to accompany him. The lantern's uneven swaying light abandoned the room to death and darkness.

At last the Paraguayans were bled dry and the war crept to a slow, faltering halt. Alvis was invited, along with other officers in the Count's favor, to sail down the Parana River through Argentina, where they paused briefly in Buenos Aires to receive an assortment of toasts and congratulations for their victory. However, even in the wake of the hostilities, onboard a ship filled with comrades, the devastation of the war continued to move stealthily among them, reminding them of its presence—imparting the knowledge that it would remain with them all, always.

So it was that a man who had successfully spied for the Paraguayans over the course of four years and at great financial benefit to himself, suffered a breakdown on deck, laughing wildly at the officers around him as he betrayed all. He was still laughing when a colonel stepped up from behind him and cracked his head with a heavy oar, knocking him into the river. They all watched the body as it bobbed for a few moments before the water around it grew agitated at the arrival of the creatures for which that river was named, attracted by the smell of the man's wound. As the ship drifted on, officers jostled one another at the rear of the vessel, taking turns peering though a spyglass in the hopes of catching a glimpse of the quickly-receding feast.

Despite that dark incident, the days were brilliant and golden as they continued down the Parana and then out into the Atlantic, where they continued to hug the coast, bearing northward toward Rio. Onboard, rough jokes and elaborate lies ensued regarding the war's events or the nature of the demure damsels and gorgeous whores who were said to await them in Rio.

Yet Alvis shut out such talk and spent his time mostly on deck, looking out over the sea, anxious at the thought of Lavinia's circumstances and wondering idly how Evandero had fared in his absence. But he tempered these thoughts with a hard-earned patience, for he had learned long ago that the skies smile no matter who frowns. They remain unmindful of the ways of men, as do the waters. This knowledge notwithstanding, in the evening when he closed his eyes and abandoned sight to the sensation of the ship's steady swaying motion, the warm images of loved ones would give way to the persistent inquiry he perpetually made of sky and water, that he seemed destined to ask always: why he should have lived and others died on so many different fields and occasions, and so live on now, condemned always to ask the question?

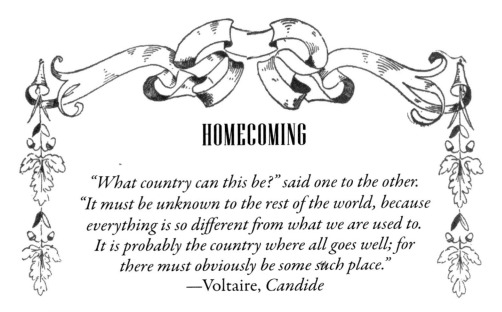

HOMECOMING

"What country can this be?" said one to the other.
"It must be unknown to the rest of the world, because
everything is so different from what we are used to.
It is probably the country where all goes well; for
there must obviously be some such place."
—Voltaire, *Candide*

W HEN the war was over, Count d'Eu, commander in chief of the allies and the Brazilian army, returned to Rio by sea, bearing Alvis and a number of other favored officers with him. It had required the death of Lopez and his refugee band to conclude the ugly struggle with Paraguay, but at last their martial duties had reached their end.

As the Count's vessel neared the city, the Emperor sailed out into the bay, the light of the west behind him, on a steamer decorated in flags, wreaths, and gay-colored pennants in the best Brazilian tradition, as celebratory cannon-fire echoed across the open waters from the forts. The Emperor boarded the Count's ship with his entourage and, having embraced Count d'Eu briefly, moved among the officers, shaking hands and bowing his head slightly as he listened to their words. When he came to Alvis he lingered an instant longer, perhaps noting his foreign features, before thanking him for his service and moving on.

The Emperor, possessed of blue eyes and a heavy gray beard which matched the color of his hair, looked to be in his mid-forties. His bearing was gentle and quiet as he continued to speak with a certain measured dignity to the Count and various other officers and officials. As they floated toward the docks, he toured the ship, greeting as many men as he could.

"*Que contentamento he o meu*," he murmured to his son-in-law.

He continued his review, remaining all the while studious in his observations, and in the ship's kitchen tasted the bread that had been made that morning and declared it good. Alvis had heard it said that the Emperor was a humble and intellectual man who had professed more than once that, had he not been destined to be Emperor, he would have been a teacher.

On the docks the Empress and another entourage awaited them, the throngs of Rio pressed in behind, waving and cheering. The Empress was large and fleshy but pleasant looking despite her somewhat macabre garb of heavy black silk. The ships came to rest at the Naval Arsenal, at the end of *Rua Dereita*. The Emperor, the Count at his side, and all their procession continued on foot to the Palace Square, built long ago in the old Portuguese style, where the Count, tall and graceful, dressed all in black, received the congratulations of the people. The crowds thronged the building for hours, cheering the imperial pair and blocking the roads, a stray, red balloon drifting up above the crowd and bobbing on the gentle harbor breezes.

Three days of festival ensued during which the city lit up and exploded into activity. Temporary buildings were erected and covered in wreaths, some of them representing forts taken during the war. In the Arsenal of War, illuminated by calcium lights, were gathered all the spoils of the long conflict: cannon, flags, the sword Lopez was wearing at the time of his death, and the lance of Chico Diabo which struck Lopez down. Festoons were suspended and structures raised high above the streets to serve as pagodas for the many musicians.

Fine quarters had been arranged for Alvis and the Count's other officers along the *Praia do Flamengo*, a beach that once had been frequented in large numbers by the bird for which it was named. There Alvis was pressed for some time by his fellow officers to join them in their sojourn to the most renowned whorehouse in Rio, but at last they relented and left him alone. From the balcony off his quarters, he watched the moon high above the palm-crowned mountains beyond the Bay of San Francisco Xavier as the faint sounds of music and shouts of nocturnal merry-making drifted on the calm harbor air. He dwelled again upon Lavinia, her image set against the moon. He had thought of her thus many times, and indeed it seemed to Alvis almost as though the moon aided him in recalling her since it had smiled upon them together and thus shared in their love. He would write Lavinia the following morning, addressing the letter in the care of Old Soriano's trustworthy eldest daughter.

Alvis lingered a long time on the balcony, listening to the sounds of the city and the inebriated racket of the returning officers. At last there was quiet, the Emperor's victorious drunken soldiery having finally sated their passions and taken to their beds. Alvis slept heavily but at first light, the sun not yet above the water, returned to the balcony, where he observed the early morning bathers arriving upon the beach, the ladies attended by servants who spread out tents for them. All along the beach, the women waded out into the surf, clad in their light-weight, dark robes which trailed behind them on the surface of the water like dark plumage.

Alvis spent the majority of his days prior to his discharge walking along the shore or the avenues of the city and visiting with his comrades or the wounded acquaintances who lay in the Santa Casa da Misericordia, Rio's largest hospital, which rested along the seaside beneath the brow of Castello Hill. He felt now—could appreciate—in the wake of two wars, that life and one's personal history are not unlike some great chain: something pulled at one end and the other end of it moved. Ever it seemed his body had been pulled and pressed, and thus he marveled at the unaccustomed pause which afforded him now the leisure of reflection.

On the afternoon he at last received his discharge papers, he bought drinks all around for his fellow officers before returning to his room in anticipation of an early departure the following day.

They were reluctant to let him go. "You have not seen the last of us, Confederado," a major said, hand resting on Alvis' shoulder. "Brazil remembers its defenders and friends."

Promised future visits and potential business ventures were exacted of Alvis before they would allow him to depart. Humbled and honored by their affection, he experienced a sobering of his spirits when he entered his quarters and discovered a dispatch from Soriano warning him that Emilio had learned of his return and boasted of riding out with a party of mercenaries to intercept the Confederado. Alvis crushed the note in his fist and hurled it against the wall when he had read it. Would he ever be rid of Emilio? Yet Soriano's note also had revealed a fragment of promising knowledge: that Lavinia had returned home. He knew now all must be determined soon as he gazed out over the harbor, expression grim. He would ride home tomorrow and if Emilio and others elected to stand in his way then look to their lives they must and woe be unto them.

Alvis had hoped to slip out the next morning unmolested. Yet his comrades, drunk and hung-over though most of them were, had anticipated his plan and risen early or stayed up all night so as to afford him their last blessings, though he saw to it they remained uninformed of the peril into which he was riding. Vergara, the old second in command of the exploradors, had brushed and saddled Alvis' horse and stood holding his halter when Alvis descended into the courtyard. Bleary-eyed in the first light, the men held their hats in their hands and watched silently as he mounted the old army horse that would bear him and his army chest the short distance to the docks. Surveying his comrades from the saddle, Alvis removed his own newly-purchased hat of leather and delivered to them all his heartfelt farewell.

"May the powers of fortune go with you."

ℬℭ

Lavinia had long since returned to Espírito Santo from the finishing school to which Mr. Ferreira had committed her in Curitiba and had resumed the routine of her prior life on the *fazenda*, reading and tending a small garden when she was not galloping about the countryside. She had heard nothing from Alvis during the long months of the war, a fact which her father and Emilio both pointed to as proof he no longer cared for her, his love having been successfully beaten from his body at last by the hands of Emilio and the hardships of combat. She knew better, of course, and during one of her longer rides strayed so far as Evandero's *fazenda* where she at last formally made the acquaintance of the good-hearted old man and learned that in truth Alvis' silence possessed an opposite meaning: that it was exercised to avoid burdening her with the dangers he faced daily and adding to her sorrows if he failed to live out the war's duration. This knowledge brought Lavinia pain as well as relief, and served also to make her fond of Evandero, whom she began visiting regularly and whose tales of famous bygone horses and the old Portuguese explorers delighted her. The elderly man made mention of Alvis but rarely, for he hoped to cheer and divert Lavinia since he knew she joined him in worrying over his circumstances. On those rare occasions his name arose, there would ensue a brief, shared interval of warm happiness and fond memories between them before an uncomfortable silence set in, Lavinia's gaze drawn inevitably to the white tooth which sat atop the mantle in an old tarnished brass candlestick holder.

Lavinia had no reason to suspect that Alvis' life was in immediate jeopardy, though his silence troubled her as much as her eagerness for his return. Yet there appeared in time a subtle sign which gave her hope. That spring white jasmine mysteriously sprung up beneath her window, causing her wonder at the miraculous occurrence until she discovered from one of the servants Alvis had sent the seeds to Old Soriano, who planted them as directed on a night after the last frost, by the pale light of a new moon. How it comforted her to look down upon the comely plant from her window. Often, when she did, a secondary curious feeling would come over her, which almost led her to believe that somehow Alvis' spirit was housed within the jasmine, quietly considering her in her window even as she dwelt upon him.

Her soft-spoken adoptive mother, whose opinion of Alvis had remained quietly favorable in the midst of her husband's and Emilio's disapproval, did her best to soothe her daughter's subtle disquiet.

"I have always liked this strange boy of yours from your homeland to the north," she said, "who has the eyes of a very old man. Immediately I took him for one who does not mind his own inconvenience so long as he can spare his loved ones. There are not many such people in this world."

Mrs. Ferreira sighed. "But when you have been married

as long as I have," she continued, "you will learn that a few days more or less of any man's society makes but little difference in the long term. Have patience then, my girl, and do not worry so."

Incredulity was the prevailing reaction when news reached Linhares in the wake of the war that the lone Confederado had served honorably in the contest, been decorated in Rio, and enjoyed the personal patronage of Count d'Eu and, by extension, the Emperor. Lavinia's father offered no comment when this intelligence reached him, since he recognized then any further plots and attempts to detach Lavinia from Alvis would be in vain and, more importantly, bad business. In seeking to destroy the young man he had instead transformed him into an honorable match for Lavinia—a fact in which he failed to sense irony and, instead, congratulated himself, beginning already to calculate the manner in which the connection, if realized, might serve any number of his political and mercantile purposes.

"She will defy you if you interfere," said Mrs. Ferreira, sensing in her husband some lingering reservation. He suspected she was correct, but remained not a little piqued at a world that placed a woman's knowledge of such unspoken things before that of a husband or father.

"Alas, this is not my kind of business," he replied at last with a sigh and deflated shake of his head, "and I fear that for me these sorts of speculations rarely have borne much profit."

However, whereas Mr. Ferreira resigned himself at last to Lavinia's will and destiny, his wayward bastard charge, Emilio, quietly raged and gnashed his teeth at the news of the Confederado's honors and impending return within two day's time. In the stables he knocked to the ground with a

curse the servant who curried his horse, saddled up and galloped off in the direction of Evandero's *fazenda*.

A steamer took Alvis as far as the little seaport village of
Santa Cruz, where a letter of introduction from the Count
enabled him to secure a good horse. Two days of hard riding
across desolate, rolling, rocky ground brought him within
several miles of Linhares. There he began studying the terrain as he rode, noting the passes which cut between slopes
covered in low bushes, stunted trees, and loose boulders.
Evandero had recounted to him tales of this desolate area to
the south: of its loose rocks, deceptive hills, and narrow trails.
He knew that his homecoming was expected and that not all
in Linhares welcomed it. One in particular weighed on his
mind as he nearly had been killed by him before. If there was
to be trouble from Emilio, as Soriano had intimated, Alvis
reasoned it would come here amid these empty hills. Alvis'
expert eye for terrain continued to rove across the landscape
as he rode on. When at last he had found and reconnoitered
the place he thought would best serve his purpose, he rode
forward to a rise in the narrow road and waited, scanning
the plain to the northwest.

Alvis Stevens knew, had learned long ago, how to wait
and let the world tell him things. Birds circled, the breeze
changed direction, a cloud drifted overhead in the shape of
a dragon. He was content to watch and let this landscape
share of itself.

He waited two hours, three, and then he saw them coming—an anomaly against the terrain: a dozen horseman
cantering across the plain, a pale dust cloud rising behind
them. From where he stood on the hilltop he and his mount
would be set out in relief against the sky for the men below.
Suddenly the riders' pace quickened and changed direction

slightly, and he knew they had seen him. Anger rose in him as they neared when he spied his beloved old mount Heliodoro with Emilio astride him, beating his flanks with a riding crop as he came on. With a curse, Alvis turned his mount and vanished down the backside of the hill.

The motley crew came on, Emilio at their head, and when they occupied the same hilltop Alvis had they glimpsed him now atop another, larger hill—a rocky outcropping—perhaps a quarter mile to the south.

"Look at the coward running," Emilio sneered to his fellows, who grinned in answer at the sight of their quarry and the thought of the reward Emilio had promised them for Alvis' death.

"He wants us to follow him; very well," continued Emilio. "Pursue him as he wishes, but I'll ride on ahead to ensure he never reaches another hill."

With an oath, Emilio delivered a vicious blow to Heliodoro's rump and then laughed as the tired horse bucked before leaping into a gallop. With a ragged shout of their own, Emilio's rough mercenaries set out for the rise where they had last glimpsed Alvis.

By and by the party of assassins came to the rock-littered foot of the hill and, noting the loose rock, dismounted in order to ascend without fear of one of their animals losing his footing. Steadily they climbed in a rough, close formation, each man gripping in one hand his horse's reins and in the other a pistol. Their eyes clung to the summit where last Alvis had been spotted, oblivious to the wild barren beauty of their surroundings.

High above them, near the top of the ridge, stood massive jagged, serrated rocks, which rose almost like battlements. The men slowed their pace as the rocks about them grew larger and the slope steepened. Could the Confederado be waiting for them behind one of those great rocks? Suddenly, a man slipped on the broken hillside shale, pulling his horse's head forward and cursing loudly as he twisted his ankle. As a body then, in the wake of their companion's fall, it seemed they all suddenly recognized their peril. They must watch closely where they stepped while also remaining wary of the terrain ahead—all while exposed in the open. They closed formation as they climbed on, their horses' stirrups brushing against each other.

What happened next must have felt to them as though it unfolded in a dream—as in a slow, terrible dream from which one wishes to awake and escape but cannot. With a reluctant scraping sound, one of the great serrated boulders high above them tilted forward from its precarious resting place and rolled toward them, gathering rocks, widening the wake of its disturbance as it came on.

After an instant of frozen terror the mercenaries let go their horses and lapsed into panicked scattering: some running forward, some back, three of them crouching in place, wide-eyed as through paralyzed. The whole hillside appeared to be moving, undulating with incredible speed and force while groaning in a low rumble. One moment there were men and horses, moving, rearing, yelling, clasping their hands about their heads. The next moment there was nothing, the hillside having washed over them, claiming and burying the occupants. Dust rose here and there from a new sloping field of loose rock, and all was silence.

Alvis waited in a draw below the backside of the hilltop from which he had launched the avalanche. He knew there had been eleven of them and knew also the identity of the absent man. He waited now where he believed Emilio would seek him out. Alvis recognized that in circumstances such as these—matters of strategy—he could see into Emilio's mind the way a skilled hunter intimately comes to know the tendencies of the wild animal he stalks. Alvis thought of Emilio as something of an animal albeit an extremely dangerous, predatory one. He patted his horse's neck absently. Emilio would come, and he knew he must kill him.

The better part of half an hour passed and then, as if answering some cue of fortune, Emilio appeared from around the curve of the hill, guiding Heliodoro carefully over the rocks. As man and horse approached, Alvis discerned the animal was nearly lame, his legs working unevenly as he stumbled on the broken terrain. When they drew closer still, he observed Heliodoro's swaying gait and noted the whip marks, resembling crimson brush strokes, about his flanks and rear.

"You are a fool, foreign trash," said Emilio by way of greeting, coming to a halt not twenty feet from his nemesis, "to have come back here. But this beaten old nag deserves a beaten rider, though I promise you that when we are finished today you will never ride again."

Alvis eyed Emilio's contemptuous countenance for a moment before gazing beyond it, letting his eyes wander up and down the barren hillside and then further, across the span of lonely hills. A light breeze filtered through the draw, raising miniature dust devils out of the earth as if some sorcerer were seeking to summon his demons. When Alvis' glance at last returned to Emilio he slowly shook his head.

"No, Ferreira bastard," he replied at last. "I fear it is you who are the fool for having come here with those poor outlaws, bearing your customary words but aided no longer by the customary allies you depend upon to realize their intent. There is an old saying in Paraguay: that when two devils come together, hell is to pay. Yet I have grown weary of killing and will spare you even now if you give me my horse and walk back down that draw."

Emilio spat at Alvis in contempt and, with a curse, drew out his knife and dismounted.

"Get down off that horse!" he yelled, voice hoarse with malice, "or I'll cut its neck open and drag you from it!"

Alvis stared at the raving bastard as he shouted anew and brandished his knife.

When at last Alvis dismounted and loosed his gun belt, wrapping it about the pommel of the saddle, Emilio let loose a string of filth, punctuated with a sneer. Yet for all the bastard's high bravado, Alvis noted that his knife-hand trembled.

Then the Confederado drew out his own knife—a jewel-hilted razor of a blade lifted from the headless corpse of a Paraguayan brigadier in the wake of Piribebuy. It was a cruel-looking, curved weapon, the nicks of which boasted it had drunk the blood of many men before finding its way into the possession of this North American whom so many had sought to kill.

Slowly Alvis walked toward Emilio, eyes locked on the wild orbs of his nemesis.

"Let these few moments," he said, raising the knife familiarly, "decide our fates forever."

Emilio's trembling increased but he gritted his teeth and spat. Alvis' mind was cool. It harkened back to days of his youth when he and Silvanus Stenson had stabbed at each other with harmless wooden sticks, the little woodsman teaching him the Monocan way of handling a knife mixed in with the rough tutelage he had received from the mountain men who had reared him. The instruction had proven useful on occasions in both wars when, while fighting at close quarters, both pistols spent, he had stabbed and hacked his way out of danger with the foot-long blade he carried in his waistband.

Alvis had possessed no knife on the last occasion the Ferreira bastard had attacked him. He knew Emilio's knifesmanship to be considerable, but he believed he had the advantage in that the bastard knew nothing of his own foreign skill.

He recalled from the last confrontation that Emilio's reach was greater than his, so that when his nemesis sprang forward with a shout and a sweeping right to left cut, Alvis sidestepped to the left. Emilio's wicked slash cut only air where Alvis had been, while the Confederado's backward cut tore cloth, scratching the skin above Emilio's hip bone, drawing blood.

Howling, the bastard turned and slashed empty air again before the two lapsed into circling each other warily, stones crunching beneath their feet. Emilio struck suddenly at Alvis' face, lunging with the agility of a cat, and the Confederado's head shifted only just in time. His knife hand out of position to strike, Alvis delivered a jab to the bastard's stomach with his left fist. Emilio stumbled back, gasping, nearly falling, dropping a hand to the ground to steady himself.

When the hand came up, Alvis failed to assess what was in it until the dirt and rocks were hurled into his face. A stone rolled under his foot as he retreated, blinking to regain his vision, and he tumbled to the ground.

When Emilio charged forward Alvis thrust upward with a leg, catching him in the pit of his stomach. Growling in rage as he recovered himself, Emilio lunged again and their knives clashed, but Alvis let his slide off to the side and, gripping the wrist of the bastard's knife hand, plunged the curved Paraguayan blade deep into the bastard's torso.

Emilio staggered back, inspecting the wound incredulously, unable to accept it, as Alvis rolled to his feet. Then he came on anew like some wild thing, cutting and slashing. Though he gasped for air like a drowning man, in his fury he did not even seem to feel his wound. Bleeding as badly as he was, he seemed as intent as ever on killing the hated foreigner.

Emilio lunged, but this time slower, his breath ragged, and Alvis, holding his knife low, sidestepped the blow, then brought his blade up hard, driving with all the force in his powerful legs and thighs. It drove in to the hilt and for a moment the combatants were eye to eye.

"You could have walked away," Alvis said quietly before withdrawing his knife with a sudden jerk.

Emilio tottered to one side like a drunken man before falling to his knees. Dull eyes fixed on Alvis; he struggled to rise but instead fell flat on his face and moved no more.

ᔕᔆᘓᘍ

Evandero said nothing of Heliodoro's empty saddle when he glimpsed Alvis riding slowly toward the *fazenda* stables, the injured Andalusian in tow. They dispensed with elaborate greetings so that Heliodoro's wounds might be seen to immediately. As they treated the horse, however, Evandero recounted in brief how Heliodoro's theft had taken place while he slept two nights previous. Alvis, in turn, revealed no details of his encounter, stating only that the buzzards in the valley of scattered bones would feast well that week.

When news of Alvis' homecoming reached the Ferreira *fazenda*, Lavinia would bear no restrictions or censure and galloped away to greet him. Upon her arrival she ran into the house in search of him, but, finding no one home, emerged breathless back into the yard. As she led Meainoite toward the stables, however, a gleam in the barn's shady doorway caught her eye and, drawing closer, she discerned the light issued forth from an object which hung at the end of a necklace, its fine links, in turn, held by an outstretched arm, the body to which it belonged obscured by the stable door.

As Lavinia reached the entrance she felt her heart flutter and released Meainoite's reins, for at last she recognized the necklace's featured ornament: a cut emerald rendering of blossoming white jasmine. Then Alvis stepped out from behind the door smiling and took her in his arms.

On the occasion Alvis requested of Mr. Ferreira his adoptive daughter's hand in marriage, the wealthy land-owner condescended as cordially as he might.

It continued to vex him that in the days following Emilio's disappearance he had sent out riders who had returned bringing neither discovery nor news. Though he suspected the foreigner's involvement in the disappearance of his volatile charge, Ferreira thought better than to mention the topic to Alvis. There were, after all, unpleasantries the Confederado might raise as well. Mr. Ferreira reminded himself too he had not enjoyed much foresight or luck in his prior dealings with the foreigner and thus pledged to refrain from introducing new business of a delicate and potentially contentious nature.

The talk instead during these slow, happy days was the pleasant murmur of marriage as preparations unfolded, and Mrs. Ferreira talked excitedly of expensive dresses, old friends, and elaborate meals. Meanwhile, the priest to perform the ceremony, an amicable young fellow from Rio, met with the lovers and began advancing Alvis through the ponderous and bulky machinations of the church. Having witnessed too many grand, yet ultimately empty, military ceremonies in his time, Alvis placed little stock in the religious variety. And since his arrival in Brazil, he had remarked, not always without amusement, the church's pompous and corrupt priests, tedious processions, gaudy tinsel shows, and meager firecracker displays. In spite of this, however, he thought it possible he might come to believe in the scriptures again some day—those same passages which had brought him to faith long ago and, later, to the Portuguese language.

As the day of the wedding approached, there were memorable words of counsel and well-wishing: words of love.

"You will learn that love is a great joy," Mrs. Ferreira informed her daughter, "but it is also work. Young people must take love seriously and learn it as a discipline. So many young people believe play is happier than work, but work is more satisfying, and love born of work is stronger stuff, better made."

The night before he was to be wed, Alvis was somber as he sat with his old friend. "I doubt seriously I am good enough for her," he said. "I have fought wars on two continents, killed more men than I can recall, abandoned the family that raised me, and done all manner of questionable things."

"There is an old saying," Evandero replied after a moment, his mouth lapsing into a sly smile, "that when a man is about to travel, he must pray once; when he goes to war, twice; and when he is going to be married, three times."

They laughed together before Evandero's expression grew serious. "Men and stones," he said, "are always to be found in this world, Alvis. Men live because they are born; men live to die. Life holds no promises, though the expectations of men often lead them to believe that it does. It merely moves on, life. I tell you this now, my son, but you have lived more than enough to know it for yourself. Live your life, Alvis. Let this woman love you."

When the wedding was over and they were alone, Alvis and Lavinia took a short walk beneath the white, shapeless mass of a full moon obscured by clouds and danced a soundless *serenar na dansa* before returning to the Ferreira house. Pausing at the door, Alvis kissed Lavinia and, as he did so, was struck by the notion that perhaps it would suit him well to mingle now with things that never pleased him—that indeed were never possible—before. Perhaps, he thought, as she lay her head upon his shoulder, there is a chain of events after all that leads us to a place in the world.

Inside the house, in the richly-decorated great hall, still inhabited by members of the wedding party, Evandero, stoked by high spirits and cachasa, had endeavored to explain the background of Alvis and the Confederados to a group of Ferreira family guests from the coast south of Rio.

"These were people," he said, "who would not die in their own war, nor submit in its wake. Their country went down in flames, yet they rose from the ashes and found their way here among us across thousands of miles. Alvis Stevens was one of their number."

He paused before continuing, his voice breaking with pride and too much rum. "I say was, for now he is one of us, a Brazilian: *coronelismo* of the *fazenda* Pallanteo and husband to a beautiful and virtuous woman."

The old man raised his glass and nodded in the direction of the newlyweds, who were just then entering the great room arm in arm: "May the powers of fortune go with him!"

All who heard the toast drank to the health of Alvis Stevens.

Acknowledgments

CONFEDERADO, like all works of historical fiction, claims a material and cultural heritage of the history and mythology of its time expressed through narrative. Its facts, such as they appear, come back to us altered by the funhouse mirror of fiction.

Stories of ancestors' experiences, of how a sword cut or an embedded bit of lead came to mar the doorframe of a family home, are nothing new and serve as reminders of how close we still are to this novel's time period. Alvis Stevens emerged as an embodiment of those artifacts and stories, yet it was his unusual migration to Brazil—his identity as a Confederado—which fascinated me and made him something more than a one more clichéd Civil War protagonist

I am indebted to many books (too many to list here), period and recent, as well as primary materials from the Library of Virginia, the Universities of Virginia and South Carolina, and libraries both in Rio de Janeiro and the state of Espirito Santo.

In addition, readers whose literary journeys have paralleled my own will have recognized the inspirations for certain portions of the book: nods to writers as diverse as Poe and Ovid. It is my way of attempting to do them some small justice and keep their legacies vital and alive.

As with my other books, too many people to list contributed to this novel in one way or another. They know who they are and carry with them my deepest gratitude.

Lastly, I thank the fine staff at Ingalls for bringing the book into being.

CASEY CLABOUGH is the author of the creative non-fiction work *The Warrior's Path: Reflections Along an Ancient Route,* the scholarly title *Inhabiting Contemporary Southern and Appalachian Literature*, and four other scholarly books on southern and Appalachian writers. He serves as Literature Editor of the Virginia Foundation for the Humanities' *Encyclopedia Virginia* and as Editor of the *James Dickey Review*. Clabough teaches at Lynchburg College and also manages a farm in Appomattox County, Virginia.

A SHORT TIME TO STAY HERE

by Terry Roberts
ISBN: 978-1-932158991
Publication: Sept. 1, 2012

War changes everything that should have been in the summer of 1917.

The U.S. enters WWI and Stephen Robbins' beloved Mountain Park Hotel is pressed into service as an internment camp for over 2,000 German nationals, including Hans Ruser and his men. Feisty Anna Ulmann, seeking her independence in a male-dominated world, flees south from New York to devote her life to documentary photography in beautiful Hot Springs, North Carolina. Haunted by demons both past and present, these people face heartbreaking tragedy. Yet together they discover the true meaning of imprisonment and escape.

"Brilliantly plotted and rendered in a style both lyrical and concretely realistic, flawless in characterization and with an authoritative command of the history that enfolds it." —Jerry Leath Mills, Editor Emeritus, *The Southern Literary Review*

"Thrilling story of the clash of cultures, of mystery, espionage, revenge, and love. … a riveting story … bringing to life a particular Appalachian time and place, by one of the exciting new voices of Southern fiction." —Robert Morgan, author of *Gap Creek* and *Brave Enemies*

"Roberts brings to life both the historical circumstance and much more." —Doris Betts, author of *Souls Raised from the Dead*

TERRY ROBERTS was born and raised near Weaverville, NC. His ancestors have lived and worked in Madison County, NC since the 18th Century. Roberts is the Director of the National Paideia Center at the University of North Carolina.

WITHDRAWN

CPSIA information can be obtained at www.ICGtesting.com
Printed in the USA
BVOW040025020512

289072BV00001B/8/P